Blood Roses

By Chloe Testa

For the people who supported me throughout this work, from

inception to completion

Prologue

On the top of a hill in the old Yorkshire town of Aysforth stands a beautiful Victorian house, with a shingled roof and picture windows looking out across the moors. It has a large, ornate black door and a small porch with intricate carvings made into the woodwork. Beyond this sprawls a magnificent garden bursting with colour and light as thousands of red roses bloom.

But this beautiful house has a hideous past.

It once belonged to a rich couple, their son and two young daughters. The father bought the land and built the house from the ground up, choosing that part of town specifically for the fantastic views across the countryside and then filling it with everything money could buy. It screamed of money.

For two years the family lived there in quiet contentment. A perfect home for a perfect family. But after their two year period of peace, something strange took over.

The garden around the house had always been plain; an endless stretch of lawn. One summer, roses began to bloom; bright red roses which seemed to spring up overnight. No matter how many times the father cut, trimmed and uprooted the unwanted roses they would simply return, bursting into life faster than he could cull them.

Now the roses in themselves were indeed nothing more than a nuisance. Until they started appearing around the house. A rose on each pillow, three spread across the kitchen table, endless petals filling the rooms. Nobody knew how they were being brought in, each family member adamant it was not them. Rumors of ghosts were spreading through the town of Aysforth, but the family resigned themselves to believing it a childish prank.

One night, however, their son was in the bath. He closed his eyes briefly and when he opened them, the bath was filled with rose petals. As he looked, they began to wilt and die, turning black, filling the water with decay, maggots, bugs. He screamed and the father came bursting into the room to see his son thrashing around in crystal clear water. But he could have sworn, when he opened the door, a tall, pale woman had been looming over his son. The woman had turned as he'd flung open the door and her blood red eyes had locked on him briefly before she disappeared.

By summer's end the father had seen the figure and her burning red eyes many times. He began to lose his mind as he saw her wherever he went. He found himself avoiding his family, unable to endure human contact. He would lock himself in his room and refuse to open the door for anything, desperately trying to create barriers she could not cross. One night, he was locked in his room, trying to get those eyes out of his mind when a single, red rose dropped into his lap. The next morning, he was found dead; body mangled and blood covering the room.

A trial was held and the jury found his wife guilty of murder, sentencing her to execution with the official verdict being she had gone into a jealous, murderous rage over her husband's psychosis and obsession with the red eyed girl. And she, they deemed a figment of his imagination.

With the family now torn apart by tragedy, the two daughters went to live with an aunt on the other side of the country but the son continued to live in the house, unable to truly believe his mother could do something so cruel. The roses withered and died and he lived in solitude, the horror of his mother's supposed crime the only thing to haunt him. He spiralled into obsession, searching for information about the red eyed girl to no avail. Months passed and she further slipped away from him, becoming nothing more than a terrible memory.

But one night, the garden burst into full bloom as every rose bud sprang to life, opening up into a brilliant red rose. He stood by the window and looked down into the garden, amazed by the roses' strange behavior. At that moment, he felt a pair of arms snake around his waist and pull him back into the darkness. The last thing anybody ever heard of him was a single scream. Police went to investigate the next day and the house was untouched save for rose petals scattered across the floor while the roses in the garden continued to bloom.

They say at night you can still hear his screams echoing through the house. And the roses never die. You can still see the woman, standing by the window, looking down into the garden. Her skin is so pale she glows in the moonlight and you must never look into her eyes. For the moment you see those eyes, you are lost to her. To the girl of Rose House.

Chapter One

Tom had done some pretty stupid things in his life. He'd jumped out of the window of year seven science because somebody convinced him that, as it was only on the first floor, he would be completely fine. His subsequent broken leg and dislocated shoulder proved this theory incorrect. He'd eaten two raw, whole chilies on a dare. As if that wasn't stupid enough, as his mouth started to burn and his eyes watered, he rubbed his face and eyes vigorously in some ridiculous attempt to soothe the pain. He'd had to use eye drops for a week and his mouth still burned at the memory. And then of course there was the time in year nine he'd asked out Jenny Williams at break in front of all of her friends. Not only did she turn him down with a sneer, but for the rest of the school year, every time her or her group saw him, they'd burst into hysterical laughter. The memory still made him cringe today.

But nothing could quite compare to this terrible decision he had just made. No matter how many stupid things he'd done in the past, nothing was quite as stupid as this. Nothing would ever compare to the stupidity he was about to embark on.

It's a well-known rule that when something's meant to be haunted, or even remotely scary, unless you're staring in a Hollywood blockbuster movie and getting paid more money than Tom ever actually hoped to see in his life, you don't go anywhere near it. Ever.

Unless of course, it's Halloween and, on a stupid dare enforced by a high amount of peer pressure, you're goaded into it. By your two best friends. Who refuse to accompany you.

And that's how Tom found himself standing outside Rose House on a dark and cloudy October evening, surrounded by people eagerly anticipating the idiot he would soon make of himself. Nobody expected him to be in there for more than five minutes and, if not for the fact Tom was a complete sucker for peer pressure – it wasn't as if he'd started smoking due to the appetizing smell of cigarettes – he'd be backing out faster than anyone could think.

He was nervous, though he would never admit it to anyone, preferring instead a cool nonchalance. Butterflies had filled Tom's stomach all along the walk here, itching and twisting their way through his gut. Now, staring down the barrel of a potentially loaded gun, the butterflies had vanished, only to be replaced by lead. He looked up at the house before him and imagined having the courage to turn to the group, refuse to go through with this bullshit idea and then go eat his body weight in pizza. How he fully believed every Halloween should be spent. He'd just take a deep breath, grit his teeth, and say no. This was ridiculous. Just say no.

"Couldn't have asked for a better day to do this," a voice mused from beside him, bursting through his happy little distraction. "Dark, cloudy, chance of rain in the air. It's like fate."

"Of course it is," Tom snipped back; his default response when dealing with any emotion was sarcasm. It had served him well so far. "Or it could be the fact it's the middle of Autumn. In Northern England. It's not as though rain's an anomaly here."

"Somebody's testy. Scared, perhaps?" Sebastian replied eyes gleaming with mirth. And it was in moments like these Tom questioned why he and Sebastian were still friends. Tom glared back at him, not wanting to say anything more, hands balling into fists; Sebastian had a way of knowing exactly what Tom was feeling without him ever having to say anything. It was the most infuriating thing about him.

"Are you ready for this?" a second voice finally piped up diffusing the tension that had developed between the two; it was Oliver, the level headed one.

The house before them was massive with enormous

picture windows and an old, shingled roof. The garden stretched around the house, wide and deep and overgrown. It was full of blood red roses, blooming brightly in the twilight shadows of an autumn evening when roses really shouldn't bloom. Their vibrant red colour stood out against the charcoal grey of the house behind them, looking dingy in comparison.

"Yeah, I'm ready, it's just a house, right?" he said, looking back at them casually, his voice belying his true fear. "Nothing to be afraid of."

"Rather you than me, boy," Sebastian said, patting him on the back and grinning.

Oliver handed Tom a long, metal torch. He and Sebastian also had torches, for when the sun fully set and they were left waiting for Tom in darkness. "Rules of the dare are as follows: spend an hour in Rose House and you will receive a collected amount of £50 from all of us, any less, and you don't get a single penny."

"And what if I stay in there longer?" Tom asked cockily.

Sebastian snorted rather unattractively as laughter exploded through him. "You get a pat on the back. Don't be greedy! Tom, you won't even last an hour. And we'll never let you forget the time you came out of Rose House, screaming like a little girl."

"Don't hold your breath," Tom said, rolling his eyes. "Can I go now?"

"None of us are holding you back," Sebastian pointed out. "Whenever you're ready, head on in."

Tom nodded and turned to the house, eyes scanning the façade, glancing into every window briefly. He opened the iron gates before him, half expecting them to creak ominously as if to signal the start of a terrible horror fest. Surprisingly, they didn't. Either they weren't iron or the 1800s had some top quality way of preventing rust. He shook his head at the ridiculous thoughts racing through his mind and stepped into the garden. The moment he entered the

9

pungent scent of roses bombarded his senses, overwhelming him. He wrinkled his nose, attempting to block out the sickly sweet smell filling his nose and throat, cloying and heavy like treacle.

"We'll miss you buddy!" Sebastian cried out dramatically, as Tom took a few more steps into the garden. "Be brave!"

Tom flipped him off and released the iron gates. As they swung shut behind him an anxious voice wailed out into the night, stopping the crowd's farewell. "Wait!" A loud pounding filled the street rivalling the pounding of Tom's heart in his ears, and the group were momentarily distracted by a harried figure racing towards them, coat flapping and scarf trailing out behind. The girl came skidding to a halt just before the iron fence, dark hair plastered to her forehead as beads of sweat clung to her flushed skin. "Hey," she panted, bending over slightly to try and regulate her breathing, pulling in deep, gasping breaths, hand jammed in to her side. "Um...b-be careful, ok? Try not to. Die. I'd rather you. Weren't dead."

Tom had turned back to see Mariana as she raced towards them, her flapping coat and rather wobbly run very distinct, even in low light, and the butterflies in his stomach returned with full force, dancing a rather enthusiastic jig. In true Mariana style, she was late to the event and he had half wondered with ever increasing disappointment whether she simply wouldn't turn up. Ten years of knowing her had forced him to accept her terrible time keeping and he shared a half smile with her, all traces of disappointment forgotten. "Trust me, it's not something I'm planning on doing tonight," he said. "Feel free to come to my valiant rescue though, if you see a guy in a black robe with a sceptre wandering about."

She attempted to giggle around gasps in response and shook her head, strands of hair whipping with the movement, sticking to her slightly slick, still very red cheeks. "Always will," she replied, poking her tongue out at him. She was uncharacteristically jittery this evening Tom noticed, as she wrung her hands together and bounced from foot to foot, despite the harsh exercise she had just endured. But then, she was never good with anything remotely horror related, so being so close to Rose House was probably having an effect on her. Again, another reason he was surprised to see her here. She normally refused to even walk passed Rose House in the middle of the day. It took several bribes of ice cream and money to get her the next street over.

"As riveting as this is," Sebastian cut in, disrupting Tom's rapid, somewhat disjointed, train of thought. "Maybe we could continue this awkward moment when you're done? Think about the poor fools waiting for you out here in the freezing cold. Hurry up and get on with it."

Tom glared at Sebastian. He let his eyes sweep across his friends a moment longer, memorising the sanctity of their group, before turning and strolling up the path casually. His stance belied the fact he was absolutely terrified and would do anything to leave this place immediately. Forget the bet entirely. Skip away into the nonexistent sunset and have a merry old time elsewhere. It wasn't the £50 which kept him going, it was the fact that he was too proud to admit he was afraid.

Tom dug into his pocket and pulled out a slightly crushed packet of menthols, violently jabbing one into his mouth and attempting to light it with shaky hands. After the third attempt the end glowed soft red and he took in a deep minty breath of nicotine. As the smoke filled his lungs, he relished the brief calm that worked its way outwards from the pit of his stomach to the tips of his hands. Reluctant to relinquish this moment of calm even for a second he sucked hard on the cigarette, inhaling all that he could until the filter remained. With a heavy heart, he crushed it into the ground. There was nothing else to do but make his way forward through the garden now.

Twisted, brown branches covered in thorns jutted out into the path, blocking his way, creating a maze-like effect which left him dodging and ducking branch after branch. The effort required was almost enough to make Tom forget the lingering fear pooling in his stomach, as overgrown rose bushes tested his reflexes and ninja-like skills. The roses bloomed incandescent in the watery dusk light, larger than any roses he had ever seen. Just before the door, the roses were so wild and overgrown he was unable to pass without physically moving them. Reaching out, he brushed the branches out of the way. The thorns from one of the roses dug into his arm.

He wrenched his arm back with a string of curse words so profane they'd make a sailor blush as an electric shock of pain forced its way through his arm. Blood was pooling in the corner of a long cut steadily growing angry and red as the skin reacted to this devastating betrayal of ripping and tearing. As Tom stared, blood trickled out of the cut, travelling down over his skin and dripping onto the floor. Bunching up the corner of his shirt and muttering another string of profanities Tom pressed the material to his torn skin and stemmed the blood flow. Applying pressure helped stop the cut from throbbing though it left one of his favourite shirts stained with blood. He desperately hoped his mum could sort it out in the morning.

Viscous fluid appeared to be forming on every thorn along the guilty rose's stem. He flicked on the flashlight and bent closer to the stem, curiosity urging him to examine this bizarre sight further. The fluid shimmered red in the flashlight's beam, resembling blood in colour and thickness, if the way it was pooling at the tip of each thorn was any indication. He knew he wasn't bleeding that badly so the blood on each thorn could not have been his own. Blood beaded on the thorn closest before dripping off and falling to the ground. Almost instantly, another bead of blood-like fluid appeared in its place, as though the roses were bleeding themselves. The sharp, metallic scent of blood filled his nostrils and he bit down hard on his lip as bile raced up his throat, jerking away from the rose. Blood made him queasy.

Tom took in deep, desperate breaths of fresh air, holding on to the contents of his stomach as he tried to rid himself of the overwhelmingly nauseating smell. Once sure he wouldn't projectile vomit the moment he moved, Tom hurried forward, away from the bleeding rose and towards the front door, tentatively walking up the rotting, wooden stairs, holding onto the railings for dear life as they creaked under his weight. Perhaps if they crumbled now and he fell and twisted his ankle, he could walk, or, more likely, crawl away from this dare with some dignity, without actually having to enter the house. He secretly prayed for the stairs to collapse.

Of course, luck wasn't on his side.

Tom stood before the front door, staring up at the ornately carved wood and wondering if he'd have to pick the lock. They hadn't considered whether or not he could actually get into the house when they'd concocted this terrible dare. Now Tom was faced with the very real possibility of being denied access - which, of course, would be absolutely terrible. Cough. He prayed the door would be locked. He didn't have a key or anything on him so actually picking the lock would be out of the question, and there would be no point heading back to the group, only to make this treacherous journey again.

Tom's stomach dropped as the door swung open with a creaking groan, dashing his hopes of escaping his fate. It seemed tonight destiny had her own games to play.

It was so dark he could barely see a foot in front of him, even with the powerful beam of the torch leading him further into the house. Tom stepped across the threshold and into the dark and dingy corridor despite the fact every fiber of his being was screaming at him to turn and flee

Tom entered a room and swung the torch beam around, illuminating random pieces of furniture. An armoire, an elegant coffee table, a massive fireplace. It was so bare, so old, like walking into a museum's display. For the first time since the idea of entering Rose House had come up, his fear subsided. Though creepy to imagine people had lived and died in this room so long ago, its silence and its emptiness were almost comforting. There were no photographs, no mementos, nothing to even suggest anybody had lived here, created a home here. It was bare of any emotion and any attachment. Evidently the house's valuables had been cleared out once the son had vanished.

Tom headed over to the massive armchair which sat in the corner and flopped down on it. A cloud of dust burst up around him and he coughed violently, feeling as though he'd inhaled sand as his throat scratched and tickled. Dots of light burst around him as coughs tore through his chest, pulling at it tightly. First the rosebush attack and now a coughing fit – part of him wondered whether this house was trying to kill him.

Finally, the coughing subsided and he was able to breathe somewhat normally once more, despite the burning in the back of his throat. He leant back into the chair, running his fingers over the worn upholstery, enjoying the feeling of the soft, dusty material against his fingertips, picking at small holes and pulling out strands of graying gold fabric, hypnotically focused on the way it twisted through his fingers.

It was as if he'd suddenly remembered he was all alone, in a dark and potentially haunted houses as shivers ran down his spine. The eerie silence, once comforting, now weighed heavily on him, suffocating him and the longer he sat in silence, the more his mind played tricks on him, conjuring up noises and movements that weren't there. He knew they weren't there. They were only in his head, a product of fear and the unknown, but it still didn't stop the rapid pounding of his heart, and the way his ears seemed to prick at every slight imagined sound.

He threw himself up out of the chair and decided exploring the house may be a better way to ease his nerves than sitting in the desolately quiet room waiting for fear to literally kill him.

Tom wandered from sitting room to study, exploring dusty, old books stacked high on bookcases and ink held in ink wells that had coagulated into black tar. Out of the study he found himself in the kitchen at the back of the house, where empty cupboards and a cracked, porcelain sink were all that greeted him. Though the kitchen was bare and uninteresting, it provided a very good view of the garden.

Tom turned from the window and kept exploring. He refused to go down into the basement. He reasoned with himself it wasn't because he was scared, but because the stairs were probably rickety and old and would crumble beneath his weight sending him spiraling down to a painful and lonely death. The fact that the rest of the house appeared to be in good condition did not factor into this musing. His decision was further aided by the quiet, menacing voice in the back of his mind choosing to incessantly whisper about the killer hiding in the basement, beneath the stairs, in the darkest corners waiting to attack.

Tom tentatively made his way upstairs instead, flashlight illuminating wooden railings eaten away by termites and woodlice. He made his way up onto the landing and walked along, glancing into rooms, the flashlight's beam swinging wildly around, picking up various objects of little or no interest.

The last bedroom he walked into was obviously the master bedroom from its size and the enormous bed in the corner of the room. Tom ran his hands along the bottom of the bed tentatively, not wanting to mar the white sheets, feeling soft silk beneath his fingertips, crinkling with dust and age. The bed had been made for the previous occupants but nobody had had the chance to sleep in it.

Tom shuddered and quickly stepped back away from the bed, goose bumps bursting across his skin as his thoughts raced. That the room stood perfectly made, waiting for the last occupant to come back as though he had never left, was unnerving. Tom looked up from the pristine sheet and found himself looking out of the window down into the enormous garden below. He wasn't sure how he knew it, but he knew this was the room from the story. This was where the son had slept until his disappearance.

It was well known that the story about Rose House was partially true. After all, legends often spring from dark moments in history.

It was one of the young town's darkest hours and had come to be immortalized as a horror story over the years though nobody truly knew who began it. A family had lived there and the mother had killed the father. The daughters had left but the son had remained until his disappearance a few years later. It was in all the town records though the fact that it was a true story was not often mentioned, as many preferred legend over truth. Truth marred a perfect historic record; legends simply added a factor of interest.

As the years progressed it had become less history and more urban myth. Despite the fact the son's body was never discovered nobody actually believed a mysterious creature had dragged him into her realm for all eternity. Rather, that he had committed suicide somewhere in the vast woods or surrounding moors. It wasn't uncommon for that to happen.

Glancing though the large, ornate glass panes, Tom realized he could see passed the gate to his friends who lingered beyond the property line. He fought with the window to open it, pulling on the handles until finally, after much heaving and straining, the window flew open, almost taking him with it.

"Hey!" he called, waving wildly at his friends standing below. They looked up, shocked to see him hanging so far out one of the windows.

"Tom! What are you doing?" Mariana called, eyes widening almost comically at the sight of Tom leaning out the window.

"Oh, you know, just hanging about, taking in the scenery," he said nonchalantly, grinning at his own terrible pun. "It's a pretty nice house, actually."

"Have you seen her yet?" Sebastian asked playfully. "Don't suppose you've looked into her eyes, or been seduced to join her dark army, have you?"

He continued to grin down at them, raising both thumbs as he spoke. "I am intact thank you very much! But my forearm's a bit cut up. I caught it on one of those bloody rose bushes and practically ripped it to shreds. Hurts like a bitch."

"Aww, I'll kiss it better when you come out." Sebastian puckered his lips, blowing dramatic kisses at Tom.

"No thanks, I might get some nasty disease off you," Tom replied, scrunching his nose up.

"Screw you."

"Seb, have you ever considered the reason why you're so sexually overt with Tom is because you harbor a deep seated desire for him?" Mariana cut in, loud enough for Tom to hear. The group around her burst into fits of laughter as Sebastian glared.

"Speaking from experience, Mari?" he retorted darkly, quiet enough so only she could hear. He took glee in the blush which spread across her cheeks.

"It's ok Seb, I don't judge you," Marianna continued, attempting to ignore his comment. She hated the way he always resorted to taunting her about her feelings, resented him for using them against her. "I accept you for who you are. Now you need to accept yourself."

"Yeah, go on Seb, you know you love me!" Tom grinned. "I wish I could share the sentiments. Don't get me wrong, I love you, just more like the brother I never wanted than a potential partner."

Sebastian turned to glare at Tom who could just about make out the daggers being fired in his direction. He curled his hands into a heart and winked at Sebastian who flipped him off in reply.

"Hey, how much longer till this hour's up?" Tom asked.

"It was up ten minutes ago," Oliver replied, still chuckling to himself.

17

Tom punched the air triumphantly. "Winner! Ok see you guys in a few."

He shut the window and turned back towards the door, glad to finally be leaving this house. He had just reached the doorway when movement out of the corner of his eye caught his attention. Turning slightly, Tom scanned the darkness, sending the torch beam into the corners of the room. Finding nothing, he shrugged, putting it down to a trick of the sparse light.

Turning forward, fear jolted through his body at the sight of a tall, pale person standing before him. Tom managed to scan her entire being within the space of a millisecond. Her skin was luminescent in the sparse moonlight spilling in through the window. His blood ran cold as his eyes wandered up over pale, pink lips and he looked into her eyes; her blood red, piercing eyes.

A shrill screech wrenched itself out of his mouth and he turned to run, forgetting he was in a room where the only exit was the door currently being blocked by the figure. Before he could flee backwards, the figure had darted around him, blocking his path. The speed and agility with which she moved was completely impossible. Tom's eyes were drawn to her crimson orbs which glowed even in the darkness. A smile graced those impossible lips.

Tom felt weak. His knees turned to jelly and his mind blanked. His eyes rolled back and the last thing he saw before he blacked out was her large, red eyes.

"Where the hell is he?" Oliver asked looking at the front door for the hundredth time that minute, hoping it would have swung open between glances. They had been waiting for Tom to come out for over twenty minutes now, and still no sign of him.

"Do you think something might have happened?" Mariana asked, looking anxiously at Oliver. He could see genuine fear radiating in her eyes. Mariana considered herself to be something of a mother figure, herding the misfit boys along, keeping them safe. In truth she was as incompetent as they were, spending more time tripping over her own feet than anything else. She genuinely cared about them though, and hence would worry herself sick at the very idea of them being hurt. And right now, Oliver could see just how nervous she was at the thought of Tom possibly being hurt.

"If something had happened, he would've let us know," Sebastian replied confidently. "A scream, a phone call, a cry for his mummy, something."

"Do you think he's just messing around with us?" Oliver implored, looking at Sebastian.

Sebastian rolled his eyes theatrically. "This is Tom we're talking about. He probably wants to make us sweat. I bet he's there, looking at us through a window somewhere, laughing his ass off. Then we'll go in to look for him, he'll jump out of the shadows, he'll scare us silly and make us look like the idiots, again. And if I'm forking out money, I'm keeping my dignity at the very least!"

"He has done it before…" Oliver mused.

"Of course he has. He always does this," Sebastian replied. "I say, we leave."

"What?"

"We leave," Sebastian said simply. "We just go, leave him in there. He can come out and find us when he's ready."

"Are you sure that's a good idea? I mean, what if something does actually happen and we're not around?" Mariana pressed. "It's not like something bad happening is impossible. He may have done this before but, I'd feel awful leaving and then finding out he was actually hurt"

"What's going to happen, the creature will come and get him?" Sebastian scoffed, rolling his eyes at her. "Come on, it's just a story. All that's in that house is dust and old furniture. The most he'll get attacked by is a hungry moth, or the biggest dust bunny known to man. Let's go, I need some food."

As if on cue, his stomach rumbled dramatically. Without waiting for anyone to say anything, he turned on his heel and walked away from Rose House. One by one, his friends followed, turning their backs on Rose House and Tom, until finally Mariana and Oliver were the only two to remain.

"Do you think Seb's right, he **is** just messing with us?" Mariana asked nervously.

"I don't know," Oliver replied. "He has done it before. And we've fallen for it before."

"But he could really be hurt."

Oliver nodded. "Yeah, he could. So what do you want to do? Go in there and search? Or wait here until he decides to come out?"

"I'm not going in there," she replied, without needing to think about the situation. "I can't do it, I'm sorry. I am scared and I'm not afraid to admit it."

"It's ok. I wouldn't go in that house." Oliver smiled at her gently. "Tom's fine, I'm sure he is. He's got his phone on him so if anything does happen he could call us."

"What if he-"

"Mari, stop." Oliver sighed. "Let's go home, I'll walk you. You can't wait here for him to buck up his ideas and come outside. And I've got a curfew to eventually make."

Mariana glanced back at the house, unease settling deep within. She didn't want to leave, knowing that if she did something was going to happen. Something had happened. Rationality couldn't explain how she knew this, though, and without rationality she couldn't begin to understand, and then make Oliver understand. She had no reason to fear anything. Sighing, Mariana turned away from the house and allowed Oliver to walk her home. Unknowingly, by turning away from their comatose friend, who was most certainly in danger, they were setting the wheels of fate in motion.

Chapter Two

Inside the house, Tom began to stir. His head hurt and he could barely see as he tentatively opened his eyes. The room was pitch black, but he knew it was not his own and his heart began to race, not remembering where he was. He blinked rapidly trying to bring his vision back into focus when an image swam before his eyes. Deep red eyes in a face of porcelain filled his vision and he sat bolt upright, heart pounding as he now remembered where he was. Dread coiled in the pit of his stomach, hissing and spitting like any angry snake as his eyes darted around. Relief hit as he realized it was completely empty save for the antique furniture he knew should be there.

Tom sighed and leant back against the soft, overstuffed corner of the mattress, breathing deep, trying to calm his racing heart as his mind soothingly whispered thoughts of dreams and his imagination getting the better of him. He didn't know how he had ended up on the bed, sure he hadn't been there before what he assumed was a fainting spell brought on by his lack of dinner had hit. Throwing his hand out to the side he searched for the flashlight, colliding with its smooth metal surface and flicking it on. A small circle of light now illuminated the wall opposite, chasing away darkness and fear.

Until he felt the bed dipping beside him.

He shot up, leaping halfway across the room before even turning to glance at why it had dipped. His heart hammered violently against his chest, beating an angry rhythm and his breath hitched in his throat. Thoughts raced furiously through his mind eagerly telling him it had been a sensory trick, his imagination once more playing cruel jokes on him. He refused to turn and look.

The hairs on the back of his neck seemed to stand on edge further as electrical waves of fear danced across his skin. Every nerve ending was on fire and he could hear the slightest of sounds as loudly as a gunshot, as his fight or flight instincts kicked in.

He bit back a scream as what felt like fingers trailed up his back, ghosting across his neck, ice cold in their touch but leaving burning fire in their midst. Unable to move, he glanced down as fingers slowly danced across his shoulder and down his arm. Into view long, thin, skeletal fingers appeared, barely touching his exposed forearm but feeling as though they were tearing at his skin.

He closed his eyes, praying it was a trick of the light, an overactive imagination, anything but reality. As much as he wanted to, Tom found himself unable to move, rooted to the spot, trapped in his own body as fear quelled inside him. Adrenaline pumped through his body and all he could hear was the beating of his own heart as his mind screamed at him to run.

He turned his head to the side as best he could, body quivering as his mind desperately tried to rationalize everything that was happening. As he turned, Tom found himself staring into the same blood red eyes he had seen just moments before his collapse. They glowed ethereal.

She, for he could see that it was female, glared burning fire into his soul, face inches away from his own. Her hot, sickly breath ghosted across his cheeks, causing strands of hair to whip about and the smell of death and decay to overwhelm him.

He was afraid to blink, convinced that in the split second it took for his eyelids to open again she would come closer, would hurt him. He fought off the instinct for as long as he could until tears pooled at the corners of his eyes and blurred his vision. No longer able to fight off the impulse his eyes drifted shut and snapped open barely a millisecond later.

She sat upon the bed watching him, eyes trained upon the way he moved. Bolt upright, her hair fell loosely around her shoulders, partially covering her face though unable to mask her gleaming eyes, pools of blood in which he felt as though he were drowning.

"W-Who are you?" he finally managed to ask, the words forcing themselves out from between his lips. Realizing how dry they were, his tongue darted out to lap at the chapped skin, tasting blood, having worried his lip to ribbons.

A grimace formed upon her red lips, almost half a smile. There was no warmth in it; instead Tom felt ice quelling inside, turning his blood cold. He never thought he'd be warm again

"Who are you?" he asked again, louder this time, feeling as though he was gaining some momentum.

She opened her mouth as if to respond, giving Tom a glimpse of razor sharp, elongated teeth. Her tongue darted out instead, running across those teeth as if to test their sharpness and strength. A low growl formed in the base of her throat and the only response Tom found himself able to conjure was a short burst of laughter, more of a bark than anything, born of fear.

Hissing spilled forth from her mouth and he shuddered at the sound. His skin began to crawl and he desperately wanted it to stop, unable to understand what she was doing.

"Stop!" he finally cried out, putting his hands over his ears in an attempt to block out the sound. She was silenced immediately. Almost against his will, he lowered his hands back to his sides.

"You should leave," she hissed, words forcing their way out of her mouth. Her voice was raspy, seeming to echo around the room coming from everywhere and nowhere at once. He couldn't even be sure she had said anything, her lips barely moving to form the words.

"Who are you?" he asked once more

"You will come to understand," she continued. A thousands voices echoed the words like a hall of mirrors producing a thousand reflections, reverberating off the walls and filling the room with the sound.

"Tell me now."

"No," she replied. That was enough to halt any question half formed and half forgotten. "You know who I am. You shall see all. Soon."

She stood up off the bed and slinked across the floor towards him, moving with catlike grace, seeming to barely touch the ground as she walked. "Go," she whispered into his ear, breath burning like fire across his neck and down his back. The echo had vanished from her voice and now all he could hear was menace. As if his body was acting freely from his command, he slipped out of the room, barely registering the movements he was making. Flashlight forgotten, he made his way blindly down the stairs, aware of the fact she was following close behind despite the lack of noise the wooden floorboards made under her weight.

Tom glimpsed behind him, catching sight of her a few meters away, eyes trained upon him, boring into the back of his head. As he stepped outside he fully expected her to follow, but the instant relief he felt as the cool night air wrapped itself around him revealed she hadn't followed. Turning around, she was nowhere to be seen.

He shivered as the cold hit him, numbing his exposed cheeks. Out of the maze of roses just before the iron gates he turned to look at the house, searching for and dreading seeing her again. A shape seemed to exist in the darkness, adding another dimension which he could hardly see but knew was there. Tom slipped through the partially open gate and walked down the empty street, half in a daze. Though no longer feeling her there, part of him knew she was still watching, her eyes trained upon him, even as the house disappeared from view.

Chapter Three

When Tom awoke next, he was in his own bed, wrapped up in his own duvet, looking up at his own ceiling, completely alone. Sitting up carefully, not wanting to shatter his precarious grasp on his own life, he glanced around taking in the familiar, blue walls. Clothes were scattered across the room, expertly thrown signifying their need to be washed and books were piled across a large desk in the centre of which rested a partially open, grubby, black laptop.

He looked around nervously, searching for large red eyes and porcelain skin sure he would find the demented creature from what he hoped was a dream hiding somewhere. When he didn't find those eyes, he let out a sigh of relief and hopped out of bed, feeling considerably lighter. Without physical evidence of the strange girl, Tom could easily pretend he had dreamt the whole thing, despite the fact he could still partially feel his skin tingling and burning where her fingers had been.

No matter, Tom considered it a vivid dream and nothing more. He had entered Rose House, that much was clear, but the horrifying girl was nothing more than a nightmare. It was over now.

Getting ready that morning was a bit of a chore for Tom, however. Pretending last night hadn't happened and actually believing it were two different things. Every shadow he saw flitting across his room caused his breath to hitch and every noise he heard no matter how slight made him jump. He expected to see the girl every time he turned around and his heart was continually in his throat. As the morning wore on, he began to calm down, pushing all thoughts of the strange girl in Rose House out of his mind. By the time he arrived at school, after a hearty breakfast consisting of half a slice of toast gulped down between rapid glances around him, he was back to his cool, confident self and his dream had been forgotten.

Walking through the gates and into the crowded

common room where half the college sheltered from the rain, Tom glanced around, searching for his friends.

Sebastian was sat on a table in the corner, a smattering of people surrounding him, roaring with laugher at something he'd said. Oliver sat beside him briefly scanning a book, not really reading but attempting to absorb something while Mariana was nowhere to be seen, probably running late.

"Tom, you are alive!" Sebastian called out, his loud voice booming across the room to where Tom stood. Students turned to look at Sebastian, some wincing as his voice burst through their sleep addled minds, others, particularly those who had heard about the bet, grinning wildly. Though their town wasn't that small, good gossip spread rapidly, as it is wont to do, and most had heard about the Rose House bet.

"Alive and kicking, Sebastian," he replied, striding over towards his friends, smiling at random students as he passed. "Touch and go, for a while there, but I survived, just like I told you I would, so...pay up!"

"What are you talking about?" a girl Tom had seen hanging around before asked, looking up at him with pretty blue eyes and a questioning smile.

His tongue darted out between his lips and he smiled coyly at her, instantly slipping into flirt mode. "Didn't you hear? I spent time in Rose House."

Her eyes widened to the size of dinner plates and Tom was sure that, at any moment, they may just pop right out of their sockets. "You spent time in Rose house?" she asked, voice full of awe and incredulity.

"You know it," he replied, winking at her. "I spent a good hour in that house, all alone, just wandering the empty halls."

"Weren't you afraid?!" she asked.

"Of course not. What's going to hurt me in that old,

empty place?" he asked, raising an eyebrow.

"What about…the thing?" she said, eyes darting from left to right conspiratorially. "If you look into her eyes, well, you know. Going into that house is like…suicide!"

"Nothing in this world frightens me," he replied with a cheeky grin. He bit his lip flirtatiously as the girl in front of him seemed to melt on the spot.

"Come on Romeo, it's time for class," Sebastian said, grabbing Tom by the arm and dragging him away from the girl who's cheeks were flushing scarlet. Tom was exceptionally good at flirting with girls but terrible at even attempting more.

"Spoil my fun, why don't you," Tom said, glancing back over his shoulder at the blushing girl giggling with her friends.

"What happened in Rose House, yesterday?" Oliver asked as they walked to class, eyes trained upon the ground.

"What do you mean?" Tom said. "Nothing happened, took a walk around, looked at a few things; nothing spectacular really."

"Why did it take you so long to come out, then?" Oliver replied. "Mariana was really worried about you."

"Not enough to hang around and wait though," Sebastian cut in. "We left."

"I noticed, thanks a lot guys," Tom replied, rolling his eyes. In truth, he hadn't actually noticed they'd left. He couldn't quite remember leaving Rose House at all, a rather worrying. "I don't know. It's weird; time seems to pass so differently in that house."

Oliver scoffed. "What, are you going to tell us it was like a time warp?"

"Hey, it **is** just a jump to the left!" Tom replied, smirking. Oliver punched his right arm, hard, at his stupid retort. "No, it wasn't a time warp, more like you don't really notice time passing. There are no clocks, it's really dark and all the windows are grimy so you can't see much out of them and before you know it, an hour has passed and it feels like a few minutes. It's like you're stuck in time."

"How very poetic of you, Thomas," Oliver remarked dryly.

"Freaky," Sebastian said, shivering dramatically.

"Eh, it's not so bad. If only some other things could be more like that, the world would be a better place!" Tom replied.

Tom flung his locker open, and dug around inside for his books. The general disarray of the metal box was such that actually looking inside wasn't worth the effort. It was easier to simply feel around for his textbooks. Tuesday was always a fantastic day for him, he had a free period and he finished early; nothing could be better than that. As he reached for what felt like his Organic Chemistry textbook pain flared through his fingertips and he pulled his hand back; he'd brushed against something sharp hidden within his locker. A small bead of blood was forming on the tip of his finger.

Unaware of anything other than textbooks hiding in his locker, Tom squinted into the darkness, searching for the deadly culprit. His heart stopped as his eyes landed upon a vibrant, red rose.

"Did you guys do this?" he asked angrily, gesturing wildly at the rose resting against his textbooks.

"What are you talking about?" came Oliver's muffled reply, still buried deep in his own locker.

"Aww look, Tom got a rose!" Sebastian cooed as his eyes landed upon the flower. "Who's it from, lover boy?"

Nerves bubbled up inside him and he bit his lip. "You're telling me neither of you did this?"

"No, of course not," Sebastian continued. "It would've been a pretty good prank though. Any idea who it's from?"

Tom's voice caught in his throat. "I-I don't know."

"Someone has a secret admirer," Sebastian said. He grabbed the rose out of Tom's locker, careful not to skewer himself on one of the many thorns along the stem. Tom's heart leaped into his throat and he all but bit his tongue to prevent himself screaming at Sebastian to drop the damn thing. "There's no note on it. That's no good!"

"That's the point of a secret admirer...by definition, you don't know who they are," Oliver commented dryly, rolling his eyes. "How did it get in your locker? Did you give someone the combination?"

Tom shook his head in response. His locker, like every other locker in the school did have small slits in it at the top but these were much too small to slide anything other than pieces of paper through. There was no way a rose could be shoved through and much less so for it to appear inside his locked in perfect condition, resting against his books gently. It had to have been placed there purposely, there was no other explanation. It's placement among his books, right in the centre of the shelf directly in front of the book he need first period was a sure indicator of this. "S-someone must have figured it out. I'll need to go and get it changed."

"Yeah," Sebastian said. He looked at Tom skeptically, noticing the way his voice hitched as he spoke. "Something wrong, Tom?"

"No. Everything's fine," Tom replied, biting his tongue, trying to sound calm despite the fact he felt so far from calm it was almost impossible to ever remember what calm had felt like. "We better get to class."

"Yeah, let's go," Oliver said, turning to leave.

"Don't forget your rose," Sebastian mocked, handing the red flower to Tom. Cautiously, Tom took it from Sebastian's grasp, expecting something terrible to happen the moment his fingers wrapped around the long stem. Nothing did.

Tom's wary behaviour didn't go amiss. "You sure you're

30

feeling ok?" Oliver asked.

"What?" Tom snapped. His temper was flaring. "Why do you keep asking?"

"You're acting really weird," Sebastian said, none too gently. "I mean, come on, it's a rose not a bomb, grab it like a man and let's get to class already!"

Tom gaped at Sebastian. There was no way he could explain his wariness to his friends, he could barely explain it to himself. He grasped at excuses. "I-It's covered in thorns! I don't want to cut my hand to shreds on a dumb rose."

"You know, somebody probably went to a lot of trouble to sneak that into your locker," Oliver replied tartly. "It's not as simple as magically opening it and putting it in. You should be nice about these things; your admirer might be a bit on the insane side."

Tom rolled his eyes at his friend and, ignoring his inward revulsion, grasped the rose properly, mocking the request. It wasn't as though they knew he was beginning to wonder, deep inside his mind, whether it had been placed there using some kind of strange magic. "Happy now?"

Oliver stuck his tongue out at Tom before all three resumed their march towards first class. With the other two barely noticing him as they immersed themselves deep into conversation, he allowed his front to slip and fear clouded his mind once more. The rose seemed to shimmer in the light, as though it were glowing with vibrancy. There was no way this could be a simple coincidence after his trip into Rose House the night before. As crazy as it sounded, he also knew this particular rose was from the garden surrounding Rose House. It was impossible to prove visually of course, all roses looked the same to him, but he just knew this one was from that garden. Tearing his eyes away from the damned thing, he glanced up to see they had reached their first class of the day.

Before entering class, Tom dropped the rose into the large, black garbage bin by the door.

Shutting the door behind him, he shut the rose out of his mind and focused his attention entirely upon their current topic, Alcohols and Ethers.

Chapter Four

That morning seemed to drag by. Time ticked like sand through an hourglass and every minute lasted hours. By the time Chemistry ended, Tom felt as though the entire day should've ended, when in fact he had more lessons to endure before he could even stop for lunch, let alone head home. He had started the day rather pleased with the fact it was Tuesday and now, he hated that it was this awful day.

After Chemistry came Mathematics, one of his worst subjects and one he knew he would probably do horribly in and yet somehow needed to pass to get to University. No matter how hard he tried his mind could not wrap itself around the infinite amount of numbers, letters and strange symbols squiggling across his text book. He often spent most of his Maths lessons with his head placed upon the desk, putting his text book to much better use, as a pillow. Though he sat in between both Oliver and Sebastian, during Maths, neither was exactly talkative. Oliver himself was never very talkative during lessons, preferring to concentrate and hang upon the teacher's every word. Sebastian concentrated so hard during Maths for a number of reasons, not least his own struggles with the subject.

Tom had barely been in class for more than 5 minutes when his mind decided it had had enough for one day, and shut down, refusing to even concentrate on the equations upon the board, let alone attempt to puzzle them out. Resistance was futile and Tom soon followed his mind, giving up entirely and placing his head upon his desk, doodling on his open text book to keep his hand busy.

It appeared though that his mind did want to think, it just wanted to focus on other things. Algebra vanished from his mind's eye only to be replaced with visions of the scarlet rose and those deep red eyes. Though he had managed to convince himself the girl was nothing more than a dream, the moment he had seen the rose all thoughts of it being a dream had vanished. Fear gripped his heart like ice causing his entire façade to freeze and crack and he knew it hadn't been just a dream. Confusion only enhanced his fear, as he could honestly think of no logical explanation as to who she was or why she had been there and the more he thought about her the more confused he became.

He desperately needed to think about something other than the rose and that awful girl. He sat up, eyes roaming around the room, trying to find something visually stimulating to keep his mind occupied. His classmates were dull, and the room was dull, and nothing could keep his attention for more than a few fleeting moments. As his eyes roamed they swept over his best friends, one buried deep in a textbook, the other scribbling frantically across pieces of paper. The rhythmically scratching and swirling of the pen was hypnotic and Tom found himself drifting into a sort of calm as he watched blue inked words form on slightly crumpled paper.

Suddenly, both Sebastian and Oliver rose to their feet and, with a start, Tom realised the lesson was over. His slight hypnosis had caused the lesson to slip by without a single thought of the girl and the rose, or so he thought.

As he hurriedly gathered his books, he glanced down briefly at his open text book and his heart skipped a beat. Though his mind hadn't consciously focused upon the girl and her roses, subconsciously it must have done for all along the page he had drawn detailed roses. In the centre of the page covering half of the formulae written down leaving it mostly illegible, he'd drawn a pair of piercing eyes, dark and penetrating. They were the eyes which had haunted him last night.

He threw his books roughly into his bag, not wanting to see those eyes any longer. Tom ran out of the classroom tailing Oliver and Sebastian to their next lecture.

Unable to concentrate from that moment he spent the rest of the morning jittering uncomfortably, trying to keep both his hands and his mind occupied. The morning ended after what seemed like a hundred years and he hurriedly left, glad it was finally time for his only free period of the day.

Making his way outside, he searched the grounds for the one person he knew would be out here, Mariana. Oliver and Sebastian both had classes during this period so it was the only time Mariana and Tom were truly alone.

Mariana and Tom had grown up together, their parents having been close friends 'back in the day'. They'd been each other's first friend, and, for a long time, each other's only friend. Their parents would fondly recount their mischievous childhood years, often getting into trouble, which Mariana blamed Tom entirely for.

Mariana was never hard to find during their free period considering she was always perched under the same tree she favoured, always heading outside unless it was too wet and cold, then she'd spend time in the library. With her back against the trunk of the tree she held a book in her hands, nose buried deep within it. Though from here he couldn't see clearly he knew she had her tiny headphones jammed into her ears, blasting music loud enough to burst her ear drums.

The anxiety bubbling away in the pit of his stomach slowly intensified as he made his way across the grounds. Though he'd never admit it, being alone with Mariana always sent shockwaves racing through him. Plopping down beside her, she didn't look up barely even noticing he had sat down, her absorption within the pages so great. Finally tired of being ignored, he tugged one of the earphones out of her ears and jammed it into his own.

He winced and ripped it out after a few seconds of listening to the impossibly loud music. "How can you listen to this?"

"What?" she said defensively.

"Aren't you worried about going deaf?" Tom replied. "You can hear it just fine on a lower volume, you know."

Mariana scowled. "Hey, if I choose to deafen myself, that's my business. Besides, it means the outside world never bothers me."

"Fine, suit yourself," Tom grinned. "But I will not be

learning sign language for you when you can no longer hear the sounds of my beautiful voice."

She smirked. "Thomas, the day I no longer hear your voice, it will be a blessing!"

"You'd miss me too much," Tom replied petulantly. The banter continued for a few moments, as they took jibs at each other until both drifted into silence. Pulling a slightly crushed packet of menthols out of his pocket, he lit up a cigarette and breathed in deep, enjoying the way the smoke filled his lungs. Though there weren't supposed to smoke on school grounds he was far enough away from most authority figures to not be caught.

"You feeling alright today, Tom?" Mariana asked, breaking the silence, her voice full of concern.

The question caught him by surprise and his breath hitched, coughing as he inhaled the smoke wrong. "W-what? Why does everybody k-keep asking me that?"

"You've been silent for an incredibly long time. Too long for you. So, what's up?" Mariana replied matter of factly, once his coughing had subsided.

"It's nothing, Mari, just a bit distracted," Tom replied with a raspy sigh.

"Want to talk about it?" she asked, folding the corner of the page down and closing her book as she spoke. "I don't mind listening to your incessant ramblings."

He hesitated, weighing the idea of confiding in Mariana in his mind. "You'll just think I'm insane," he replied, stubbing the cigarette butt into the ground and hurriedly lighting another. "I'm starting to think I'm actually insane."

"If it's any consolation, you are insane," she conceded with a smile, grabbing the newly lit cigarette from between his fingers and taking a long puff. "But, aren't we all? Surely that's why we're friends, above all else? We're all a little mad."

Tom grinned, glad for the distraction Mariana could

offer his thoughts. He leaned against her shoulder and she stroked his hair gently, comforting him in a motherly manner, giving him the time he needed to word whatever was on his mind, if he even would tell her what was wrong. They passed the cigarette back and forth between them - Mariana was still adamant she wasn't a smoker so she never just took the entire thing herself or bought her own. Her cold cheek rested against his forehead and he knew her skin would be flushed the most delicate shade of pink from the frozen air and nicotine rush.

"I've been feeling weird all morning," he finally said, finding it hard to word his thoughts.

"Weird, how?" Mariana questioned once Tom had fallen silent and refused to continue, her voice was raspy from the nicotine and it sent slight shivers down Tom's spine; he'd always felt like it added something…interesting…to her voice. "Sick, or something else?"

"No, not sick, just weird," he said. "Somebody figured out my locker combination and left a rose in it this morning and, well, ever since, I've felt as though I'm being watched."

"Oh," Mariana replied, not quite sure what else to say. "Well, have you noticed anybody actually watching you?"

"Not more so than usual," he whispered. "It's been the usual number of stares and glances; a grand total of none. This is different though. I feel as though wha-uh, whoever is watching me can see right through me, can read my mind or something."

"You feel an invasion of privacy," Mariana murmured.

Tom nodded. "Yeah, but more than that."

"Tom, it's only natural to feel like that," she said, voice low and soothing. "Somebody broke into your locker, something which, ok may belong to the school but is essentially your private property, at least for the school year. It's a complete violation, despite the sweet and, rather creepy, gesture made. I'm sure the 'watched' feeling is because of this. Nobody is watching you."

Tom knew she was wrong; everything she said contradicted how he was actually feeling. It was more than being watched. It felt as though eyes burned straight through him wherever he went and he was completely unable to hide from the piercing gaze trained upon him despite being unable to see them. He was slowly driving himself insane. Instead of contradicting Mariana however, he allowed her to prattle on about his feelings being completely normal without needing to say anything more himself. By the time she had exhausted her arsenal of comforting words, their free period was over and the best part of the school day loomed…lunch.

Mariana and Tom made their way into the cafeteria ready to grab some lunch and wait for the rest of their group at a table somewhere. Being the first few students to enter the cafeteria certainly had its perks and the two easily slid into a short line, able to grab their pick of the food selection before students descended like locusts and touched everything.

Grabbing their snacks, they headed to an empty table and ate in silence, Tom still lost in thought. Mariana watched him intently, wanting to say something but unsure what exactly she could say to comfort him that she hadn't said already. She placed a hand on his and squeezed gently, reminding him she was there. Tom looked up and locked eyes with her. Staring into familiar, emerald eyes, he felt a wave of calm descend over him. Though she could be sarcastic at times, she was his biggest comfort; not that he'd admit it to her. She smiled gently and he watched the way her eyes seemed to brighten with that simple smile, her cheeks turning a deeper shade of pink. He couldn't help but smile back and he allowed himself to stop thinking entirely, becoming absorbed with looking at her. His hand flushed warm where her fingers rested upon his and goose bumps erupted across his skin.

It wasn't long before Sebastian, Oliver and a handful of others joined their table, breaking the calm Mariana had helped create. Chatter broke out around them and Tom slipped back into his musings, discretely withdrawing his

38

hand from hers. Shivers ran down his spine and his arms dimpled with thousands of tiny goose bumps despite the relative warmth of the cafeteria the longer he sat in silence and the more his mind raced.

He picked apart a bread roll as his eyes scanned the room, constantly on edge, expecting to find brilliant red eyes staring right back at him from some hidden place. The calm that had washed over him when he and Mariana had been alone seemed to vanish almost immediately once other people began to join them – as though a spell had been broken.

"Hello, Earth to Tom!" Sebastian called, waving a hand in front of his friend's eyes. Tom jumped as the massive hand cut off his line of vision. "Did you even hear a word I said?"

"What? Oh...uh, yeah," Tom replied distractedly

"Liar," Sebastian scoffed. "Go on then, tell me what I said.

"You admitted your undying love for Oliver," he said with a shrug, a cocky glint in his eyes, trying to hide his distraction once again. Hiding behind sarcasm was easier than admitting just how distracted he was. Talking to Mariana in an empty field was one thing, discussing his fears with Oliver and Sebastian surrounded by people he barely knew was akin to social suicide. "I always knew something was up between you two. Should've made a bet on it to be honest, I could've gotten some more money out of some unsuspecting sap like you."

"Not even close to being funny," Sebastian deadpanned. "No offence, Olli, but you're not exactly my type or anything."

"Likewise," Oliver replied, barely looking up from the coursework he was putting the finishing touches to, as he did every lunch period. "Sorry Seb, you're handsome and all, but not the kind of guy I normally go for."

"Hey, I could give any of your potential suitors a run for

his money." Sebastian winked at Oliver and raised his eyebrows suggestively. A slight blush graced Oliver's cheeks and he lowered his head even further. The movement didn't go amiss, and Tom grinned to himself. "Back to the point at hand, where's your head today, Tom?"

"On my shoulders," Tom retorted dryly. "Yours?"

"Oh haha," Sebastian replied, feigning amusement though his eyes remained cold. "Seriously, you've been spaced out all morning, what's up?"

"Nothing at a-" Tom began, but before he could finish, Mariana cut in.

"He's been feeling weird," she said. "He reckons he's being watched. I told him it's nothing but his mind playing tricks on him. But I guess nobody listens to me."

Tom groaned. "Oh come on Mari, I listened to you! I spent an hour listening to you tell me that, and I know you're probably right," he conceded, biting back his anger, willing to tell her what she wanted to hear to keep the peace at the very least. "I just can't shake that feeling, alright! It's nothing, I know that but I can't help it."

Mariana huffed in response, focusing upon her iPod instead, pressing the 'next' button so violently Tom was sure she'd press right through the screen at any moment. He couldn't understand the sudden anger that burst forth out of her. Moments before she'd been tenderly keeping him calm.

Ignoring Mariana's odd behaviour, Sebastian turned to Tom. "It's probably your secret admirer you know, the one who left you the rose. Looks like you've got yourself a bit of a stalker!"

"Just what I need," Tom sighed in response. If his current performance was anything to go by, Tom was sure he could add acting to his list of creative talents; the way he was hiding his fear which simmered so close to overflowing he was sure at any moment it would explode out of him, truly astounded even himself.

"You never know, she might be hot. It all works out for you in the end, if she is," he said, trying to look on the bright side of things.

"Or it could be that greasy girl with the lazy eye who sits behind me in English and picks her nose." All three grimaced at the thought of that unfortunate girl whom nature, it seemed, deemed it fit to make the butt of so many jokes. "I'm definitely not hungry now!" Tom exclaimed, pushing his uneaten lunch away.

Chuckling quietly to himself Sebastian returned to his sandwich. "Tom, I think your rose is losing petals," he said around a mouthful of mushy bread.

"What?" Tom asked, looking at Sebastian in fear. The rose had been on his mind for quite some time now but not because he still had it; he knew he'd thrown it away. He couldn't bear to actually keep the damn thing which he was sure would be cursed in some horrible way. "I-I don't have it anymore. How do you know it's losing petals?"

Sebastian picked up something red and shimmering from Tom's forgotten tray, holding it up by thumb and forefinger for Tom to glean a better look. "There's a rose petal on here."

Tom's heart stopped as he looked at the petal, unmistakably from the rose he'd thrown away earlier. He wasn't sure how he knew the petal belonged to that rose but then he wasn't sure how he'd known that rose came from Rose House's garden, he just knew. It was impossible though, that much he also knew to be true; he'd thrown it away. Yet here was a part of it sitting before him. He wondered whether it was possible for his secret admirer to have seen him throw away the rose only to fish it out of the bin and taunt him with a pristine petal. The thought was most disturbing as the petal hadn't been on his tray when he'd picked it up, nor had it been there while he was eating; he wouldn't have missed it if it had. It was impossible for a person to place it on his tray, even if they'd walked by and tossed it across –he would have noticed that - which only

41

seemed to enhance the idea that the only person who could be behind this was the one person Tom's mind tried so hard to deny existed. And it also meant she was here, now, somewhere.

"Tom, are you ok?" Oliver asked worriedly; Tom had gone as white as a ghost and his breathing was laboured. "Tom?"

"I-I don't feel so good," he said, standing up quickly and taking a few shaky steps back. "I'm going to the bathroom."

Before either of them could get up to follow, he had scampered out of the cafeteria, much to the confusion of a number of students watching Tom's harried escape. Practically running down the hallway, dodging to avoid the few students walking aimlessly, he threw himself into the bathroom. Dashing into a stall, he bolted the door and sat heavily upon the plastic toilet seat, feeling his head spin as thoughts rushed towards him. His breath caught in his throat and he felt himself panicking, his throat constricting and preventing him breathing. He began to feel light headed, his vision swimming before his eyes as the sound of static completely blocked out the outside world. He dropped his head into his hands and willed himself to calm down, sucking in large gulps of air in a desperate attempt to relax.

"Am I going crazy?" he asked out loud. "I threw that damn thing away, I know I did!"

He shook his head, eyes still closed, trying to dislodge the image of that perfect rose shimmering translucently before him, taunting him, if that were possible. As the image faded, another popped into his mind taking the rose's place; a garden full of blooming, brilliant red roses, a garden he was looking down upon. Red eyes, the same colour as the roses, looked deep into his, burning straight through him.

His eyes snapped open, heart beating erratically once more, so violently shoving itself against his ribcage he was sure it would burst out. The moment he opened his eyes he instantly regretted it, for actually staring back at him were those red eyes, penetrating straight into his mind. A sharp intake of breath brought more than those red eyes into focus; a slanting nose, high cheekbones, stained crimson lips behind which gleaming, sharp teeth hid.

Unable to speak, unable to move, Tom remained powerless as she slinked closer towards him, completely invading any semblance of personal space he may have held. Her face so close to his her features blurred. Unsure of what she would do, he was frozen, unable to feel anything more than the electricity crackling through the air as she moved. Her tongue darted out and she ran it across his lips, causing Tom to shiver in fear and revulsion.

It was only one sweeping, fleeting movement but it seemed to last forever. Her tongue, running against his bottom lip, burning, searing into his memory, causing his stomach to jolt unpleasantly with unspeakable, unthinkable emotions. Tom, still frozen in place, could do no more than stare vacantly at the spot where she had stood, barely aware of the air suddenly rushing around him.

She growled at him and he looked up, watching her crimson eyes as she glided backwards out of the stall towards the sinks.

As much as he wanted to remain in the stall, or perhaps even shimmy through what constituted for a window, his body refused to comply. Instead, Tom followed her as if in a trance, eyes locked with hers.

"Do you understand yet?" she asked, voice as repellant and heavy as he remembered it. He knew rather than felt goose bumps erupting across his bare forearms.

"I don't understand anything, just that you must be crazy," Tom said, though he could barely form the words, his mind unable to formulate even the simplest of thoughts with his tongue too heavy to spit them out. "This is all crazy."

She hissed at him, a frighteningly cat like response causing the hairs on the back of his neck to stand on end.

"What do you want from me?" Tom asked nervously.

"You," she replied simply, her voice clear and void of the echoy, gasping, raspy quality it had once possessed. The simplistic response seemed to unnerve Tom more than anything else.

"What? Why?" Tom countered after a few moments, having been shocked into silence.

She smiled forebodingly. "Such curiosity. Such stupidity."

She stretched out a hand towards him, allowing her fingers to caress through his soft, tousled hair, before grabbing a few strands and pulling hard. He gasped in pain and suddenly found himself completely alone in the bathroom, staring at nothing, rubbing the spot on his scalp where she had violently yanked a moment before.

Before Tom could do anything, the bathroom door swung open and Sebastian and Oliver cautiously entered the room.

"Hey, Tom, you-" Sebastian stopped as his eyes landed upon Tom, stood in the centre of the room, rubbing his head, face flushed and eyes wide. "What are you doing?"

Snapping out of his daze, Tom shook his head briefly. "Um...nothing...just...daydreaming, I guess."

They both watched him, skepticism and disbelief clearly obvious through the way they stared, Oliver raising an eyebrow – his trademark expression. "Honestly," Tom countered, hating the way they seemed completely able to read through any terrible lie he could produce. "Just got distracted with my own thoughts."

"Because that's not strange," Sebastian retorted.

"Yeah well this entire morning's been a little strange," Tom snapped. He felt a migraine beginning to form just above his right eye and he pressed two fingers against the spot, attempting to massage the pain away. Or perhaps burst through his skull and deaden it completely – either would be better than the searing pain he was rapidly overcome with. As the pain built, he closed his eyes against the bright light and bent over. Even with his eyes closed, blindingly white light seemed to fracture through his clenched eyelids and bore into his skull. He felt movement beside him and despite the rising panic, he knew it was Oliver. Comforting, warm, safe Oliver.

"Tom, you ok?" he asked gently, not knowing exactly why Tom had gone from staring into space to suddenly bent over double, clutching his forehead.

"I'm fine," he said through gritted teeth, the pain building. "Just a headache"

"I think you should go home," Oliver continued. "Let's take you to the nurse. She can sign you off, especially if it's this bad."

"No, I'm fine, seriously," Tom replied, though he could barely keep the pain from clouding his voice.

Oliver grasped his arm. "Tough, you're going home, no complaints." Sebastian grabbed his other arm and they helped him stand, almost dragging him out of the room.

"You really do like that rose, don't you?" Sebastian mused, looking passed Tom to where sinks lined the wall, upon which a brilliantly shimmering, scarlet rose sat.

Chapter Five

Having frog marched Tom out of the bathroom and into the nurse's office, the two sat beside him like iron guards until she was ready to see him. Though Tom was adamant he was fine, the fact that he was unable to even look at her without wincing in pain had the nurse agreeing with Oliver and Sebastian and Tom was sent home.

The moment he walked out of the school building and into the quiet, comforting solitude of a Tuesday afternoon in a small town his headache rapidly diminished and he found himself glad of the few hours alone.

Instead of returning home however, he headed in the opposite direction, wanting to walk rather than sit enclosed within the confines of his room and his own musings. He made his way over to a large park which, at this time of the day, would be completely empty. The idea of this open space was already helping to completely calm his mind and he eagerly picked up the pace, wanting to finally find peace in what felt like a continually chaotic day. He always found himself coming here in times of great turmoil. When his father fell ill, this had been the place he instinctively ran to, to escape the crying and the pain at home, to escape watching his father waste away. And when he finally passed, this is where Tom had come to cry and take out his anger on himself.

Perching on one of the free swings - a rarity in this park where children actually queued to use them - Tom gently swayed back and forth, enjoying the mind numbing, repetitive motion. Staring out across the park and beyond at rolling hills and lush, wild greenery, he seemed to hypnotize himself with the swinging motion. His mind fell blank and visions of red eyes faded away into nothingness.

While he swung, the sky darkened; heavy, pendulous clouds rolled in, blocking out the sun and bringing on an early sense of twilight. Fat droplets of rain began to fall, splattering the ground and bringing Tom back to his senses with a start. Time had passed by rapidly as he sat there, mind delving into nothingness and he realized the streetlights had flickered to life. His bag sat, mercifully, albeit soggily by his feet; it was obvious he had dozed off during that time and anybody could've walked over and taken his precious bag without so much as a batted eyelid from him.

Cigarette butts lined the floor around him and he kicked them to the side hastily, burying them under the grass and wood shavings, just in case. He'd seen kids pick up the strangest of things and put it in their mouth so leaving glorified death sticks hanging about probably wasn't the most responsible of decisions.

He slung his bag up onto his shoulder and slowly walked out of the park, letting the rain wash down upon him, slicking his hair against his cheeks and forehead. Winter was truly here he came to realize as rain lashed his skin and the wind whipped around him, tugging the scarf lightly slung around his neck into a noose like grasp. Though it was cold, in a way it was also refreshing, pleasant. The drop in temperature seemed to wash a thousand fears away and wipe the slate clean, bringing his thoughts back to him, fresh, clear, sharp. He would not let this sense of clarity cloud his thoughts completely though; the last time he had done that she had appeared to him, taken him off guard and played tricks with his mind.

Not that he believed her to be some form of supernatural creature. Though…some things that had happened in the last twenty-four hours were enough to make him irrationally question this, such as her odd coloured eyes. Of course this could be explained in a completely logical way; her eyes were not red – unless she happened to have a very rare condition. No, the redness was simply produced by coloured contact lenses which could be bought at any fancy dress shop along the high street.

In fact, every single strange thing that had occurred directly relating to her was explainable. He knew she was human, possibly insane but human nonetheless. That she had only been in his life for less than twenty four hours was disconcerting to Tom; it felt as though so much more time had elapsed between then and now. Time seemed to be joining her in this weird attempt to drive him to the brink of insanity.

Thunder clapped and the rain fell harder. Picking up speed, Tom began to jog home, now wanting to get out of the frigid cold and into the warmth. Though it had initially been comforting a chill was beginning to nestle itself deep inside of him, forming a little nest of frost and ice where he'd never be warm again. He turned a corner and suddenly realised exactly where he was.

Having walked this way home a thousand times before he had allowed his feet to guide him, not paying attention to where he was walking, focusing upon his crazed thoughts and their sane outcomes instead. And guide him they had. Looking up, he found himself gazing upon Rose House, its brilliant garden shimmering even in the twilight gloom. Each rose stood out stark against the overcast sky. Looming menacingly behind the brilliant roses was the house itself, glowering down at him. He felt his heart stop; he hadn't meant to come here and yet here he was, a wrong turn and an entire half mile away from where he wanted to be. This time yesterday he had just been entering the bloody thing, none of this had even started and she did not exist to him. He desperately wished he could go back in time to that point and never go into that house at all. His dignity was a small price to pay for a stable frame of mind.

Barely noticing the icy rain drenching him, Tom bit his lip nervously, watching the house, waiting for something, anything to happen. He half expected it to pounce, drag him inside, further drive the point that he was going insane. Or perhaps one of the roses to talk to him; he wouldn't mind a nice conversation right about now, it had been a rather long time since he'd spoken to someone else.

Sudden movement caught his eye and he glanced over at the lowermost window. He was sure he had seen a flash of red and the shifting of curtains out of the corner of his eye. He scanned the front of the house, trying to see if anything else would move. He felt eyes burning into him and the hair on the back of his neck stood on end. Shivers having nothing to do with the frosty weather ran down his spine and his body began to tremble violently. His hands curled into tight fists, nails cutting in to the soft flesh of his palms.

His eyes caught sight of something and he turned to look full on at that thing. His heart, which had been hammering violently, suddenly stopped as he saw a pair of gleaming red eyes staring back at him. It was her, stood in that house once more, as though she belonged there. She smiled at him, teeth gleaming brilliant white and her eyes full of dark promises of what was to come. He gasped and took a step back.

His body collided with something soft; another body. Whirling round, he half expected to see her standing behind him in a grotesque parody of the slasher movies he used to love watching. His heart skipped a beat as his eyes landed upon some unknown person, breathing a sigh of relief at the fact that it was not her he had bumped in to. From the look upon that person's face, they had not seen her…there was no fear, only slight annoyance at Tom. Glaring, they walked on as Tom muttered a brief, nonsense apology. That slight movement had broken the spell he had been under whilst staring at Rose House and he turned around once more, ready to face whatever he had seen. Those red eyes were nowhere in sight. Each window stood dark and empty against the gathering dusk and even the roses seemed to have dimmed in the darkness. It all seemed so normal.

Turning on his heel, Tom hurried down the road back the way he had come, concentrating on nothing more than the way home, lest he find himself back there again by some cruel trick of fate. By the time he had skidded up his driveway the rain was beginning to let up. Not that he had noticed, as he was soaked right through so in actual fact it made no difference. Night had gathered completely, veiling the world in darkness and this, coupled with the terrible weather left Tom with an ominous feel. He still couldn't shake the feeling of being watched though he had left Rose House far behind.

He thrust his key into the lock and all but threw the door open, jumping as it banged loudly off the wall, slamming and locking it tight behind him. Pressing his back against the door, he gulped in as much air as he could, reveling in the warmth which enveloped his frozen limbs. Feeling began to rush back into his fingertips, leaving them to tingle and burn and blood rushed to his cheeks as they warmed up. His hair and clothes dripped, leaving puddles in the entrance hallway and he just knew his mother would throw a fit the moment she saw them. Dumping his sodden bag upon the ground and kicking his sopping wet shoes off, he padded down the hallway in search of said parent, hoping to glean some hot food and maybe a touch of pity.

"Mum?" he called out, walking quietly down the hallway. He could hear the television echoing out from the front room and knew somebody had to be in there. "Mum?"

Once again the hair on the back of his neck stood on end. It was weird for his mother not to answer his calls and he knew somebody had to be in; his family was obsessed with trying to do their bit to save money so leaving the television on when nobody was watching it was a big no. A sense of foreboding washed over him and instantly he dreaded walking into that front room, sure he would see something he never wanted to see. A shadow flitted along the wall and his heart hammed violently in his chest. He couldn't breathe as each cautious step down the hallway took him that inch closer to something horrific he knew would be there, waiting for him. He wanted to close his eyes, run away and hide, wait for somebody to come and find him.

"Tom, is that you?" his sister called, stepping through an open doorway on his right. Tom leaped a foot in the air, his heart stopping completely as he shrieked in a rather girlish manner. Looking at him in confusion, his sister Darcy shook her head, not quite sure what to make of Tom's odd behavior. "Are you ok?"

"I'm fine, Darce," he replied, breathing a sigh of relief at a familiar face. "Where's mum?"

"Working late as usual," she replied with a shrug. "Where have you been? You're soaking wet!"

"Well…it is raining outside," Tom remarked dryly.

"I would've thought you'd have enough common sense to get out of the rain," she said. "Or called someone, I could've picked you up."

He sighed once more, his cheeks still flushed in embarrassment. "I was fine walking, it's only rain. It never killed anyone."

"Until you get pneumonia or something, no…it never killed anyone!" she replied sarcastically. "Go get changed, I'll take pity on you and heat some leftovers up."

He grinned; sympathy was exactly the way to go. "Thanks Darce."

"Whatever," she replied, disappearing into the kitchen. Her disappearance was followed by the fridge being thrown open then the microwave starting up. He hurried upstairs, avoiding all uncurtained windows, keeping his eyes upon the ground for fear of catching sight of someone he'd rather not see. Once inside his room, he forcefully shut the curtains and slid out of his wet clothes into warm, dry sweats, making as much noise as possible to keep all thoughts at bay.

The sound of the microwave pinging as well as the faint smell of food wafting into his room made him practically leap down the stairs. That and the fact he did not want to be alone right now.

Sitting beside Darcy on the lumpy, familiar couch, eating lasagna and watching some unknown TV show he truly did not care about, Tom began to relax. It was another one of those moments where he could almost pretend every strange thing which had happened since his venture into Rose House had been nothing more than a dream; out of sight, out of mind. Without something actually happening, Tom could push it all to the back of his mind and go on pretending as though it never had. His thoughts were free to be his own. Having his sister so close, someone so familiar, someone older, he felt safe. It was outside, alone, in the real world where whatever was driving him to the brink of insanity could actually get to him that he needed to be on guard.

As midnight approached, fatigue began to consume him. His eyelids drooped and he struggled to focus more and more upon the TV. Light snoring to his right meant that his sister had fallen asleep too. Deciding he would rather drift into oblivion down here with his sister as opposed to in his room alone, he allowed his eyelids to flutter shut and his mind to drift deep into sleep.

Instantly his mind rebelled and the thoughts he had been repressing since he'd come home surfaced in the form of strange and terrifying dreams. The red eyed girl haunted his mind and those awful eyes followed him as he tried to run away, trying to flee but never escaping. Wherever he went, she would always appear, smirking at him, eyes glimmering with something terrifying. Coming to a dead end, he found her towering over him, menacing, determined. The world around him glowed red, pulsing, beating, a living thing filled with rage and fury and fear as though the world itself had burst into flames, consuming and transforming with him at the heart of the blaze.

The more he looked at her, the more entranced he became. He found himself unable to look away, as though he had been hypnotized. He knew he didn't want to approach her yet his body craved it so desperately and he found himself unconsciously moving towards her. Emotion washed over him, emotion he had never felt before, a primal desire, pure instinct and nothing more, controlling his mind, leading him towards her against his will. Though the distance between them closed, if anything, it seemed to grow; he needed to be closer to her, needed to feel her and yet, no matter how much he tried, she was just out of reach. It felt as though his entire body pulsed for her, existed solely for her.

He needed her and the longer they were apart, the more he would need her. But as the need for her grew strong within him, it was battled by an overwhelming sense of repulsion at everything she was.

"You see," she began, her raspy voice enveloping him, wrapping around his mind. "You cannot escape me. I belong here. In your mind. Beside you. Watching you."

He could not respond; the words would not move, his vocal chords refused to produce them. Not that he had a response prepared. The rational part of his mind, that part which remained conscious even within these depths of sleep desperately wanted to contradict her, to run, to keep away but the other part of his mind, so absorbed within the dream, knew she was right.

With strength he hadn't known himself to posses he rushed forward, closing the never ending gap between the two, unsure what he would do once he reached her but knowing he had to try. As the gap closed between them he realized he had no intention of stopping but rather of racing headlong into her. Perhaps by causing some form of impact he would break himself out of this madness.

"Stop," she commanded, and instantly he did, though not of his own accord; it felt as though the ground had turned to tar and he was stuck within it, held fast mere inches away from her. "You cannot stop this. It is nothing more than a dream. So wake up."

With that, the fiery world around him began to fade to black. Brilliant red and splashes of burning orange fading into a blurry half vision of what he knew should be his home. Blinking rapidly to erase the dream and bring his own vision back, he motioned to stand up, knowing he had fallen asleep curled up on the couch. It was a shock to find himself standing, leaning against a rather cold wall. The world came sharply into view and for a few moments Tom looked around in confusion. He knew he'd fallen asleep on the couch and yet here he stood face to face with an open window through which wind and rain lashed, chilling him. It seemed the weather had not cleared up from earlier; if anything, it had gotten worse and, without thinking why the window was open, he reached up and tried to slide it shut. For the moment the dream, along with the emotion felt, was forgotten and he focused all of his attention on desperately shutting the stubborn window which refused to give. Taking a moment to rest, he looked down involuntarily, eyes scanning the garden as he caught his breath.

Taking his breath away once more was the sight of something ethereal, ghost-like in its luminescence. She stood in the garden, looking directly at him, those eyes gleaming like the Cheshire Cat's, standing out starkly in the darkness. Though the moon was hidden behind dense cloud, her skin glowed as if bathed in moonlight. Despite the pouring rain and gale-like winds, she remained perfect, untouched, as though the elements did not affect her.

He wanted to scream, to cry out, to do anything, but just as he had been during his dream, he remained frozen in place, unable to do anything more than stare.

Suddenly, the window descended, slamming closed with a resounding bang shocking him out of his stupor and momentarily drawing his gaze from her. Though not wanting to consider it, a part of him felt as though this unknown girl had closed the window. Somehow, despite the distance separating them, she had forced the window shut. Raising his eyes back up to look at her once more, he caught nothing more than a fleeting glance as she disappeared backwards into the dark foliage of his garden.

Heart hammering as though it had been shocked back to life, he could feel the blood rushing through him causing his entire body to pulse with fear and repulsion, both emotions conflicting for dominance.

He heard footsteps but could not muster the strength to turn around and see who was coming up behind him. A hand snaked up onto his shoulder and its warmth seeped through the thin shirt he wore. He realized that, once again, he was completely soaking wet, and incredibly cold.

"Tom, what are you doing?" his mother's voice wormed its way through the haze which had come over him upon seeing the red eyed girl, and he felt an odd sense of Déjà Vu. "What was that noise?"

"Nothing," he replied meekly. "I left the window open, the wind caught it and it slammed."

"You're soaking wet; what's going on? It's absolutely freezing in here!" she asked, voice full of worry - there was nothing quite like the sound of a mother's fear at being shocked awake in the middle of the night.

"Nothing, mum, seriously," he barked, suddenly filled with anger. "Everything's fine, go back to bed."

She faltered at his strange tone. "Is everything ok, Tom?"

Tom turned to properly look at her for the first time since she'd entered his room. Her eyebrows knitted together as she took in the sight of him. He was deathly white, as though having seen a ghost but his pupils were dilated, almost frighteningly so. Thick, black rings hung beneath his eyes as if he hadn't slept in days and his lips were bruised and swollen red. "I'm fine." The anger leeched out of him, having been replaced instead by a strong feeling of fatigue.

She found she could not argue with him. Whether it was the look in his eyes or his tone of voice she knew he would not tell her what addled his mind. If nothing else, she knew her son well enough to know this. She placed a comforting hand upon his cheek, his skin icy to touch. "Get into some warm clothes and under that duvet. You're going to be freezing for weeks."

"Ok mum," he replied, voice taking on a dream like quality. She lead him away from the window and over to his own bed, carefully coaxing him out of his soaked clothing and into warm pajamas. Fatigue heavy on him, he let her tuck the duvet tight around him. It was as though, in his cold and tired state, he had reverted back to the small child he had once been. The child who was only safe within his

55

mother's arms.

Satisfied that all was well and wanting to get out of the frigid room and back into her own warm, safe bed, she placed a gentle hand on his forehead in an attempt at comfort before turning away. As she left his room, she turned the thermostat controlling the heated floors up, noticing that it had been turned right down. This explained the extreme chill in the room and perhaps, she reasoned, it was what was making her feel so strange. Indeed, closing the door behind her, she felt a sudden relief wash over her. The chill which had consumed her soon vanished once that physical barrier stood between her and the frigid room.

As the door slowly shut behind his mother, Tom felt the spell which had come over him start to wear off. Everything was becoming too strange; his mind could not work it out and though he tried to explain what was occurring in some rational kind of way, he couldn't. No form of rationale could explain what was happening. He needed to understand; it was just how Tom was. Never one to believe in myths and fairytales, Tom relied heavily upon fact, truth, corporeal beings and real life; he wasn't even spiritual, choosing to believe in nothing, neither confirming nor denying any form of religion for the simple fact that he had no proof of each individual god's existence. The fact that he could not make any sense of what was happening perhaps frightened him even more than anything which had occurred so far. The modern world was built on sense and understanding and without that, he felt completely lost.

Chapter Six

Sleep would not return that night though he remained huddled up under his duvet, shivering as his temperature steadily rose. Tom could feel her eyes still trained upon him, watching him intently though where she was he did not know. Every noise, every shadow, every slight movement would have him on edge, waiting for her to appear and this paranoia coupled with the thoughts racing through his mind meant that sleep was far from near.

As the sun began to rise chasing away the shadows of night and bringing the world into focus once more, the only rational thought he'd finally focused on was that he was completely and irrevocably insane. Everything that had occurred existed solely in his mind. Perhaps the insanity had come from Rose House. Being exposed to some horrible, madness inducing pathogen would indeed make all of this that bit easier to swallow, though the thought itself was bordering on the insane. Like a never ending circle of madness he couldn't escape from.

Deciding his mind was too frazzled to attempt school, he hid under his duvet, falling into fitful sleep plagued with strange half dreams and motionless images, things he had come accustomed to seeing since entering that awful house.

He awoke a few hours later and the heavy quiet of the house let him know his sister and mother were out. But more so than this, for what felt like the first time in much too long he felt completely alone. Padding downstairs in search of food, he reveled in the feeling of not being watched. It was almost like relief, as though a weight had been lifted off of his shoulders. It was only without that weight that he realized just how crushing it was and just how long he had been carrying it around. Without that feeling, he now felt bare, almost naked. It was euphoric, though how long it would last, he wasn't sure.

His mind could not stray from the red eyed girl though, despite the fact that hers had seemed to stray from him, for the moment at least. He just could not grasp what was happening, what had begun this insane descent into madness. Perhaps his old friend the internet could help. If nothing else, it may support his 'insane' theory, which was starting to look more appealing as the hours ticked by.

Sitting behind his desk, he pulled his slightly battered laptop towards him. The familiar tone rang out as it started up and the light from the screen was almost a comfort in its own right, albeit blinding in the dim room. He had debated opening curtains but that felt a bit too much like effort.

Opening up a fresh page once the internet had done all it needed to, he headed to a search engine and stared at the white search bar. In truth, he didn't quite know what to search for. What was he supposed to type in, 'crazy red eyed girl stalking me'? Time ticked by as he stared at that empty bar, hoping the answer would literally smack him in the face. In all honesty he had nothing particular to search for and though search engines were incredibly accurate when finding things he doubted even the most advanced would find something relating to whatever was going on.

He decided to begin with the most obvious of searches. Typing in Rose House, he pressed enter and waited. 62,000,000 hits relating to his query. Not narrowing things down in the slightest. Reading the brief descriptions, he could tell instantly that not one of the links matched his query in any way. For the most part, they were about hotels, salons and spas; certainly not what he was looking for, though perhaps a spa day at Rose House would help him forget about Rose House. He giggled inwardly, wondering if, perhaps, madness really was taking over and he was becoming hysterical.

Entering the name of his town, Aysforth, into the search bar, he prayed it would refine the search. It did.

Clicking on the first link - which appeared to be the most promising if the little description was anything to go by - the page turned black and a rose appeared followed by a short flash animation of the rose wilting and blooming over and over. Finally the irritating image disappeared and a page full of text appeared, with a picture of the house. Reading through it quickly, Tom gleaned it was a simple historiography on the house and the legend he knew so well. His eyes scanned the text, searching for something he might not know. No dice.

Frustrated, he returned to the homepage and typed in 'Red roses, meaning'. Scanning the pages, he discovered that red roses represented love, passion and lust, sometimes even obsession. Red roses were also a popular topic amongst the vampire subculture with every other page seeming to be some site containing vampires and vampiric mythology. He never did understand why vampires were considered so attractive, he mused, whilst browsing page after page of nonsense. According to lore they were nothing more than parasites and hence not something to become enamored with. It was the equivalent of falling in love with a leech. It only served to prove his belief that these superstitions and ideas could not be real; the inconsistencies and their ability to evolve enhanced his skepticism.

Red, Blood, Roses...it was all so unreal. Tom felt as though he had been plunged into a movie; even his own thoughts seemed too absurd to be real. But he couldn't help the way his mind raced, absorbing each and every thought. His rational mind could barely make heads or tails of what was being written and yet...

He returned to his trusty search engine and typed in 'Red Roses, Aysforth, Rose House'.

The first website he opened up was quite obviously a horticultural one, with flowers and various leaves adorning the page borders. As the main body of text came into view, along with a number of pictures, Tom's heart almost stopped. There on the screen before him, shimmering scarlet with what appeared to be silver edging the petals was a full sized image of the rose that had been haunting his dreams. The text loaded up and he found it almost impossible to focus, his eyes continually drawn to the rose which, he now knew to be a Blood Rose. Finally, dragging his eyes away from the image, he scanned the text.

'Known as the Blood Rose (Rosa Sanguinem), this rare, endangered species is hard to find and almost impossible to cultivate. Native to Northern England, it grows abundantly in areas of little to no industrial development where nature seems to have been undisturbed. Preferring cooler climates, Blood Roses are mainly found across Northern Europe – particularly the United Kingdom and Scandinavia, Alaska and North Canada. Curiously, this Rose is unaffected by changing seasons and will bloom all year round, unlike other species of rose which are prone to one flowering season per year. Blood Roses are also more durable than other rose varieties, taking longer to wither and die in comparison. The reason why it is called a Blood Rose has to do with the strange colour of sap contained within the stem. Scientists have yet been unable to identify why, curiously, the rose will often secrete red liquid from its prickles, or thorns, as well as from the broken end of the stem when cut. Some speculate it is a form of defense mechanism, as it is an irritant. In strong enough doses it can also cause hallucinations and strange visual/aural phenomena and hence it is advised the Blood Rose should not be handled for prolonged moments. This liquid resembles blood in thickness and appearance, lending itself to the rose's name.

Due to its strange properties, the Blood Rose has often been used in Folklore, with particular regard to the common myth of the witch who became the rose [origin unknown]. This myth is further enhanced by the rose's odd secretions, as it is said that this liquid is the blood of the witch.

Currently undergoing delicate scientific exploration, it is hoped this beautiful, rare species will soon be cultivated on a large scale, allowing further understanding of this mysterious species.

At present, these roses bloom in the following areas:'

Tom scanned the list of places where the rose could be

found. Each town had a date beside it, written in brackets, stating when the rose had first been observed. His eyes landed upon Aysforth and the date within the brackets, 1805. According to the town records that was also the same year in which strange things began to affect the family living in Rose House, the same year in which the mother murdered the father.

Tom couldn't help but stare at the rose. It certainly explained why, when he had caught his arm on the rose at Rose House it had appeared to bleed; he must've triggered it somehow. Though, it cast further confusion when he considered the rose found in his locker. There had been no traces of these red secretions on the rose, even around the cut end of the stem. Despite his manhandling of the awful thing it had remained secretion free so this did not coincide with the argument. And it also explained his strange behavior over the past few days. Considering he had been exposed to a small quantity of the rose's sap, it must have been the cause for the visions that had been driving him to insanity. It was a relief to know he wasn't going mad, but seemed to be under the influence of the worst drug possible. Or maybe the best. This might be worth looking into…

The article had calmed his rational mind slightly by giving logical explanations. Things were less supernatural and more scientific, he realized, as he read the article once more.

The final part of the puzzle, he thought, rested in the myth the article had briefly mentioned.

Going back a page, he modified his search terms one last time, yielding few results. He disregarded the first few results, and settled for the fourth link. Despite the poor layout, he found it to be a detailed description of the myth, along with crude drawings of what he presumed to be the girl in the myth. Once again, he let his eyes scan the text.

'In the darkest of hours, long before Western culture as we now know it had engulfed the world with technology and modern evils, when all was still new, there existed a village in the Northernmost edge of what is now known as Yorkshire. A village where people worked the land and lived serenely, before the heavy layers of coal smothered this soon to be most industrialized of areas.

It begins with Alyse, a beautiful girl, as stories so often do. But beneath the beauty lurked darkness. Wrath flowed so perfectly through her veins and the lust she felt was unbounded. Uncontrollable, Alyse used her beauty to her advantage which was often the downfall of even the strongest of men. Unable to resist her, she could charm anyone, for anything, presenting them with red roses in exchange for their hearts, and beware the fool who tries to deny her what she desires, for her wrath was like no other.

Many feared this girl. Her beauty seemed almost unnatural, unbelievable in its strength and many of the villagers began to question how she came to exist. Living alone, her parents had vanished at a young age, presumably dead in the fields they worked. Alone she had blossomed into this vision. Never seeming to leave the house to work the land or hunt or fish, it became unknown as to how she survived. Her time was spent capturing the hearts of young men and leaving them in ruin.

It happened, of course, that she came upon a man whom she could never have. He existed happily married with one of the newest members of the village. Though Alyse had lured married men before, he was unwavering to her advances for he felt the one thing she never could, pure love. She became obsessed with the man she could never have, visiting him often and attempting to lure him back with her. She presented him with the red roses to emulate her affection. The more roses he received, the more he seemed to turn towards her until finally, after enough roses had been given, he followed her away from his home and out into the darkness. His fair wife, upon returning to their home, found the roses he had been given. Recognizing the vines wrapped around the roses and the smell of herbs filling the house she knew Alyse to be a witch. Borne out of darkness Alyse's soul had been sold to evil, and now she had cast a

62

cursed spell upon the wife's beloved. She understood now why Alyse carried roses with her wherever she went, and why the sickly, cloying smell of those most awful of flowers seemed to cling to her – her wicked power stemmed from the roses.

She called the villagers together, revealing to them the girl's true form as the most wicked of witches, having used her dark and lustful powers to tempt and destroy the souls of the men in the village. Together they vowed to end the witch and as one made their way towards the affluent cottage in which she lived, on the outskirts of town. Here they found her, cauldron brewing upon the fire as hideous smells filled the night air, sickly sweet, cloying and heavy, causing many of the villagers to cough and choke in its wake.

The husband lay slumped against the house, a rose tied around his neck as the witch finished the most potent of love potions she could conjure. Seeing her husband in such a way caused an unknown rage to fill the fair wife and she demanded they capture the witch. After a struggle, the men captured the witch and dragged her back to the village where they sought to burn her wicked body to cinders and ash.

Placed upon the pyre, they set the hay alight as she cackled and gasped into the night, her words of anger and promises of hatred to come reigning down upon them. She who stood once beautiful and strong now became a horrific vision of nightmarish evil, showing her true dark form. This caused the husband to snap out of the spell she had cast upon him and he looked on at her with revulsion and disgust. He placed the final torch upon the pyre as high as he could and watched with triumph as the fire rose higher and began to lick at her porcelain skin.

Eyes filled with rage she cursed in tongues, promising unknown darkness upon the villagers and the world as she knew it. As the flames engulfed her, hideous shrieks filled the air and she seemed to double in size and stature. Blood trickled from the corners of her eyes as the demon within revealed itself. Wings made of flame and fire spread out behind her, illuminating the village in a brilliant, terrifying orange glow as though the fire were spreading and consuming everything. The last of her to burn into ash was the brilliant rose attached to her hip, the final destruction of her power.

When the fire began to die back and the witch had truly been burned to ashes, the men doused the final flames and stamped out the embers. As they did this, a rose began to grow from the remains of this funeral pyre. It was the deepest of reds, the darkest of scarlets, like the blood that had dropped from her eyes as she welcomed the fires of hell into her. The men backed in fear, knowing this rose to be the curse she had left behind. As they turned to leave she appeared behind them, eyes blood red and reflecting the darkness within. She plunged her hands deep into the chest of one, dragging his heart out and crushing it in one fluid motion. The other she manipulated, confusing his mind and controlling his thoughts as she had done in life. She used him as an example to the village, before destroying him too and massacring those who had sacrificed her.

More than vengeance, she now sought to fulfill her desire for death and pain. Luring men as she did in life, she drives them to the brink of insanity, capturing their minds and their hearts, destroying them in the process until they succumb to her wrath and she devours them in the most painful of ways. She has become known for her eyes, as red as the rose which bloomed in place, signifying her arrival like warning bells. Wherever this rose appears she is soon to follow. This rose became known as the Blood Rose, so called because of the darkest of blood which seems to stain the roses, to cling to this flower once representing love and happiness, perverting it to the darkest evils. The blood which flows through the witch.

Tom blinked, staring at the screen, having finished reading through the morbid text. Scrolling down through the rest of the site, he found pictures, hand drawn images of the girl, both when she was alive and during her burning transformation. Perhaps what struck him most was the fact that, even through these badly drawn, imitations of the girl he could see a resemblance to the girl he knew, the girl pretending she was this creature. Some of the images depicted her as an incredible beauty, just as the story had said she was, with long, black hair, and soft, almond shaped eyes. Though simply dressed, showing her lower stature, subtle changes had been made to emphasize her sexual appearance, perhaps to show that, as the story had stated, in life she had been lusty.

Other drawings were not so pleasant. These were obviously of her after her transformation and in many she was unrecognizable. Her face was twisted into a permanent scowl of anger and anguish as she decapitated humans around her. Her eyes had been stained blood red and her teeth had elongated into sharp, devilish points. In some, large, bat-like, leathery wings unnaturally bent at odd angles sprouted from her back; in others, these were missing. Every single picture, he was loath to admit, was frightening and he could not look at them for too long.

Perhaps it was the pictures themselves, or the fact that some strange girl seemed to completely believe she was this mythical creature, but Tom found himself covered on edge. It wasn't that he believed her to be this creature, for myth was nothing but that; myth. It was more the fact she believed she was this creature and who knows what else she would do if she thought she had such powers.

Feeling that his research for the day was done, Tom shut his laptop off and headed to the kitchen in search of a cup of tea to perhaps calm his jumbled thoughts. Of course, it didn't, and he was once again struck by the idiocy of people offering hot drinks in time of crisis to calm the situation; it hadn't helped in the slightest. It occupied his hands though, which was a slight relief he supposed.

He wasn't quite sure what to make of it all, he mused

as he sat down on the battered sofa in the front room, tea in hand though soon forgotten. It was all a bit too insane for his liking. Never mind the fact that this girl thought she was this mythical creature, what was he to do about it? She could be an extremely dangerous person with who knows what thoughts running through her mind so whatever Tom did, he had to tread lightly. Depending on how deranged she actually was, his life could be in danger, though he doubted things could progress to such a state. It felt almost laughable to even consider it but after enough reruns of numerous forensic crime shows Tom understood just how capable people were of doing anything horrific if they put their minds to it.

He knew he should tell someone about what was going on but he didn't know who. His mother though absolutely loving always seemed to become too heavily invested in anything he tried to speak to her about and something like this would only send her off on a complete tangent. Tom could already here the deep worry in her voice as she prattled on about murder and his safety. She'd probably end up shipping him off to stay with Aunt Eileen in Cumbria and god knows he couldn't put up with that for long. His sister would most likely have him committed to a mental home so she was out of the question and he highly doubted his friends would believe him. He knew if it was the other way round he wouldn't believe them. It was all too farfetched for *him* to grasp, let alone someone who hadn't had the...pleasure...of meeting the red eyed girl.

Though...maybe they would. They had seen the roses left in precarious places specifically for him and he had told them about feeling watched. Though strange at first, it could come to make sense to them, after all it wasn't as though he wanted them to believe the myth, just believe that a girl stalking him believed the myth. Perhaps they'd come around. It wasn't as though they could help in any way but just having somebody believe him would be better than nothing.

Shaking his head at his own ridiculous thoughts, Tom

sighed heavily, glancing around the room as he did so. Time seemed to have flown by while he was doing his research and he was surprised to find it was very late in the day. It was then that he noticed just how dark it was in the house; the sun had begun its long descent and darkness was rapidly gathering as evening approached. It seemed, since meeting the red eyed girl he knew to now be called Alyse, at least in myth form, Tom had lost precious hours thinking of nothing but her. Time seemed to warp, as it vanished in a heartbeat and yet dragged by, minutes becoming days. Though he hadn't known Alyse long, it felt as though she had been a constant annoyance for as long as he could remember and imagining life before this began seemed impossible to comprehend, though it had only been three days previous. Where time went, he did not know.

He felt a vibration run up his leg and he leaped in shock, sloshing stone cold tea down over his arm and on to his jeans. Swearing, he put the now horribly cold and completely undrinkable tea down on the table and pulled his phone out of his pocket, only to find a short, rather blunt, filled with profanity text message waiting for him. Sebastian. That jolt had brought him back into the real world though and the moment he became aware of his surroundings once more, something else became obvious to him. That creeping, loathsome feeling of being watched had returned and a jolting sense of fear was clawing its way deep under his skin. It seemed as though his day hidden from Alyse's view was over and, once again, he was prey to her watchful eye.

It was about that time that something else became painfully obvious to him; he was completely alone. Though not unusual in that base respect, it was unusual for this time of evening. He was sure by now that somebody would have been home, especially as winter had fallen with the harshest of vengeances and the weather was not pleasant at the best of times. His mum hated leaving the house in blue skies and sunny days so being out in what sounded like a small hurricane would have been her idea of absolute hell.

Standing up, he began to walk through the connecting rooms just to double check whether somebody had come home or not. The house was indeed empty and completely silent. Digging in his pocket once more to retrieve his phone, intent on calling his mum and perhaps hassling her to return, its flashing green light caught his eye. There was a voicemail message. Tom looked at it oddly. Though he had been falling in and out of his own world all afternoon he felt sure he would've heard his phone ring, particularly as a simple text had been enough to half throw his tea around the living room so seeing that somebody had called and he had missed it was odd. Dialing his voicemail number, Tom listened intently to the beeping that followed.

Chapter Seven

"Tom," his mother's voice floated out through the speakers. "I'm stuck at work again so won't be home till late tonight. Some ridiculous training thing they've decided to do. It's all pretty last minute so goodness knows how well it will go down. Don't order any more pizza, our bill is long enough as it is. Darcy shouldn't be home too late but she said she was studying with a friend in the library. We all know she isn't so why she insists on lying is beyond me. Anyway, don't burn the house down, I'll be home soon. Get some sleep, you were dead to the world this morning and burning up! If you're feeling ill when I get back we'll consider calling a doctor, k? Love you."

Well, that was a comfort, Tom mused as he deleted the message. Home alone was certainly something he hadn't bargained for and something he did not want to embark on, particularly as he felt Alyse was watching him intently at that precise moment. "Thanks, mum," he muttered dryly, shoving his phone angrily into his pocket and heading back to the living room, turning on every single light as he passed. By the time he reached the sitting room once more the house was ablaze with lights and could rival Blackpool Pier.

Sitting back down on the couch, he turned the TV on and put the volume up as high as it would go, though not so loud as he couldn't hear if somebody was around. He felt on edge, guarded, waiting for Alyse to appear and drive him further to insanity. Though he knew she wasn't the creature he had read about, she was a deranged girl who was more than likely willing to cause harm to him unless she got what she wanted. He wasn't quite sure what she wanted, per se, or how she'd go about it. In fact, he couldn't fathom what she could possibly want or even be doing but he assumed she wanted him, and that was frightening enough.

Every noise made him jump and in an old house made mostly of wood and brick, noises were not a rarity. Every floorboard seemed to creak menacingly and the wind whipped against the windows causing them to rattle. The house came alive with a thousand different sounds, each one more sinister than the last until his nerves were so shot that even the TV would cause him to jump with every unnaturally loud noise. Unable to stand much more of this induced solitude and completely irrational way of reacting, Tom once again grasped his mobile out of his pocket and dialed the first number he could think of.

"Hello?" a familiar, groggy voice answered after a few rings.

"Sebastian! It's Tom!" Tom called out happily, finally feeling slightly calmer at hearing a familiar voice. "How are you?"

"I'm fine, Tom, how are you?" Sebastian replied, and Tom could tell his voice was full of concern. "Didn't see you at school today."

"Yeah, felt a bit ill still, couldn't sleep much last night so thought, what the hell, just take the day off," he laughed nervously.

"Tom, you sure you're ok? You sound kind of strange," Sebastian said. "Everything alright?"

"Oh yeah, all's fine," Tom replied though he couldn't quite get his voice to stop wavering nervously. "Hey um, so I'm home alone, fancy coming over? Bring Olli and we'll get pizza?"

"I dunno," Sebastian replied. "I have a huge history essay I really should do before I fail this class completely and mum's somehow managed to talk me in to helping Sally with her textiles homework. Like *I'm* the one most suited to that task."

"Oh come on, really? Sebastian, you know you want pizza," Tom coaxed. "It might be fun, haven't seen you in ages!"

"You saw me yesterday," he replied, sounding confused. "Ok Tom, what's going on? Something's up, I know it, so just tell me what it is and let's be done with this whole 'I miss you' thing."

"I just feel like hanging out," he replied nonchalantly though his voice wavered once more.

"Ok, fine, I'll be right there. I'll drag Olli out on the way over," Sebastian said. "But I still say something is wrong and whether you like it or not Tom you will be telling me what it is. Even if I have to hold you down and drag it out of you."

"Thanks Seb...I appreciate the care," Tom replied sarcastically. "See you in a bit."

Hanging up, Tom sighed heavily. It was a relief to know that his empty house would not be empty for much longer. It seemed that the more time he spent alone, the more this entire thing drove him crazy. He hated this feeling and he hated this Alyse girl for doing this to him. He wasn't accustomed to fear so his behavior was almost childish and pathetic to him, something he used to make fun of Mariana for when they were children, but he couldn't shake the feelings. He felt panic rising within him at the slightest of things and though it was unnecessary panic, he couldn't stop himself from feeling it. Even the comfort of knowing reasoning behind the strange occurrences couldn't control his fear; it only seemed to fuel it.

Relief washed over him as soon as the doorbell rang, its chime clanging loudly throughout the house and dispelling all semblance of silence. Leaping up, he raced to the door and happily flung it open, glad to finally have some company to chase away the lonely fears.

"Hey guys!" he said cheerfully, ushering them into the house and shutting the door quickly behind them, locking it twice.

"Hi Tom," Oliver said gently, looking at his friend with a raised eyebrow. "You ok?"

"Absolutely fabulous," Tom replied, smiling broadly, overcompensating the charade of normalcy. "I'm great, you?"

71

"Yeah, good," Oliver said, obviously confused at the way Tom was acting but not quite sure how to react.

"So, Tom, pizza was mentioned?" Sebastian said, cutting in and directing all attention towards him.

"Yeah, you know where the phone is, get ordering. Tell them to put it on Angela Leeson's tab," Tom said, pointing to where the phone was.

"Why can't you do it?" Sebastian asked, not really feeling comfortable enough to phone up and use Tom's mother's account to pay for the amount of food he wanted to order. He knew either way she'd still be paying for it, it just seemed even more out of line to order it himself. He'd been coming here and eating her food for years so it wasn't as though her feeding him was something new but it felt right to keep slight barriers up.

"Oh well...uh..." Tom stuttered, not quite sure how to explain why he didn't want to call to his friends. In truth he wasn't sure himself; it wasn't as though Alyse had infiltrated his phone lines and so there was no need for his mind to associate the phone with her, especially as they were phoning a number he was more than familiar with. An awful sense of foreboding had just come over him at the mention of using the phone and so he didn't want to do it. Ridiculous of course, as he had just called Sebastian and nothing bad had happened there but still, it seemed his rational mind had taken a break this evening and so he was left to deal with his fears instead. "I've got a bit of a sore throat. Besides, you know what your bottomless pit of a stomach wants better than anybody, so go on, get to it."

He headed down the hallway and away from the phone, leaving there no room for Sebastian to argue with him. Mumbling to himself, Sebastian picked up the phone and proceeded to order copious amounts of pizza, sides and drinks, which would hopefully satisfy his growling stomach.

Oliver followed Tom down the hallway and into the living room. Seeing Tom sat stiffly upon the sofa as though nervous about something, he took the seat directly beside him. "Tom, what's going on?"

"What?" Tom asked, eyes wide, "Nothing, seriously I'm just having a bit of an off day, that's all."

Oliver silently looked on at Tom, eyebrow raised. Tom inwardly groaned; he knew exactly what that look meant. Oliver was unusually perceptive about people. He could tell just by listening to someone exactly what was going on and he very rarely used this gift for good. Well actually, he did use it for good by providing emotional and moral support such as now, but that was beside the point. "Not to get after school special on you or anything Tom, but we're here, we're your best friends, all of that stuff. Talk if you want, we'll listen."

"Seriously, it's nothing, I'm just going a bit insane is all," Tom shrugged.

"Well, I could've told you that from the start," Oliver quipped. Tom glared at him before cracking a grin which seemed pained but Oliver refrained from commenting. "Ok, ok, so I assume whatever is going on is making you go more insane than usual."

"Yeah that's it," Tom said, shaking his head. "Honestly, it's nothing big."

"Sorted!" Sebastian cried out, bounding into the living room, causing Tom to jump. "Pizza ordered, here in 30 minutes or so."

"Good, maybe your stomach could shut up then, it's so loud I can barely hear myself think," Oliver said dryly. "Seriously, Seb, do you do anything but eat?

"Growing lad like me needs sustenance on a regular basis," Sebastian retorted.

"Most people need sustenance on a regular basis," Oliver pointed out. "They tend to die without it."

Silence fell as both waited for Tom to jump in with some witty remark which would end up in all three bursting into fits of laughter. When no jibe came, both turned to look at their friend in wonder.

"Hello? Earth to Tom?" Sebastian called, waving his hand in front of Tom's face. This was turning into a habit of his. "Is anybody in there?"

"What?" Tom said in confusion. "Seb get that hand away from me, no idea where it's been!"

"Ok, something is definitely wrong," Sebastian said, plopping down onto the floor in front of Tom, sitting cross-legged and looking straight into Tom's mahogany orbs. "You have 30 minutes of me actually listening before food gets here and nothing else matters."

"Why thank you Sebastian, I am so glad your priorities are sorted," Tom muttered. "Nice to know your stomach does come first."

"Well, it is a lot more vocal than you are!" Sebastian accused. "You bottle everything up and lie, quite badly I might add, about being fine. It, on the other hand, lets me know when something is wrong."

"I'm glad you both have such a close relationship; when's the wedding?" he retorted.

"We got hitched last week, thank you very much," Sebastian replied, poking his tongue out childishly as he did so.

"Ok will you both shut up?" Oliver called out, silencing them both. "Back to the matter at hand. Tom, something is wrong. We know this, you know this, everybody in the entire world must know this, so talk to us."

Tom bit his nail. "Seriously, it's nothing. There is nothing wrong," he said, around a partially chewed nail.

"You're an awful liar," Oliver replied with a roll of the eyes. "Just tell us. We won't stop until you do, and you know Sebastian can hassle for hours, days, if need be."

Tom threw his hands up in surrender. "Ok fine! It's this whole stalker thing."

"Oh, so did you find out who it is?" Sebastian asked. "Is she fit?"

Tom shook his head. "You're going to think I'm insane when I tell you."

"We don't exactly think you're normal now," Oliver pointed out, still trying to illicit a hint of a smile from Tom. "May as well tell us what's going on anyway, you never know, we might just understand."

"I know for a fact you won't...but, I'll tell you," he continued quickly, knowing both Oliver and Sebastian were getting ready to continue their patented hassling of him. "Yeah, I do know who it is. But it's nobody we know."

Sebastian looked pointedly at his wrist, tapping where a watch should have been. "Start from the beginning, Tom, this cryptic stuff doesn't make us understand and time is ticking."

"Shut up, Seb," Tom said testily. "When I went into Rose house, somebody was there. It scared the crap out of me because it was a girl and I thought that maybe the story was true. Obviously it's not but I thought it was at that moment in time. Anyway, this girl is a psychopath, she honestly thinks she's the girl who's supposed to be in that house; she has red contact lenses in and all. She's the one who's been leaving roses all over the place for me. She's the one who's been watching me."

"Do you have proof?" Sebastian asked cynically. "I mean, that she's the one doing this."

"Yes. Everywhere I go she's always there. She was in the bathroom when you guys came in. I don't know where she went but she was there. She was here last night, in the garden, she is everywhere I go," Tom said, voice rising in panic as he spoke. "Roses are everywhere, she's driving me insane and she honestly believes she is that bloody girl from the story."

He paused, looking at his friends, gauging their reactions. From the cynical looks both were giving him he knew they didn't believe him but he continued anyway.

"I did some research today; I couldn't face school because I knew she'd be there, somewhere. She really knows her stuff," he continued. "The story of the house ties in with an old myth and the roses are a special species of rose; nobody knows why they grow here. This twisted girl did her research and has really come to fill her role as Alyse."

"Wait, who's Alyse?" Sebastian asked, momentarily interrupting Tom's rapid storytelling.

"Alyse is the name of the girl from the myth. Its spelled funny but I think it's just an old sort of spelling for Alice, like, y'know, Alice Morgan from the year above. That's what it looks like anyway," Tom said, waving his comment away. "This girl really believes she's Alyse. And she has deep, red eyes, obviously contacts but they're still red. She's driving me insane. Wherever I go, she's there. She keeps leaving roses everywhere. I can't do anything without her being there somehow, I'm even dreaming of her!"

"Tom!" Oliver called out sharply, the edge in his voice halting Tom's tirade and allowing him a moment to breathe. "Calm down, you're turning hysterical."

"Sorry, it's all just a bit weird," Tom replied with a sigh, trying to release the panic that had been rapidly building within him. "It's really pissing me off and at the same time, it's kind of frightening. This nut bag won't leave me alone. Who knows what she could do; she really does believe she is the girl from the myth. The girl who, might I add, tore people to shreds and decimated villages because she was supposedly a witch who was burned at the stake for using love potions on men."

"Oh," both Oliver and Sebastian murmured in unison. Silence fell as neither really knew what to say and Tom's angry rant had reached an end.

Eyebrows knitted together as he attempted to work things out, Oliver slowly mulled over what Tom had said. "Ok, let me get this straight, there is a girl stalking you and she believes she's this mythical creature or something? And not only that but…you met her in Rose House?"

"Yeah," Tom nodded.

Sighing almost dramatically, Oliver wrung his hands together. "You know, I don't actually know what to say. It sounds completely insane."

"Yeah, I know that," Tom replied sarcastically. He grabbed his packet of cigarettes off the table and lit one up with shaky hands, deciding to break his mum's no smoking in the house policy. It was under special circumstances. He was sure she'd understand. "I've spent the past few days genuinely convinced I must be slowly losing the plot and it's why I didn't want to tell either of you."

Oliver glared at the cigarette resting gently between Tom's fingers, smoke curling up towards the ceiling and the heady scent of menthol tobacco slowly filling the room. His stance on smoking was no great secret and he'd tried many a time to support Tom in kicking his habit.

"Ok I get you didn't want to tell us before," Sebastian cut in, not nearly as fussed by his friend's bad habit as Oliver was. "What I don't get is…why are you telling us now?"

"Because," Tom paused. "I don't know, I guess because you both wouldn't shut up until I did and I needed to tell someone. This chick is driving me mad. Seriously, I feel like I'm going crazy."

Sebastian lowered his head, voice barely an audible whisper as though ashamed when he spoke. "Maybe you are."

"Gee, I hadn't thought of that," Tom replied dryly, fingers tightening around the paper filter. "Maybe I am just a little bit on the mad side and I've dreamt all this up."

"Not helpful, Seb," Oliver chided. "I'm sure Tom's considered the possibility that he's going mad without the need for you to suggest it too."

Tom inhaled deeply on the rapidly burning cigarette. "I

have, and it's a scary thought."

Sebastian and Oliver glanced at each other, sharing one of their Looks. The kind of look that frustrated Tom to no end as he knew they were somehow communicating without him. And, in this case, about him.

Oliver hadn't actually believed Tom seriously considered he was losing his mind. It was one of those things people joked out – they'd misplace their keys or think they'd seen something that wasn't there and mutter 'I must be losing it', but nobody every truly thought they were developing some form of mental illness. Knowing that Tom had genuinely considered the possibility of having something wrong with him however intensified the magnitude of the situation.

"You know, Tom," Oliver began slowly. "If you are worried about your mental state, maybe it'd be best if we spoke to a professional. Somebody who could help better?"

Tom rolled his eyes at Oliver. "I don't actually think I'm losing my marbles, Olli. I can still tell with almost complete certainty what is real and I know all of this is. The stalking, the roses, all of this nonsense about the myths. It is real. There really is this strange girl out there. And you know, the worst part is, she can always see me."

Oliver raised a skeptical eyebrow. "What do you mean?"

His eyes dropped to the floor. "I feel as though I'm being watched, continually. I can feel her eyes burning into me, as though she's standing right there looking at me."

"Tom, she can't always be around watching you. That's just paranoia," Oliver reasoned.

Tom glared at Oliver, anger biting at his tongue. "No, it's not. She really is watching me, I know it! Earlier the feeling went away, so I know when she is watching me and when she isn't. I feel it! And then most of the time she does end up appearing so either I'm going psychic, psycho or she really is there. Take your pick."

"Ok, Tom, just calm down, take a breath," Oliver said, trying to ease Tom's anger and rising panic. "Let's say she is watching you, where is she?"

Tom's shoulders slumped forward as he dropped the cigarette butt into his discarded, cold tea from early. "I don't know. I really don't know and I can't understand how she can be everywhere and nowhere at once. I just know she is."

Sebastian, who had been quietly listening to the debate and slowly pulling out loose threads from the worn carpet, glanced over his shoulder at the curtained window. "So she can see us, right now?"

"Yeah, I can feel her watching me. I don't know where she is, or what window she's looking through, but I know she is," Tom nodded, voice grave. Sebastian shivered theatrically as the thought of somebody hidden, watching them unnerved him. "I don't mean watching me in a supernatural sense. I mean like, she hides and actually watches me. She was in my garden last night, I saw her out there in the dark around 1ish, I guess?"

At that moment the bell rang and Tom, forgetting they were waiting for pizza delivery, jumped to his feet in fright, his fight or flight reflexes on high alert. Oliver and Sebastian looked on, shocked, as their friend overreacted so completely to something so insignificant.

"Tom, relax, it's just the pizza!" Sebastian exclaimed. Standing up rather ungracefully, he bounded out of the room and down the hallway to claim his prize. The slamming of the front door made Tom jump once again but he tried to hide his involuntary response with a cough. Sebastian appeared moments later, carrying a mountain of pizza boxes, Styrofoam boxes and bottles of fizzy drinks. "Gentlemen, our feast has arrived."

Somehow, he managed to collapse to the ground without dropping a single box and soon the three were sat munching quietly, absorbed in the food.

Tom hoped that now the food had arrived the other two

would forget what they were discussing and perhaps move on to something less traumatic for Tom. Of course, that would be far too kind of the world. They had not forgotten and the last thing either were willing to do was move onto another topic of discussion.

"Ok so, let me get this straight," Oliver said, grabbing another slice of pizza and tearing off a bite sized piece of the dough. "Basically, this girl thinks she's a myth?"

Tom chewed thoughtfully, not quite sure how to reply. "Well...I think so. I think she thinks she's actually the myth?"

Sebastian shook his head, desperately trying to swallow a rather large mouthful of pizza. His eyes watered as he forced it down his throat. "Can I just interrupt and say, what myth are you on about? I have never heard of a myth with roses and a red eyed girl called Alyse who fancies herself a very elaborate peeping tom."

"Well neither had I till I looked it up," Tom replied, "You know, you really can find anything online these days."

"What was the myth?" Sebastian pressed, knowing Tom was about to attempt to change the subject.

It had been a long shot, but Tom had hoped someone would've taken his badly disguised subject change. "It's really cliché. There's this myth of a witch who used to cast love spells over the men in her village using roses. When they found out she was a witch they, of course, did the most normal thing in the world and burnt her alive. With her final breath she cast a spell, or sold her soul to the devil, or something of that caliber, determined to bring revenge on those who had killed her. She lives on in the roses. They are meant to be her, or connected to her in some way. It's not very clear; myths never do explain all the facts. But apparently she uses them to control people. So I'm guessing, they must do something with her powers?"

Sebastian nodded in understanding. "Oh, now I get it."

"Do you really?" Oliver asked, looking at Sebastian questioningly, a small smirk upon his lips but a genuine smile in his eyes.

"Not in the slightest, but I figured we'd understand a lot quicker if I said I did," Sebastian replied, before taking a huge bite out of another pizza slice.

"Smart boy," Oliver conceded, tearing apart a piece of garlic bread and popping a small chunk in to his mouth.

Sebastian winked at Oliver. He ran a paper napkin over his mouth, attempting to dislodge the crumbs stubbornly stuck to his lips. "What I really don't get, though, aside from the majority of this evening, is how this myth has to do with Rose House? I mean, we've never heard it before so I'm guessing it's not from around here. What's the link?"

"Oh I don't know!" Tom cried in frustration. "Because she happened to wander into Aysforth and liked the scenery so much she decided to stay? For the stellar weather? Cheap house prices?"

Sebastian choked on the coke he'd been drinking, coughing and spluttering as laughter bubbled up inside him. After the seriousness of their conversation this answer was not one Sebastian had been expecting. Oliver thumped him on the back as Sebastian continued to splutter and Tom tried to hide the grin he could feel forcing its way onto his lips. Sebastian did kind of deserve that. And it felt good to laugh.

Tom took a deep breath once the coughing and laughing had subsided. They'd been going backwards and forwards over this information for far too long now and Tom knew why. "You don't believe me do you, either of you?"

Taking a moment to judge his answer, Oliver mulled over the words. "It's not that we don't. It's just...it's hard to swallow and it all seems quite coincidental. I'm not doubting she exists, I'm just saying it is a very well thought out plan."

"Well it's either that, I'm going insane, or the myth is actually true and I'm being haunted by some ancient demon witch who was burnt at the stake hundreds of years ago and just happens to be a psychopath," Tom replied. "You pick the easiest option to deal with."

"Insane!" Sebastian piped up around a mouthful of onion ring. Both turned to glare at him. "You wanted the easiest option to deal with, well, that's it."

"Stop helping!" Oliver exclaimed. "Seb, can't you take anything seriously?"

Sebastian sat up straighter, wiping his hands on his jeans as he moved. "You want me to take this seriously? Ok fine, I will. Tom, you're crazy. But, if it makes you feel any better, why don't we stay the night and see if she decides to stalk you in person. We'll all keep an eye out and if we see her, we'll grab her and find out what the hell her problem is. If nothing else, you won't be alone."

Both Oliver and Tom looked on in shock at Sebastian after this little outburst, wondering if their normally calm, if not a little heavily spoken, friend was feeling alright. "Uh...thanks, Seb," Tom murmured after a few moments of silence, not knowing what else to say.

Sebastian's comments felt like the closing of the conversation and so, from that point on neither the myth nor Rose House were mentioned. Reverting to their stereotypical role of teenage boys, they spent much of the evening consuming what was left of their take out whilst making small talk, with the TV's incessant hum in the background. Though the idea of being watched continually by some potentially insane girl was unnerving to both Sebastian and Oliver, neither had seen Alyse so neither felt much affected by her presence. They could quite easily push the thought of her to the back of their minds unlike Tom whose mind refused to focus upon anything else.

He knew both Sebastian and Oliver hadn't taken his thoughts on Alyse seriously. He had known they wouldn't all along which was why he had refrained from confiding in them about her. Indeed, he could understand their point; if one of them were to come to him with the same story he had fed them, he would think them insane. The fact of the matter was though, he was not insane. He had seen Alyse with his own two eyes and while he knew she could not be this mysterious, mythical creature, he still believed her to be deranged and possibly dangerous. It frustrated him so much to know they wouldn't believe him; just because they hadn't seen her, didn't automatically mean she was in his head.

Though Tom still felt on edge about Alyse and the entire explanation of her, it was easier to relax with someone else in the house. He was able to lose himself in idle chit chat despite his heart racing at every unfamiliar sound. They set up sleeping arrangements in the living room, with blankets and pillows covering the sofa, both armchairs and most of the floor. It was something they hadn't done since they were children, transforming Tom's living room into a soft fort and it was oddly comforting to do now, on a Saturday night, as teenagers who perhaps should have been out drinking or doing whatever else society expected them to do. Not that Aysforth was the most happening of towns in the UK.

Though conversation continued for a while, Oliver's soft, snuffling snores soon let Tom know he was the only one wide awake. It was a small comfort, having his best friends so close to him, though it did little to quell his fears once they were both asleep and there was nobody to directly engage and distract him with conversation. Closing his eyes, Tom quickly came to realize, only brought back visions of Alyse and the odd dreams he had been having. A part of him knew that when he did fall asleep, nightmares would hit. Whether it was his mind's way of reacting to the fear or she was subliminally controlling him he didn't know. He did know, however, that the nightmares were because of her. Last night, the moment she had turned and fled his garden he had been able to drift into a peaceful sleep. He felt sure that would not come tonight.

Time seemed to slow down as minutes became hours and the dark night stretched on. Late night television was as bad as it had always been and both of his friends were by now completely immersed in dreamland, for which he envied them. His eyes kept drifting to the clock above the television and his heart would sink with every glance, as it became obvious that time really was warping around him and sleep did not seem any closer than it had at last glance.

His mother returned home at around 2.30am, tiptoeing into the quiet house so as not to disturb anyone. Well, her version of tiptoeing in high heels which involved a strange sort of shuffle click every step she took. Tom assumed the fact that both the television and the living room light were on hadn't been something she was expecting, if the faint, burning tang of vodka as she came into the room was anything to go by. He heard her stumble slightly as she kicked her shoes off, swearing under her breath - the three motionless bodies spread about her living room obviously having been another surprise. Not that Tom sat up to talk to her, choosing to feign sleep instead. Her drinking was a rarity, but his mother had always been a soppy drunk and right now he didn't want to deal with her hugging him, stroking his hair and mooning over how proud she was of him.

Assuming the boys were immersed in sleep, she almost painfully slowly crept across the living room, picking her way gingerly over the mess they had created, to switch the television off. Grabbing her shoes and awkwardly fumbling for the switch, she turned the light off and pulled the door to. As her now muted footsteps slowly disappeared up the stairs, fear rose within Tom, the darkness pressing down on him. Part of his mind tried to reason with him, as this fear of the dark was quite new and the fact that a person whom he barely knew had caused this irrational fear was mind-boggling. The other part of his mind could do no more than silently scream, banging its way dramatically against the inside of his head, desperately trying to find a way out, a hidden exit sign or emergency escape button, babbling almost incoherent ideas on what could be lurking within the shadows.

Knowing his rational side was right Tom lay completely still, hidden beneath the blankets, eyes screwed tightly shut, refusing to so much as peek into the darkness to prevent the irrational, frightened side of his mind from going into hyper drive. The darkness was so heavy he could barely make out anything in the gloom and for the few brief moments he had glanced around, every half visible shape became Alyse hiding in wait, red eyes burning through the darkness. Closing his eyes was safer.

He willed his breathing to slow down, become deep, feigning sleep, hoping that this would somehow make it come true. How long he lay like that, Tom did not know and eventually he assumed sleep did come for him as he found images scrolling through his mind, so vividly they could have been right in front of him. Though not unpleasant, they consisted of things he didn't want to see; roses, and old, battered houses, stained deadly shades of red. When the pictures faded from his mind, the impulse to open his eyes became overwhelming. Unable to stave it off for much longer he allowed his eyelids to part a crack, noticing the watery light filtering into the room beginning the process of banishing shadows. The sun was slowly starting to rise; night was gone and the nightmares had not returned.

He blinked rapidly a few times to clear his eyes of sleep. Having had so few hours sleep meant his eyes ached from tiredness and he desperately wanted to return to slumber, even if it meant being bombarded by images of Alyse.

Rolling over, trying to find some comfort on his now horrifically uncomfortable, makeshift bed, he found his eyes drawn to the coffee table beside him. His eyes widened and his heart stopped completely as a splash of red caught his sight. On the table within touching distance was a brilliant red rose, its stem facing towards him, red blood-like liquid dripping slowly onto the cherry wood surface.

Chapter Eight

Tom sat bolt upright, looking around, hoping to see Alyse but at the same time dreading that he might. The liquid dripping from the stem was still fluid and had not dried into a gloopy mess meaning the rose had recently been placed there and the person who had brought it - Tom knew it had to be Alyse though how she got into his house he didn't know - could perhaps still be around. If either Oliver or Sebastian could just see her, get a glimpse of her, they'd believe him. They wouldn't think he was crazy. He wouldn't think he was crazy.

Reaching across the gap between him and Sebastian, he frantically shook his friend awake. "Seb, wake up! You have to see this!" Tom called anxiously, hoping his voice would rouse his friend.

"Later," Sebastian mumbled sleepily, shifting away from Tom and his incessant shaking.

"No! now!" Tom called, desperation seeping into his voice.

He turned and looked at Tom through puffy, half closed eyes, sleep pulling at him still, trying to bring him back into dreamland. "What's the matter?"

"Look! There's a rose o-" Tom stopped as he back to look at the table. Where moments before a rose had sat, now there appeared to be nothing; the table was completely void of anything more than empty glasses. "Um…never mind, just a bad dream I guess."

Sebastian swatted in Tom's general direction and slumped back onto his pillow. Almost instantly, light snores filled the room.

Tom's heart began to pound faster as he swung his legs over the side of the sofa sitting up properly this time, careful to avoid kicking Oliver in the leg as he did so. Shuffling to the end of the couch where the coffee table had been moved to the night before, he looked closer at the tabletop, inspecting its surface, almost as if he expected the rose to pop back up, appearing through the wood itself. Though no rose did appear a small drop of red liquid caught Tom's eye. Gently, with a shaking finger, Tom touched the drop; the crimson liquid felt thick, gelatinous. Bringing it to his nose he sniffed gingerly, wrinkling his nose as a familiar coppery scent bombarded his senses; it smelled like blood to him.

The sudden impulse to move as far away from the table as possible overwhelmed him and he threw himself backwards into the back of the couch. He desperately wiped his fingers over the upholstery, trying to rid himself of the sticky liquid. Though he'd only touched it with the very edge of his fingertip it felt as though the liquid had spread covering and contaminating his entire hand. Paranoia crept through him and the feeling of being watched intensified. He glanced around anxiously, expecting to see Alyse, watching him, eyes trained solely upon him and enjoying his fear.

He felt something imbed itself deep within his skin and slowly slither up his bare right arm. Without needing to look down, he knew somehow that it was the vile, sticky, red liquid that had been pooling upon the tabletop. What he had once assumed was blood seemed to have a mind of its own, an entirely independent organism, a virus, an infection, angry and red and moving fast. Despite mentally screaming at himself to scrape at his flesh with his nails, his body would not cooperate, choosing instead to remain motionless as the organism slithered under the skin, burying itself deep into his flesh. His body was overcome with sudden hot flushes as the blood organism wormed its way deeper into his skin, wanting to imbed itself within his core as far as it could go. Burning, burying.

Breathing became increasingly laborious and he found himself barely inhaling enough air with each shallow breath, causing a lightheaded feeling to build. His hands contracted of their own accord, gripping on to the sofa's upholstery, tearing through the fabric as he desperately fought for something to hold on to. Heat continued to rise and he was sweating profusely, feeling the droplets trickling down his back and the blood organism continued to move. All he could see was red as a heat filled mist clouded his vision and it made it harder for him to focus on anything more than this thing. This hateful, burning thing. He could feel it, circling his heart and he knew that it had found where it wanted to be. As though playing out on a screen before him, he watched as this snaking, red, blood filled thing circled his heart, round and round. Stopping directly in front of the beating organ, he knew this was it. Taking as deep a breath as he could, he watched as the organism plunged itself deep within his heart. Red mixed with red as the organism fed on his own vital fluid, draining all he was, becoming one with him. Taking him over.

"Tom!" Oliver called, shaking Tom violently. Tom remained unresponsive, hyperventilating, eyes fixed upon some far away image that neither Oliver nor Sebastian could see. "Seb, he's having a panic attack; he's just not responding."

Sebastian looked on as one of his closest friends seemed to break down before him. Their violent shaking of him and calling his name had done nothing and they were rapidly running out of options. Sebastian felt utterly helpless, watching Tom suffer with as simple a task as breathing. Tom's lips were slowly turning blue as he struggled to take in air and, even though Sebastian's only current medical knowledge was through watching bad hospital dramas with his mother, he knew this wasn't good. Not knowing what else to do, Sebastian pulled his hand back and smacked Tom across the face, hard. The sound of skin on skin seemed to ring in their ears as the force of the blow knocked Tom back.

"Sebastian!" Oliver exclaimed. "What the hell was that for?"

"That's what they do in films when someone is having a breakdown!" Sebastian retorted, defending his actions though he himself had not intended to do that, and certainly not that hard.

Before the argument could escalate, a deep, gasping breath brought the two back to the present. Tom had moved from the rigid, upright position he had been in before, to laying slumped over, half on and half off the couch. His eyes were wide, filled with terror and he desperately took in deep breaths, scrabbling at the sofa beneath him as he fought for air. He felt as though he had been submerged in water for too long, and the ability to breathe again was a blessing as his body screamed for oxygen. His heart pounded against his chest and he desperately pressed a hand to it, eager to feel that it was indeed still there.

"Tom?" Oliver asked, gently leaning over the boy, trying to gain his attention. Tom jumped at the sound of his own name but soon realized that Oliver was the one speaking to him. "Are you ok?"

"Y-yeah," Tom stuttered, breathing deeply to calm himself. "I'm fine."

"You don't look fine to me," Sebastian replied tentatively.

Tom's breathing had finally returned to normal by this time, and his heart was slowing back down to its normal rhythm. The red mist had vanished and he could finally see clearly, the entire room now back in sharp focus, bright sunlight forcing the gloom away. The feeling of being invaded by some unknown parasite was fast subsiding and with it, his fear. Though he could still remember the feeling of having the parasite crawling under his skin, the feeling itself had vanished. As rapidly as it had started, it had stopped and almost immediately Tom's mind began to conjure up logical explanations for what had happened.

"Bad dream," he mumbled, trying desperately to wave his friends away. As he turned to look away from their imploring eyes, he glanced out of the window at the large patch of brilliant sunlight falling across the carpet. The sun had obviously risen completely during his 'dream'. He wondered briefly how long he had been lost in the haze.

"That was some nasty bad dream," Sebastian replied, voice heavy with skepticism. "You sure that's all it was?"

"What else could it have been, Seb?" Tom asked, though his voice wavered as he spoke. "It's all this stalker stuff, making me have bad dreams."

"Tom...this wasn't a dream," Oliver cut in. "You were wide awake, staring at something, completely unable to breathe. We thought you were having a heart attack."

"Well...I obviously wasn't," he countered. Despite knowing that it hadn't been just a dream, the less they asked, the more he could convince himself that it had all been a sleep deprived manifestation.

Like a dog with a bone however, Oliver would not give up. "That wasn't exactly the most normal of things to happen though. You were turning blue from lack of oxygen. Even if it was just a bad dream Tom, dreams shouldn't do that to you."

"It was just really vivid ok," Tom said irritably, biting his lip. He winced as pain shot through his lip and down his jaw, as the rusty taste of blood filled his mouth. Gently touching his bottom lip, Tom felt a ragged cut running across it. He dabbed at it with his sleeve, trying to avoid the concerned and slightly anxious looks on both their faces. "It was nothing, I'm fine, I'm over it. I've had them before."

"Bullshit you have!" Oliver cried. Sebastian placed a hand on his arm to calm him down, but he could see that Oliver was genuinely frightened by what had happened. "If this had happened before, you would've told us."

Tom shrugged his shoulders. "Well...what do you want me to do about it then, Olli?"

Instantly, Oliver deflated as he didn't have a legitimate answer for Tom. "I don't know. Maybe, see someone?"

"You mean...like a therapist?" Tom asked, raising an eyebrow and scoffing at the suggestion.

"Or talk to the school councilor," Sebastian suggested, hand still resting on Oliver's shoulder, attempting to calm him down. Sebastian could feel the anxiety radiating off him in waves and he knew how rare it was for Oliver to ever reach this stage of emotion.

"The point is, if a reaction like that is being produced from you being stalked by this girl then perhaps you should speak to someone," Oliver proclaimed. His voice shook as he spoke and his hands curled into tight fists, nails digging in to the soft flesh of his palms. "That was just really weird and kind of frightening, that's all. And you're quite clearly terrified, even if you won't admit it. "

You have no idea Tom thought as he briefly recalled what had happened mere moments ago. He shivered violently as the feelings raced through him once more. "Look, if it will make you feel any better, I'll go find the school councilor and talk to her. But only if this happens again, ok?"

Oliver looked at Tom imploringly, obviously not happy with this solution.

"Look, Olli, I'm not going to talk to someone over one bad dream," Tom reasoned. "She'll think I'm losing it and that's not going to solve anything is it really."

"He's right, Olli," Sebastian countered. Oliver glared at Sebastian for taking Tom's side, feeling as though he had been betrayed. It annoyed him even more so, knowing Sebastian had been just as terrified as he was during Tom's unexplainable episode. They'd both felt that fear, that inescapable panic of not being able to help, not being able to do anything or fix things because they didn't know what needed fixing. Oliver knew exactly how Sebastian had felt and now Sebastian was letting it slide as nothing more than just a dream.

"Fine, Tom," Oliver finally conceded, clearly still unhappy to do so but knowing there was very little he could do to change Tom's mind. "Do it that way, but do actually go and speak to her if you have another 'dream', if that's what you want to call it."

"It is...and I will," Tom replied. An awkward silence

hung heavily over the group; an after effect of the tense situation.

"So...breakfast?" Sebastian finally said, breaking the silence and easing the others slightly. Conceding to the idea of food, all three left the excessively messy living room in search of some form of sustenance. Tom's mother was, mercifully, nowhere to be found; if last night's entrance was anything to go by, he wondered whether he would see her much this morning. As it was such a rare occasion for her to enjoy a drink, her hangovers were always absolutely horrific and she'd spend most of the day with a thick head and queasy stomach, barely leaving her room to go much further than the couch or the kitchen. On a normal Saturday, Tom knew he would not have been able to deflect his mother from asking questions had she been around to see him panic as he had so he was glad for her absence and potentially painful day ahead. Even if that momentary happiness was followed by a wave of guilt at feeling slightly chipper about his mother's pain.

Despite knowing that Sebastian and Oliver could not remain with him forever, Tom had hoped they would spend at least most of the day with him. This was not to be however, as around early afternoon both boys were forced to leave. Though it was a Saturday, both had other commitments they needed to attend to and Tom could not think of an adequate reason to keep them longer – aside from the obvious, his impending insanity. Sebastian and Oliver both wanted to stay; their worry from earlier hadn't actually subsided, leaving them to watch Tom intently for any signs of weird behavior starting back up. It was silly to think either could help but they, especially Oliver, wanted to stay, just in case.

Watching his friends gather up their minimal belongings, an overwhelming sense of abandonment came over him and he desperately wished he could make them stay. Unable to come up with an excuse to extend their stay, he walked his friends to the front door and watched them reluctantly walk down the path. As he shut the door, his own isolation hit him hard. He wandered through the house in search of his mother, hoping she'd be awake by now and feeling just well enough for him to crawl under the duvet with her and watch Saturday afternoon catch up TV. Despite it being broad daylight, he felt as though he was lost in the darkness, waiting for something to come.

Chapter Nine

"Well…that was odd," Sebastian said tentatively as the two walked down the street away from Tom's house and towards their own homes.

Oliver sighed heavily as though the weight of the world pressed upon him. "Just a bit."

"Olli…you don't think there's any truth to what Tom was saying, do you?" Sebastian asked.

"You mean, you don't believe someone's stalking him?"

"Oh no, I believe that without a doubt," Sebastian replied hastily. "I mean…the story, the witch girl, Rose House, there's no way it could be true…is there?"

Oliver remained silent, not quite sure how to respond. His rational mind told him that there was no way the story could be real and yet, he was hesitating for some reason. "No Seb, the story's about as real as the Tooth Fairy, or vampires. It's a myth."

"So…the girl really is just a girl who's gone a bit nuts and taken a shine to Tom?" Sebastian asked, needing Oliver to confirm that fact, that the world was still as it should be, and nightmares weren't becoming reality, even if reality seemed to be more frightening. Sebastian needed Oliver to say this because he needed to know he was just being stupid. He needed a rational mind like Oliver's to let him know things were as they should be. For though Sebastian knew nothing could really be there, like his hidden fear of the dark it was a part of his mind that couldn't be reasoned with.

Oliver fingers restlessly pulled at a loose thread on his coat, untangling it from its woven prison, twirling the red string through his fingers absentmindedly. "Yes…that's all she is, just a girl." The thread snapped and he let his hands drop to his side.

Sebastian dug his hands into his pockets, balling them into fists, staring intently at the sky as he walked, the watery sunlight trickling through heavy clouds. "Tom woke me up this morning saying something about a rose but…there was nothing there. And then the dream or whatever it was. He's really losing it."

"Wouldn't you be on edge if someone was doing this to you?" Oliver questioned. In truth, he couldn't explain Tom's erratic behavior. Sure, there was the general apprehension around this girl and her borderline psychotic stalking of him, but Tom seemed to have gone thirty steps beyond this. Oliver had never known Tom to be so frightened by someone; and this was much more than just simply nerves. This was a deep seated, primal kind of fear, an animalistic, desperate horror too ravaged to hide behind a façade of basic calm. And what was worse is it seemed to be manifesting itself into actualized symptoms; try as Tom might, there was no way Oliver would even believe what had happened before was just a dream. If dreams could do that – stop a person breathing completely – then he'd never be sleeping again. Having always been an imaginative person, Tom had been able to easily rationalize all of the world's frightening, unexplainable oddities, it's why he was so good with horror movies and urban legends. He was a nightmare around magicians and magic tricks. Only now it seemed as though that definite line was starting to blur too rapidly.

"I guess," Sebastian replied with a shrug. "Maybe not that much but…I suppose."

"He's just freaked out, and it's making him act odd," Oliver continued, unable to say much more than that and feeling as though he shouldn't continue to analysis Tom. It wasn't as though he was qualified for the task anyway.

Sebastian stopped, having reached the point in their journey where he and Oliver would go separate ways. "It's just weird, that's all. It was all a bit too horror movie, for me."

"Seb, this isn't a movie, it's real life. There's no such thing as mystical creatures and hauntings and things like that. Like I said, Alyse the Demon Witch is about as real as a vampire or a werewolf," Oliver reasoned. Without having Tom and the physical signs of his fear in front of him, it was easier for Oliver to distance himself from the ordeal and hide his own apprehensions further. He needed to be the rational one now. Someone had to. "Remember what Ms. Brennan said in English last year? Creatures in myths were created as warnings, manifestations of fears in the physical world; a way of blaming bad things on something other than a random chance or the unknown. It doesn't mean they're actually real. But I guess…our imaginations really can run away with us when we don't know what's going on. Look at how many people believe they're being haunted. The only real thing about Alyse is that she's just a girl."

Sebastian sighed heavily. "You're right. It just freaked me out a bit is all. But yeah, you're right, as always. Do you think we should tell Mariana?"

Oliver paused, biting his lip. "It might be worth mentioning it briefly. She's known him a lot longer than we have and she might be able to help him a bit better. I don't know how, but it's worth a shot. Monday?"

Seb nodded in agreement, mulling over Oliver's words. Exchanging goodbyes, Sebastian turned and walked up his driveway while Oliver continued on down the road toward his own home. Despite both boys knowing that there was nothing supernatural about the situation, neither could ignore the tiny, almost imponderable part of their mind that whispered maybe, just maybe, there was another explanation.

Chapter Ten

Tom had hoped his mother's hangover would be one of her killer I-can't-get-out-of-bed-today ones where they could lounge in her room all day, watch her absolutely appalling and yet slightly catchy (not that Tom would ever admit that) soaps with mounds of sweet and starchy snacks they'd send Darcy out for. It was something they had done a lot when he was a child, before his dad got sick. Tom and Darcy would sneak into their parents' bedroom early in the morning and bury themselves under the duvet quite unceremoniously shaking both awake. What would follow would be some form of tickle/pillow fight, plenty of cuddles and them kicking his father out in search of breakfast, snacks and their favourite videos. For a solid three months, every Saturday, Tom had eagerly watched The Little Mermaid, brushing his mum's long, auburn hair with his fingers. It was something they'd stopped doing once his dad fell ill. For a long time Tom hadn't been able to see his mum's bedroom as anything more than sickness and death. A place where he'd watched his father wither away.

Sadly, it was one of her I've-got-to-get-up-and-do-something days, and so when he flung open the door in search of some childhood comfort, he'd found her half way in the closet, looking for a hopelessly lost brown court shoe.

She jumped as the door crashed into the wall behind it. "You okay, Tom?"

"Oh, yeah," he said, trying to hide the disappointment. "You off out?"

Angela kicked off her one brown shoe, and instead pulled on a pair of tattered boots. "Food shopping. I'm guessing from the piled high pizza boxes, our cupboards are bare."

Tom nodded. Not that he'd looked in the cupboards recently. Food hadn't been much of a priority over the impending sense of doom slowly creeping up on him. "Will you be long?"

Raking a brush through her hair, she looked at Tom through the mirror. "About an hour, probably. Why, hungry already?"

"No no," he said, shaking his head slightly. "Just curious is all. Was going to suggest a duvet day, like we used to do, but I've got homework anyway."

She stopped what she was doing and instantly Tom regretted saying anything. She had that look in her eyes, like she was about to prod and pry at him until he admitted to some deep emotional trauma. Then she'd probably tear up. "I can stay home if you-"

"No, please, go buy food. I'm starving," he said, almost frantically shaking his head, hoping to stave off the questions. Yes, he wanted distraction and she felt safe, but he certainly didn't want the emotional side of it. He just couldn't handle that today.

"You know, we haven't done that since your dad-"

"I know," Tom cut in. "I'm a bit too old to be climbing in to my mother's bed to watch cartoons anyway."

She bustled across the room and enveloped him in an almost bone crushing hug, clasping his shoulders tightly. She was a good five inches shorter than him however, and it left him awkwardly half crumpled in an attempt to fit into her arms. "Hey, you are never too old for mummy snuggles."

"You are literally crushing me," he managed to gasp out. She released him from her arms and he awkwardly tugged at his overly rumpled shirt, trying to pull it back into shape.

"Such a delicate boy." She patted his cheek before ushering him out of her bedroom. Slinging a cardigan over her shoulders she pulled the door to behind her. Slinking across the hallway to his bedroom, he muttered a quiet goodbye to his mother, after what felt like an age of her staring at him intently and asking twice more what was wrong. He just hoped she'd maybe take pity on him and come back with some chocolate.

Once alone inside his room he gave himself no time to think about anything but working, throwing himself completely into the first essay he could find. He steadily worked his way through coursework, trying to completely forget the outside world. Assuming this would not be possible and that his mind would not focus upon anything but Alyse now that he was alone once more, it came as a shock to him to find that almost two hours had passed since he began working. In those two hours, Alyse had not once crossed his mind. He had taken a small break when his mother had returned, eager to delve through the shopping and hopefully sniff out something chocolately, high calorie and full of additive heaven. Seeing her, eating everything she had brought back and then working through coursework as the sound of her putting the shopping away drifted through the house, he felt almost normal again. A strange kind of peace had come over him in these hours and it felt like the greatest relief.

With most of the work done, Tom turned his focus to the post-modern book they were studying in English. By now however, his lack of sleep was starting to wear upon him and his eyes began to droop. Desperate to stave away sleep he turned on his blindingly bright lamp, hoping the almost painful illumination would keep him awake. How foolish of him. Sleep tugged at his eyes like a petulant child before an ice cream van and soon exhaustion took over as he drifted into unconsciousness.

Chapter Eleven

With his mind so intently wrapped around Alyse, Tom automatically expected sleep to be clouded with nightmares and terror, but for the second time in a row, sleep came peacefully to him. Dreamless and empty, his mind was little more than a haze and the heavy layer of sleep that shrouded him from the world was translucently pleasant and soft.

By the time he woke up, gently this time rather than in the blind panic of earlier, the sun had set completely and his room was bathed in darkness. Having had such a blank, pure sleep, the darkness rested gently around him, comforting in its emptiness, unlike the night before where it had been a living, breathing manifestation of his overwhelming terror, encroaching upon him. Tom rubbed his eyes, shoving the last remnants of sleep away and bringing himself to full consciousness before reaching an arm wracked with pins and needles out to flick on the lamp right beside him. A niggling feeling of déjà vu scrabbling quietly at the back of his mid swept over him but sleep still weighed heavily, so he paid no mind to this. Annoyance soon replaced all feelings as the lamp refused to turn on. It was a new bulb and all.

He stood up and groggily walked in the general direction of his door, searching for the light switch, trying to maneuver his way through the mounds of stuff upon the floor without falling over and breaking his neck. Tom's foot connected with something hard and sharp as the scuttling sound of books being sent half way across the room let him know what he'd just kicked over. He swore and hopped the rest of the way across the room, his toe throbbing from its collision with the sharp book corner.

Fingers connected with the smooth plastic of the light switch and he quickly flicked it up, shielding his eyes from what he knew would be a blinding flood of light. He shook his arms violently as he waited, trying to push away the feeling of pins and needles coursing through him; a byproduct of the nap he had taken earlier. With his eyes finally accustomed to the light, he looked up and almost immediately wished he hadn't. Thoughts of Alyse and her obsessive, oppressive presence hit like an 18-wheeler as his eyes swept across the room. Hundreds of scarlet rose petals were scattered, covering every surface, their deep, angry colour resembling blood splatter.

Tom's mouth hung agape, watching as petals floated to the ground as though falling from the ceiling, raining red drops of blood. Lost in a sea of rose petals, Tom desperately felt for the wall behind him, searching for the door handle he knew would be there. His hand connected with something cold and metallic and he pulled it down, hard. The door sprung open and he fell through the gaping exit, stumbling to the floor as its swinging pathway knocked him off kilter. Leaping to his feet he made his escape, running out of the room and down the hallway, heading for the stairs. The house's incredible darkness engulfed him the moment he reached the top of the stairs and his heart stopped.

He turned, looking back at the room he had just left only to find the light spilling out of the open doorway becoming increasingly faint. Having bounced off the wall behind it with great force when he'd flung it open, it was now swinging back. A quiet click, louder than a gunshot, reverberated down the hallway as the door slid shut.

Tom found himself once more in a sea of darkness; however this time the thought of Alyse clouded his mind, clinging to the walls and clawing at hin. He knew she was watching him, he could feel her eyes trained upon him and he felt sure that she would be hiding in wait at the bottom of the staircase. He could almost see her, crouched in the darkness, eyes burning. He stood paralyzed, not sure what to do. If she wasn't down there then she would be behind him. No matter where he went she would be there, she would always be there; he didn't know how, he just knew. She would be waiting for him, watching him, here to consume and destroy him.

The ominous silence was shattered by the sound of something scraping against wood. Eyes boring into the darkness below, he desperately tried to glimpse what was making that noise. The sound increased, becoming an almost deafening roar. Instinctively, Tom threw his hands up, covering his ears, desperate to block the sound out but unable to.

Light flared, almost blinding him with its intensity. He closed his eyes as they burned from the sudden shock of light. Bright spots flickered behind his closed eyelids and a searing pain burst through him. The lights suddenly coming on had shocked him but what had caused his blood to run cold was the vision of red eyes right before him, looking deep into his own.

"Tom?" a familiar voice called. He forced himself to open his eyes, hoping the vision of her wouldn't be there. Alyse had vanished, being replaced with his concerned mother on the landing below. "Are you ok?" A small voice in the back of his mind, the part of him that was rapidly losing all sense of reality and dissolving instead into a pit of pure madness fleetingly wondered if she was tired of repeating herself. Maybe she was stuck and all she could ask him was if he was okay.

Tom tried to speak but found himself unable to. He took a deep breath, unaware of the fact that he had momentarily forgotten how to breathe upon hearing the scraping noise. "I'm fine," he finally managed to stutter out. He forced a smile though it did not reach his eyes. The questioning part of his mind was almost manically laughing at its own musings and he felt this laughter bubbling up inside himself.

She didn't believe him, he could tell that from here. He waited for another question to follow. Perhaps she'd ask how he was again. Then he could lie and say he was fine. It was an odd dance they were doing, her asking and him lying, but there really was no other way.

"Come downstairs, for dinner," she finally said, smiling warmly at him, hoping to convey to him her desperate desire to help however he would allow her to.

With utter relief, Tom watched his mother turn and walk back into the kitchen, barely registering what she had said just thankful it wasn't a question. Though he knew she'd keep asking, he'd have to keep lying. She was the last person he would tell any of this to. He couldn't bear the thought of her looking at him as Oliver and Sebastian had – like he truly was crazy. Taking a deep breath, he worked up the courage to head downstairs.

Walking into the kitchen, he leaned against the counter and watched Angela stir something gloopy and bubbling on the stove. It wasn't that her cooking was bad, quite the contrary in fact, most of the time it was absolutely moreish. It was the execution and indeed the entire cooking phase that had you questioning whether she'd really made it or snuck out back, ran down the street to the nearest take away and bought it, complete with bad 70s montage music.

"You've got something in your hair," she said, barely glancing away from her latest creation.

He wrinkled his nose and ran his fingers through his hair, half expecting some remnant of last night's feast to be tangled up in there; it was disgusting to admit but he had neglected today's shower and he would almost certainly bet he smelled like it. Colliding with something silky and delicate, he pulled at what felt like fabric.

Tom's heart seemed to slam itself against his chest once before stopping entirely at the rose petal grasped between his fingers. The panicked little voice in the back of his mind resumed its hysterical screaming and Tom's ears rung with the sound, though the room itself remained completely silent, save for the gently bubbling pot on the stove.

Clasping his hand tightly over the petal, he threw into the bin, desperately wanting to be rid of it. Moving over to the sink, he scrubbed his hands, wanting to remove all traces of the red petal after what had happened the last time he touched part of the rose. His body still tingled from where the red parasite had wormed its way over his skin and his chest burned at the memory of that pain.

If he could have, he would have bent over the sink and scrubbed at his scalp until red raw, fearful any more petals may perhaps be clinging to him. The very thought was grotesque and he held back the reflex to gag and be sick. And cut off every part of him that had come anywhere near that petal.

He could still feel the rose petal clinging to his hands regardless of how hard he scrubbed at them. Soap suds swirled around the drain as he desperately scrubbed, grabbing a nail brush from off the window ledge in front of him and using that to help. Flecks of blood peppered the water where he'd scoured away the thin skin on his knuckles, wincing as soap mixed in with these cuts.

"I think your hands are clean now!" Angela's voice floated across to him, bursting through a misty haze which had built up around him during his frantic scrubbing. Looking over his shoulder, she stood over the stove still, not looking at him, too busy averting what looked like an overflowing, almost volcanic pot incident.

The water was boiling hot and his skin was flecked red with blood and rapidly forming bruises. Flicking the taps off, he grabbed a tea towel, keeping his back to Angela, trying to hide the mess he'd made of his hands. He'd been so consumed with cleaning away the roses he'd barely felt the damage he was causing. But he felt it now. His hands throbbed as he patted them dry, specks of blood dotting the tea towel's white surface as more beaded on his hands. He pressed down harder with the tea towel, hoping to blot up as much of the blood as possible.

"We're not made of water, you know," Angela chided, still too focused on her cooking to turn and look at him.

"Sorry, stubborn ink stains," he said, too busy blotting at his hands to think up a better excuse.

Angela raced across the room towards Tom and he froze, sure she was heading in for some kind of hug and are-you-ok combination as a way of getting him to talk. Instead, she bustled around him, shooing him out of the kitchen on her way to the sink. "Dinner should be ready in ten minutes. I think. Make yourself useful and lay the table?"

He nodded in response. He hadn't expected to be pushed out of the way, much less escape without so much as a concerned stare. Perhaps she was finally starting to believe his lies, as deluded as that was of Tom to believe.

Slipping out of the kitchen and into the dining room, he set out place mats and cutlery, all the while focused upon the rose petals upstairs and how they could have possibly appeared, how *she* could have gotten in. Though initially feeling nothing but queasy at the thought of eating, by the time food was put on his plate Tom realized he was ravenous and ate with gusto, even helping himself to seconds. Clearly, fear was a great appetite builder.

With dinner finished, he found himself offering to help with clear up. Angela silently enveloped the boy in a tight hug and placed a loving kiss upon his forehead. Tom never offered to clean up. He often had to be goaded into doing the dishes, bribed with money or items, so this definitely wasn't like him. Something had to be wrong. And she'd noticed the cuts and abrasions on his hands but she'd also known asking outright would gain her absolutely nothing. In fact, she didn't quite know what to do. She just hoped that in that one movement she could convey to him how much she wished to help.

He melted into her embrace, allowing her comforting, familiar warmth to chase away the cold, sharp fear which had quelled inside him from the moment he woke up. She was safe, she would keep him safe. She always had. As she pulled away the warmth left with her and, though lessened, he once again felt cold fear gripping his mind. He was overcome with a sudden urge to tell her everything, every crazy little detail so she understood and could chase it all away with soothing words and more hugs. But he knew that wouldn't happen, that would never be the outcome. There would be people called and they would dispel any rational thought he had conjured up in place of their own. And their rational thoughts would all point to one, solid answer: crazy.

In truth, Tom's sudden interest in helping his mother was fueled by a desire to not be alone. He could fight the urge to tell her, but he couldn't fight the fear of being alone. He did not want to venture upstairs to his room nor did he want to sit in the living room alone. He felt like a child clinging to his mother after a bad nightmare, pathetic and weak. The calm he had felt whilst in the kitchen with her and the warmth from her latest hug were enough to show him he felt safest beside her. Though he knew there was nothing he needed protecting from, he still felt as though his mother could protect him. They worked diligently, doing the dishes and clearing the table, making small talk with Tom still deftly avoiding all questions to do with his emotional state.

By the time everything was sorted, Tom felt considerably calmer. They retreated to the living room in order to watch TV together. Angela disappeared briefly only to reappear moments later carrying the duvet from her bed, and they curled up beneath the soft, downy warmth, as Tom had wanted to do earlier. They lapsed into a comfortable silence, focusing upon some sitcom or other, the television's soft light acting as a comfort for Tom. Sometime later Darcy came home and soon found herself enveloped by the covers, sitting slightly squished but never the less cozy between Tom and Angela.

A sense of normality washed over Tom and he was able to push the thought of Alyse quite easily from his mind when surrounded by his family, his protectors.

But time soon came to shatter his peace. At midnight, Darcy excused herself, wanting to do some work before going to sleep. And like a catalyst setting the reaction in motion, Tom knew the inevitable would come when, sure enough, the axe fell as Angela decided to go to bed.

Not wanting to remain downstairs alone, Tom followed her upstairs, warily making his way to his own room. He swung the door open. Prepared himself for the crimson sea of luminous petals still scattered across the messy floor. But they were gone. Clothes lay upon the floor and books were spread about in odd piles but there were no signs of rose petals. The room looked exactly as it should be.

"Night Tom," Angela whispered, placing a kiss upon his forehead. "Sweet dreams. You know where I am if you need me. For anything."

And though he hoped his mother's blessing would come true, he knew this would not be so. *She* was there, watching him, and that only meant one thing; she would be in his dreams too.

Chapter Twelve

Sunday passed in much the same paranoid blur as Saturday had and, before Tom knew it, Monday morning was fast upon him.

Tom, normally a morning person, found it almost impossible to drag himself out from under the covers and force himself into something appropriate enough for school. He was reluctant to leave the sanctity of his room which, after Saturday night's rose petal fiasco had remained Alyse free. Unfortunately, he could not claim that about the rest of the world so felt as though entering it would bring more insanity, more fear. It wasn't safe out there.

He mentally forced himself out of the house and concentrated on putting one foot in front of the other, ignoring the burning desire to run back home and lock himself away in his room. Preferably with something heavy to act as a weapon.

It wasn't as though he feared her, he reasoned, as he concentrated on walking; it was more that he couldn't understand her, or what she gained from tormenting him in such a way. It made him nervous, not knowing what she wanted or what she was capable of doing. What made things worse was the way she always seemed to be everywhere and nowhere at once. How was it possible for her to cover his room in thousands of rose petals without waking him? Beyond that, how could she clear every single one of them away without alerting anybody else to her presence in the house? The floors creaked something chronic as the house was slowly aging beneath heavy feet. It baffled him and it was this which left him nervous and on edge.

It felt so much easier to remain in a place her presence hadn't tainted for a while, than to venture somewhere public where she could quite possibly have been present for who knows how long. His only glimmer of hope was the notion that, perhaps, surrounded by at least 3,000 students he would quite easily lose track of her and therefore get to spend at least a few hours without her stifling presence.

It was a pleasant day, Tom noted as his pace slowed, having reached the school gates. The sun was shining and it was relatively warm; something it hadn't been for a while. As a result, the grounds were filled with students lounging on the grass, soaking up the morning sun, catching a few minutes sleep or desperately trying to finish assignments due in for that day. There was an air of comfort; a stillness only felt on days like this, when the sky was forget-me-not blue, the sun's rays unencumbered by clouds. It felt like one of those perfect spring mornings, the ones that let you know the dead cold of winter was finally receding, and the world was coming back to life. If only that were the case and spring was upon them. Instead they still had months of icy winter to look forward to, and this day stood as a teasing reminder of what would soon vanish.

Spotting Oliver and Sebastian sat with a small group of people on the far side of the grounds he jogged over, collapsing to the ground beside Sebastian.

"Hey guys," he murmured, curling his legs up underneath him, wary of the fact that his jeans would probably be covered in grass stains by the time classes began.

"Tom!" Sebastian cried dramatically. "You're here!"

"Well spotted there," Tom commented sarcastically. A few voices muttered 'hello' in his general direction and he replied with a curt nod to each.

"So, Tom, good weekend?" Mariana cut in, leaning across Sebastian to look him in the eye, elbows resting on Sebastian's outstretched legs. Her chin rested upon her palm and she had one eyebrow raised quizzically, mirth sparkling deep within her emerald orbs.

He glared at her, then at Oliver and Sebastian. "Wow, thanks for telling everyone, guys," he sneered, the slight happiness which had started to overcome him quickly disappearing. "Laugh it up, Mariana, it's all you're good for."

"Harsh!" she exclaimed. "It's not my fault you're going a bit mad."

"Oh just shut up, you've got no idea," Tom growled, not in the mood to put up with her comments. He felt angry and slightly betrayed knowing they'd spilled his secret to others, particularly as it was so embarrassing. "I bet you've all been having a good old laugh at my expense. So much for best friends." He rolled his eyes dramatically and gathered his bag, wanting to leave the group.

"Tom, wait," Oliver said. "We didn't tell everyone, just Mariana."

"You shouldn't have told anyone!" he exclaimed loudly, causing the entire circle to turn and look at him expectantly. He sat frozen, staring back at everyone, eyes wide and deer like in their burning gaze. After a few awkwardly long, drawn out moments of silence, the eyes fell away from him. "It was just between us!" he hissed, now no longer on display.

Oliver threw hands up in defense. "She asked us about you! You were the one who told her about the whole stalker thing, she just wanted to know what was going on! And we just kind of thought, her knowing you for so long as well, she deserved to know."

Tom's eyes burned daggers at Oliver before sweeping across to Sebastian. "So you told her I was going mad?"

"We told her some of the stuff you told us," Oliver whispered so even Mariana couldn't hear them. "We never said madness."

Tom angrily tore apart a blade of grass, taking out his irritation on the unsuspecting leaf. He knew no matter how angry he was, arguing wouldn't take back them telling Mariana. He was frustrated more than anything. He really hadn't wanted her to know the extent of the situation, and just how badly he was reacting to it. In truth he felt kind of ashamed by his fear and pathetic reactions. Even if Mariana had seen him sob like a small child on more than one occasion. "You just shouldn't have said anything."

"Well, at least she knows now so you don't have to tell her," Sebastian reasoned. "And anyway, everyone thought you were a bit mental so it doesn't make that much of a difference."

Tom glared at Sebastian as the other two stifled giggles. "Fine, whatever. I'm just...I'm not insane, ok. I'm really not. And don't go telling anybody else!"

"Ok, we won't," Oliver said seriously. "We promise. Sorry."

Oliver nudged Sebastian, hard. "What? Oh, sorry."

Tom shook his head, more to clear it than anything else.

Mariana crawled behind Sebastian, pushing him out of the way so that she could take his space beside Tom. "Hey," she said, placing a gentle hand upon his arm. "I'm sorry, I didn't mean to butt in. I was just curious and they told me what you'd told them Friday night. I got a bit worried, that's all. You know I put my foot in it when I'm worried."

"It's ok," Tom said through gritted teeth. "It's fine."

"Don't be mad at me, please?" she asked, widening her eyes in a mock display of innocence.

"I'm not mad, Mariana," Tom finally conceded, looking up at her, amused by her awful attempt to look innocent, though the seed of frustration still pitted itself in his voice. "I'm just fed up of people saying I'm going mad. I'm not. I know what's going on sounds a bit insane, but it's all true."

"I didn't say it wasn't," she said with a shrug. "I was just kidding around. Like you said, it does sound a bit insane. But if you say that's what's going on, then it's true."

There was something in way she spoke and how she attempted to brush it off that really grated on Tom's nerves and he could feel that angry little nub in the back of his mind slowly seeping out. He didn't want to take his annoyance out on her. He wanted to keep sitting next to her. Maybe get to hold her hand again. But the anger burned red hot in him and he just couldn't get it to quell. "You don't have to patronize me you know," he sneered at her. "I'm not a child. You can think what you want, I really don't care."

"I'm not patronizing you," she bit back. "Stop being such an idiot. I'm just saying it's hard for us to get it, but if you say that's what's happening then it is. I **am** trying to understand, you know."

"Just shut up Mari," he glared, not wanting to listen to her comforting words. No, that wasn't quite right. Part of him wanted to listen. The other part was rapidly being consumed by a fiery frustration and he was becoming overwhelmingly irritable with the people around him.

"Oh good, you're being an absolute tosser," Mariana commented sarcastically. "Sorry for trying to understand."

"You're forgiven," he replied, grabbing his bag, standing up and storming away.

"So, remind me again why we're friends with him?" she asked Oliver and Sebastian as she too gathered her things. Her voice hitched slightly, whether from irritation or genuine upset neither could tell, though they both had a slight inkling as to what it may be. Mariana was not as subtle as she liked to believe.

"Maybe you should leave him alone, Mari?" Oliver said as he watched her stand up. "Sit with us for a bit. He'll calm down. You can talk to him then."

"Like hell I will," she retorted. "I'm sorry, but I'm not having him be such an ass to me. None of this is my fault. I was only trying to be nice"

She turned from the group and followed Tom's retreating figure into the large, whitewash building in front of her. His long strides carried him fast away from her and she had to race down the corridor dodging bodies as she went in order to keep up. He seemed not to notice her jogging behind him, so she grabbed his arm and dragged him into an empty classroom.

Tom's heart was slamming itself erratically against his ribcage, not quite sure whether to beat faster or give up completely and his eyes were wide in fear. He hadn't expected anybody to follow him so feeling a slender hand wrap around his wrist and violently drag him out of the hallway had been a shock. With everything that had happened, his thoughts had immediately sprung to images of Alyse and he readied himself for whatever new horrors the hateful girl could conjure up to torment him. Being flung around only to come face to face with emerald eyes as opposed to crimson ones did little to still his racing heart, but caused his brain to do what felt like a rather painful flip.

"Mari?" he questioned, unable to believe it was just her.

"You were expecting her weren't you?" she asked, looking deep into his eyes. He hated when she did this, it was like she was seeing right into his mind, able to read the racing thoughts there. Lately it seemed like everyone could do this, like they could all hear the crazy ramblings of a boy completely stricken with fear just as loudly as he could, but nobody was as adept at it as Mariana. "Weren't you?"

"Yes, ok, yes I was," he sighed in defeat. Though he wanted to scream at her, show his anger, he felt it dissipating. In truth he wasn't angry at her, he was angry with Alyse, and the fear she had inspired in him, so directing it at Mari wasn't fair on her. He held on to this rationality as the bubbles of irritation still rested dangerously in his stomach, ready to blow at any moment.

"She's really got you on edge, hasn't she?" Mariana asked, still holding onto his wrist.

He wriggled his wrist out of her grasp and took a step back, leaning against the teacher's desk. "Look, Mari, I'm not really in the mood for a heart to heart this morning ok. I just want to forget."

"But you can't forget?" she asked, still looking at him with those piercing eyes, like she knew everything. Sometimes, he really hated her. In that whole I-hate-you-but-not-really kind of way, of course. "You can't forget because she's all you seem to think about. Because you're rapidly becoming as obsessed with her as she is with you."

The bubbles of irritation popped and he was angry again, directed at Mariana who assumed she knew so much. "I'm not obsessed." He hated the way she almost accused him feeling anything more than fear towards Alyse. And he hated her most, in that one moment, because part of him was whispering in agreement over his obsession, and he knew he could never hide it from Mariana. "I'm terrified, ok. I'm absolutely terrified because I have no idea what's going on right now. I don't know where she is or what she wants. All I know is she keeps breaking into my house and playing with my mind. And I'm starting to think I am going mad. Like, lock me up in a padded cell and throw away the key, kind of mad. I don't know if any of this is real, and I kind of just wish it was in my head, because then I could pop a few pills, and maybe padded cells aren't so bad." He stopped himself, feeling a panicky rant building up inside of him and not wanting to break down completely into a puddle of fear in front of Mariana. "It would be so much simpler."

"You really think it would be simpler if all of this was in your mind?" Taking a step forward, she stood directly in front of Tom, an eyebrow raised.

He paused. "I suppose not. But it would make more sense."

"When has anything in this world ever made sense to us?" she asked, letting her hand move across the divide between them, entwining their fingers; a movement she'd done a thousand times before when either were gripped with fear, anger or tension.

"Sometimes it seems like it does," he sighed, enjoying the feeling of her fingers wrapped in his. Soothing. Familiar. "Sometimes I feel like I understand, then it all goes away and I'm just left not knowing anything."

"Yeah, but think how dull it would be to live in a world

where everything made sense and nothing strange happened," she said with a slight smile.

He scoffed. "You wouldn't be saying that if you were in my position." Tom reached out between them and moved a free strand of hair from her face behind her ear, having hypnotically watched it drift down across her eyes. This…it felt normal. It was the most normal thing he had felt in as long as he could possibly remember. Alyse was the farthest thing from his mind. All he really knew was that in this darkened classroom, with Mariana holding his hand and looking into her eyes, her safe, normal, emerald eyes with not a trace of red behind them, he felt normal again. He felt real. "This makes sense though. Now."

She nodded back, not sure what else to do. A bell rang somewhere far away and the door flew open breaking the hypnotic spell between the two. They pulled apart and shiftily moved out of the room, heading towards their own classrooms for the first lesson of the day. Eyes followed their departure and they avoided the questioning glances from students as they milled in. Tom muttered a quiet 'see you later' to Mariana before heading down the hallway; he wouldn't see her till free period today as their classes didn't collide.

As he walked, he refused to contemplate what had happened or the way his hand suddenly felt cold, and empty, without her fingers entwined in his. As he walked away from her though, the feeling of being watched by Alyse returned. It seemed Mariana had been able to stop his mind's constant fear of this unknown girl, at least briefly.

Walking through the courtyard, he kept his eyes downcast avoiding looking in mirrors or the reflective windows that seemed to be surrounding him, somehow sure he would see her crimson gaze. He'd never realized just how many windows and mirrors this school had, nor just how quiet and eerie the corridors were when classes were in session. He slid into class moments before their teacher arrived, thankfully avoiding any awkward 'why were you late' questions. Gladly, he saw Sebastian and Oliver had saved him a seat. Completely ignoring their questioning gaze and the many crumpled up notes they passed him he, for once, threw himself into Maths, determined to keep his mind focused on the numbers as they seemed to dance across his page in confusion.

Chapter Thirteen

Tom headed out into the grounds for free period, eyes scanning the grassy area for any sign of Mariana, spotting her immediately under their usual tree. He made a beeline for her, a slight skip in his step after having spent the morning looking around corners for somebody who, it seems, was nowhere in sight. Indeed the morning had been incredibly Alyse and rose free; even the feeling of being watched had dispersed, leaving him with the walking on air feeling flowing through him. He had also managed to not over think the strange moment he and Mariana had shared earlier, which was a rarity for him whose mind continually pulled to pieces every situation he found himself in. The sun was still shining brilliantly even after a few fluffy, white clouds had rolled in.

He slid down to the ground, landing rather ungracefully beside Mariana who had put her book away upon noticing Tom's approach.

"Tom, you're looking excessively happy this afternoon," Mariana noted. "I assume you've cheered up since this morning."

"And yet your sarcasm remains," he commented, though there was no bite in his tone.

"I do it because I care," she responded with equal sarcasm. Tom rolled his eyes at her before breaking eye contact to reach into his bag, pulling out a bottle of water and taking a swig from it. He had originally gone in for a cigarette, but he'd forgotten to buy some over the weekend – being a bit preoccupied and all - so that dull ache in the back of his mind begging for another nicotine fix would have to suffer till school ended.

A comfortable silence descended over the two and Tom leant back against the tree, glancing around the area quickly, subconsciously searching for Alyse; he couldn't relax until he was quite sure she wasn't there, watching him. Then again, with the amount of people around, spotting her would be difficult and her spotting him would be almost impossible. He finally relaxed completely and closed his eyes.

After a few moments, a tentative hand touched his and he startled awake, eyes wild. "Wow, Tom, you ok?" Mariana asked, having jumped back in shock at his rather violent reaction to her gentle touch. It was then that he noticed he had taken a swing at her before even fully opening his eyes.

"Sorry, you just startled me," he murmured, bringing his hand back towards him, cradling it against his chest. "I didn't hit you, did I?"

"No," she confirmed. "Lightening fast reflexes and all."

He raised a mocking eyebrow at this comment. He knew the truth about her lack of any reflexes, having seen her completely obliterate her team's chance of winning any game during sports on more than one occasion. Add to this the fact she often found herself ungracefully sprawled across the floor, having tripped over nothing, and the very idea of any type of reflex in association with Mariana rapidly vanished. "Did you want something?" he finally asked, avoiding the temptation to mock her further.

She blushed and looked away, tangling her fingers into the grass, playing with the cool, leafy blades beneath her fingertips. "I just wanted to say I'm sorry, for this morning. I know I said sorry already but...just don't want you mad at me."

"It's ok, I'm over it," he shrugged. "Your best friends call you insane...it's something you get over quickly."

"Well...we never said insane...a little eccentric maybe," she reasoned.

"Mad, insane, eccentric, weird. Call it what you like, that's just semantics; it all means the same thing. All three of you think I've gone off my rocker and I'm making this up."

"Nobody thinks you're making it up. We were just discussing it, trying to understand what was happening. It's just a bit odd." Mariana paused, mulling over her words. "I mean, if I told you some guy was hanging around me, always watching, leaving me roses, thinking he was some mythical creature you'd think I'd lost it too."

He pulled at a loose thread in his jeans. "Strange guy, hanging around a girl, leaving her presents? People would instantly think he was up to no good and that you needed immediate protection."

"Is this going to be one of those unfair-sex-treatment conversations you're so fond of?" she asked with a sigh. "I know, if I said that to someone it would be different because I'm a girl and all men are evil, whatever. I don't mean it like that though and you know it. Reverse the situation; I'm you and someone else is um…what was her name?"

"Alyse," he murmured, noticing how easily the name rolled of his tongue. Like it belonged.

"Yeah, her. Just imagine it. Then imagine everything you told Olli and Seb, I told you," she continued as though he hadn't spoken. "What do you think?"

"Look, I can see what you mean, and I do get it."

"Good."

"So…what did Olli and Seb tell you then?" Tom asked, out of curiosity, Oliver's previous statement of not having told her everything coming back to him.

"Just that some girl was stalking you, leaving you roses everywhere you went and that you'd found a load of information about a myth who this girl thought she was, or something," Mariana rambled. "It was all a bit hard to keep up with; you know how those two cannot relay information well."

"And it sounds insane, doesn't it?"

She paused. It did sound a farfetched, but she didn't want to put his defenses back up or offend him. If his previous reactions were anything to go by, he wasn't handling the stress of the situation too well. "The stalking and leaving roses part sounds frightening. The myth part sounds a little mental. Though, I guess it's more mental on her part as she thinks she's this creature person. It was kind of a leap for you to make the assumption though."

"But, not really that insane, right?"

"No, I guess not," she confirmed with a reassuring smile. He knew she wasn't being completely honest; Mariana couldn't ever lie to him. "Like I said, I was just making fun of you. You know I don't think you're insane. I said that earlier and I'll say it again till you believe me."

It dawned on him that Oliver and Sebastian had not told her about his episode the morning after their impromptu stay, nor did they mention his hysterical melt down the night before. Though he hadn't wanted to admit it, both situations had been incredibly embarrassing for him and the last thing he wanted was Mariana to find out. Though having grown up with her and found himself in every number of embarrassing situations with her, this he didn't want her to know about. Even the mere thought had his cheeks burning with shame.

"Tom...if you ever do want to talk to me though, you can," Mariana said after a few moments of silence, breaking through Tom's thoughts. "I know I make fun of you but...if it's something serious I won't. And you know I won't tell a soul. I do think the world of you, Tom. You're my best friend and I really hate seeing you so upset and so on edge. It's not like you, and it's not right."

He looked up at her and smiled. He hadn't noticed before but through this entire conversation she had swiveled to face him head on, resting on her knees and leaning forward slightly, now blocking his view of the rest of the grounds. For the second time that day he found himself looking into her emerald eyes and the thought slyly popped into his head that her eyes were pretty. They sparkled with light and intelligence, bright and shimmering green. Maybe it was exactly that that made them so beautiful...they weren't crimson. They were normal. She was normal.

She had a delicate smile playing across her lips and he couldn't help but notice just how comforting that smile was. He'd never realised how a simple smile could really brighten her up.

Mariana had always been the girl in the background. The one who was always there. They'd grown up together and she'd often been like the sister he had never wanted and yet couldn't imagine life without. She'd been there throughout the entire ordeal with his father. She knew everything about him, his family, his history. She knew all of him. And though their relationship may be laced with wit, sarcasm and continual humor at each other's expense, she was the one he knew would always be there, their paths through life forever entwined. His Mariana.

So, why had it taken him so long to realize she was so pretty? He'd always acknowledged she wasn't a troll, but now, sat in the warm sunlight, watching him intently, eyes radiating comfort and care as a small smile played on her lips, genuinely worried about him he couldn't help but realize she really was absolutely beautiful. And, that sly little voice in his mind said, she was completely real, completely normal, not a hint of red in sight.

He found himself running a hand gently through her hair, pushing strands back out of the way again. She always seemed to have wisps of dark hair drifting across her face and he wondered how she was sometimes able to see. It was a habit that used to annoy him, but now he was thankful for this graceless descent of strands. It gave him an excuse to touch her. "Thanks. I might just take you up on that offer of someone to talk to."

"I'm all ears!" she exclaimed with a smile, a faint blush gracing her cheeks. "I know what Olli and Seb are like – incredibly caring but as helpful as a pineapple."

"Yeah, perhaps sensitivity isn't their strong point," he conceded, with a smirk. "But they have their good points; they forced me to tell them about Alyse and, in a way, I suppose it was good to include someone else in the madness."

"And then they told me," she smirked.

"Yes, and then they told you," Tom replied, with a roll of the eyes. "How eternally grateful I am for that."

"You know you love me."

"Indeed," he murmured. He let his hand drift away from her face. She moved back and came to rest beside him, back pressing against the tree once more. Allowing her hand to descend slowly, she placed it on the grass beside his. She couldn't deny the strange moment they had just shared. She and Tom were just friends. They had always been just friends. Best friends, but never more. Their lives would be forever twined, as friends. And that was how it should be. How it should always be. They would be friends, best friends, close as siblings, but always platonic, nothing more. So, then, why did her heart beat a little bit faster in that moment? It fluttered once more as he gently placed his hand upon hers and entwined their fingers.

She smiled and they sat in comfortable silence, their hands entwined, both contemplating this one moment, the moment in which they knew something was about to happen, something was about to change. It felt as though whatever was about to happen would set the world on fire and consume them with it. They stood on the edge of an abyss and with one single moment they could fall, they could catch fire and burn and everything would change and it would all be so bright and so blinding. Or they could do nothing and the moment would pass, and nothing would change. Mariana could feel her heart beat rapidly in anticipation as Tom's hand gently squeezed her own. She turned to look at him to find him watching her intently.

There it was again, that gentle smile playing upon her lips. He could see a thousand thoughts racing behind her eyes and knew that she was trying to understand everything and nothing all at once, as was he. Her emerald eyes held his once more, no hint of crimson, no sight of scarlet, nothing to suggest she was anything more than this beautiful, normal girl he knew so well.

He wasn't sure why he was doing this but Tom found himself leaning forward, closing the distance between the two, his eyes focused upon those smiling lips. He watched as her eyes fluttered shut and he allowed his to drift too.

As his eyes closed, his mind flashed back to the image of the parasite two days ago worming its way towards his heart. He could see it now, wrapping around the beating tissue and squeezing, clamping down hard. Tom jolted in shock at this image, eyes flying open as the memory of pain and fear engulfed him.

He had briefly been lost in his own world, lost in her and in that short amount of time it seemed the sun's rays had dimmed, as though heavy, ominous clouds had rolled in to cover it though the sky remained cloudless. Goose bumps erupted across his flesh and he felt a violent shiver claw down his spine as familiar red eyes trained upon him. It was then that Tom realized he'd been gripping Marianas' hand painfully hard, causing her to wince in agony.

"Tom? Tom what's wrong?" she asked, noticing the way his pupils had dilated in what she assumed was fear, if the vice like grip on her own hand was anything to go by. She refused to think back to what had almost just happened, not wanting to consider what it could, or could not have meant. Her heart had been in her throat and her mind swirled with all the possibilities of what was about to happen. But when it never did, she'd opened her eyes to find Tom reeling back in what she imagined was shock, as his hand squeezed hers painfully. She reached out and shook him violently, trying to regain his attention.

His daze passed and he stared at Mariana, barely seeming to recognize the familiar emerald eyes. Shaking his head once, his mind regained who she was and where he was. And what had almost happened between them.

"Ok, that was insane," she said, voice dropping an

octave as though worried they would be overheard. "What happened?"

"I-I don't know," Tom stuttered, tongue stumbling over his words, feeling as though it had been filled with lead and lined with cotton. "She's watching me again."

"Where is she, can you see her here?" Mariana asked, getting to her knees and dragging Tom with her, forgetting he was still clutching her hand for dear life. She scanned the area, looking for somebody shifty staring at the two. She wasn't quite sure what she was expecting to find but somebody with a trench coat and heavy duty binoculars was on her list.

"No, Mari, she's not here," Tom responded, dragging Mariana back down to the ground and releasing her hand. "Well...she is. I just know when she can see me and when she's watching me. I can feel it."

"What do you mean, you can feel it?" she asked. "Like, as though someone's walked over your grave or something."

He shook his head at the analogy. "It's worse. It's like a million people have walked over my grave. And...I just know she is, I can feel it, like no matter what I do or where I'll go she'll always be able to see me."

"Tom this is absurd, how can she see you if she's not here?"

Tom's eyes darted across the grounds, examining every corner, searching for her but dreading finding her eyes. He could feel her burning through him, the red hot heat of her presence clawing its way through him, burying itself deep in to his mind. "I don't know, she just can. She can see me in my house even when she's not near it, I know she can. She's everywhere and she's watching me and she won't ever leave."

Mariana moved as if to place a hand upon his shoulder but then thought better of it and withdrew back. The time for touching and intimacy had long since gone and it felt wrong for even such a basic gesture as this. "Tom, be reasonable. I know this is really frightening, but if she's not here, then she can't really see you. It just feels like she can because she's been following you. I promise you if she's not here she can't see you."

"But...she can."

"She can't," Mariana said firmly. "I promise you that. You're ok here. And if she is watching you, then we can find her. Please, Tom, please listen to me, it's ok."

He noticed her voice hitch in her throat and it was then he realized her eyes were shining with unshed tears. Not knowing what to say in response, Tom remained silent, hating that he had made her feel like this, feel afraid of something, worried about him and who knows what else. But...Tom knew Alyse was there, somewhere, and she could see him, somehow. He rested his forehead against hers, looking deep into her eyes again, bringing that level of comfort they had shared mere moments before.

"What's happening, Mari?" he asked quietly, defeated. "Why is she doing this to me?"

Lost for words, Mariana desperately fought for something to say. Her mind was in overdrive as her heart almost ached at the broken defeat in Tom's voice. She could feel the fear radiating off him but she had no answers for him. "I don't know. I really don't know. I wish I could help. I wish I could find this girl for you and just, knock some sense into her. I hate seeing you so on edge."

"I hate being on edge," he replied. "It really isn't fun."

"You take it better than I would," she sighed, resting back against the tree, the two having pulled away from one another again. Whatever else had been about to happen, that moment had passed and, as moments so often do, may never come around again. This thought, along with the way Tom was being treated by somebody they had never even seen, caused anger to rise in her. Her moment had been stolen and, until now, she hadn't realized just how much she'd been hoping for it. "I'd be furious."

"You're not the calmest of people, though," Tom replied with a grin. "You're short and scary, you know this."

"I'm serious though, Tom," she said, and he could hear anger in her voice now. "I mean, who does she think she is? Following you, leaving you strange gifts, even though it's very obvious what she's doing is frightening you. Who does this stuff? You don't even see this in the movies because it's just too insane. And it's been going on for too long to be a stupid joke. She just needs to stop!"

Mariana's anger shocked Tom. He had never thought of it in that way before, as something to be angry over. She did have a point, though, and the more she talked about the anger she would feel, the more it felt as though it were his anger. Her fury towards this unknown person radiated off her, almost overpowering and that she had gone from barely believing him to feeling so emotionally invested resonated within Tom. Nobody else had become so passionate and it was blissfully refreshing to have somebody who seemed to finally believe him about Alyse. Plus, she had a point; who was this girl and why did she think she deserved to impose on his life so phenomenally? Why was she targeting him and, most importantly, why wouldn't she just leave him alone? It had gone beyond a practical joke and was bordering on obsessive. So, why wouldn't she just leave?

By the time the end of their free period rolled around, Tom's fear had been replaced by resentment. Indeed he still felt fear and intimidation, but white hot fury was rapidly consuming it.

Grasping his hand tightly, Mariana squeezed, letting him know she was there for him. "I'll see you later k," she said with a smile. Leaning over, she placed a chaste kiss upon his cheek. "For good luck."

Grabbing her stuff, she raced off across the grounds, heading to the building on the far side of campus for whatever her next class was.

Tom's was stunned, unable to move. The kiss had

shocked him, as what felt like bolts of electricity radiated across his cheek where her lips had briefly been. His heart beat a little faster as he watched her walk away, enjoying the feeling of warmth spreading through him. As he did so, he felt uncontrollable laughter bubbling around him, coming from nowhere and everywhere at once and it took him a moment to realize it was his own. The emotions Tom had felt, the thoughts racing around inside his mind, had left him feeling a little delirious.

Chapter Fourteen

The rest of the day passed by uneventfully and Tom hoped that Alyse had either disappeared or decided to give up. Knowing this was too hopeful of him to believe however, he settled for enjoying what he knew would be brief alone time.

Mariana, Sebastian and Oliver avoided the topic of Alyse, choosing to keep things light whenever the opportunity to talk presented itself so by the time school was out, Tom was considerably happier. Having pushed the memory of that fear firmly aside, he found it easy to once more forget about her. Despite this, he was still grateful to his friends when, at the end of the school day, they walked home with him without needing to mention why. Light conversation flowed about tedious topics, though Tom's mind was unable to focus on anything more than the way his and Mariana's hands kept brushing as they walked side by side, sending jolting bolts of electricity leaping along his skin, tingling and tantalizing. Letting himself get wrapped up in Mariana was rapidly becoming his favourite way to forget about Alyse.

His heart stopped as they turned the corner and his house came into view. Leaning against a leafless apple tree in his front garden stood Alyse, eyes trained upon the group as they approached. Her eyes gleamed ruby red in the dying sunlight, full of unknown emotion – wrath, fury, directed towards him. He felt the Rose Parasite within him twitch and twist in response to her presence and his breath hitched, trapped by the moving, convulsing creature.

Without realizing it, he came to a halt, unable to force himself to keep moving. Mariana was the first to notice he'd stopped. Her entire body had become acutely aware of his, so close to her, almost in tune with his every movement, and the sudden lack of warmth almost immediately signaled his disappearance from right beside her. Grabbing hold of Oliver's elbow, halting he and Sebastian mid conversation, she dragged them back towards Tom, worry etching itself in lines across her forehead.

"Tom, what's wrong?" Oliver asked as Mariana placed a comforting hand upon his shoulder.

"She's here," Tom whispered. Hearing his voice he hated how pathetic he sounded; how childlike and afraid of something so insignificant yet able to cause incredible, irrational fear to consume him.

"Where?" Sebastian asked. Before them stood an empty street, barren of any kind of life; still and silent as only a winter's early evening can be. Though all three did believe his story, its fantastical nature had left a shadow of doubt. Finally seeing the girl he continually saw, they would be able to expel this doubt and maybe do something about it. There was an eagerness that rippled among them as they quickly scanned the street ahead in search of their mystery culprit.

"There," he murmured, not quite sure how they could miss her, she stood out incredibly against his bleak front lawn. Her scarlet eyes burned against the dull, white expanse of his house and the entire world seemed to pale around her as she stood stark amongst a grey expanse of nothingness.

Following his line of sight, they turned as one to where his eyes rested.

"I can't see her anywhere," Sebastian finally conceded, after looking at the same, barren apple tree for what seemed like an age.

Mariana bit her lip, willing herself to see something, anything. But there was nobody to be seen. "Neither can I."

"Tom, where exactly can you see her?" Oliver asked, confirming that he, too, could not see Tom's stalker.

Tom felt the burning need to glare at his friends for not seeing what was so obviously right in front of them but he found himself unable to tear his gaze away from her. "There, by the apple tree."

Silence fell once more as their gaze returned to the leafless, pitiful apple tree. Brown branches reached towards the sky as the dead, rotting corpses of forgotten leaves littered the grass beneath it. A lone, brown leaf clung desperately to a branch, swaying precariously in the gentle breeze, grasping at life in an attempt to avoid the fate that had overcome its fallen brethren. So much to see about one apple tree. But she wasn't there. Nobody was there.

"Tom, I'm serious, I can't see her," Mariana murmured after a moment or two.

"She's there," he muttered, barely able to speak. "She's there and she's watching me. I told you she's always there. You have to believe me. You have to now you've seen her. Her eyes."

Glancing at one another nervously, they silently debated how to proceed. Unspoken, thoughts raced between them. They could not see her. All they saw was an apple tree, stripped of its leaves. There was nobody there, certainly nobody with bright red eyes.

"Um…Tom, maybe we sh-"

"You have to be able to see her!" he exclaimed suddenly, voice shocking them into silence. "She's walking towards us, she's right there! Are you all stupid?"

Alyse moved with cat like grace, slinking across the grass. She grinned, sending a quiver of fear running through Tom, sharp teeth glinting in the weak sunlight.

The instinct to run hit Tom. Some part of his mind rationally explained running would not solve anything but the desire to flee remained steadfast. His body screamed with the desire to run, begging him to move. To flee. To leave. Why wouldn't his body move? He felt his mind banging furiously against the inside of his skull as it pleaded with him to run, all the while watching her slink towards him.

Mariana's grip on his shoulder tightened. His breathing hitched and it seemed as though he was struggling for air. "Tom, calm down. What's wrong? Olli?"

130

"I don't know," Oliver said, running a hand through his hair, not knowing what to do to help his friend. He reached out and knocked Mariana out of the way. Grasping Tom's shoulders he shook him violently. "Tom!" he called, hoping to shock the taller boy out of his almost catatonic state.

"We have to move," Tom replied, voice quivering. "We have to move, now! She's coming here!"

Alyse stood a few feet away from them, a small smile gracing her rosebud lips as she watched in amusement. Tom hated that smile. He hated her for everything she was doing to him. But he was still afraid. He took a step back, needing distance from her.

Unfortunately, his coordination seemed to have vanished and what he thought had been a step back was nothing more than an ungraceful wobble backwards. Mariana, Oliver and Sebastian reached out automatically, grasping hold of his arms, holding him upright.

A high pitched, screeching noise pierced through the air and all movement ceased. Ringing filled Tom's ears as the sound penetrated through him and he looked on in shock. The awful, ungainly noise was her, laughing.

Shiver's chased their way down Oliver's spin as a cold splash of fear filled the pit of his stomach. "What was that?"

"Car crash?" Mariana asked as the hairs on the back of her neck stood on end. "It was awful whatever it was."

"That was her," Tom cut in, having heard part of their conversation. "Her, laughing at me."

"Tom there's nobody there!"

"Yes there is!" Tom screamed back. Striking out, his hand connected with Sebastian's temple. A loud thud followed his outburst and ringing erupted in Sebastian's ears. He moved back in shock, not quite believing that his best friend had hit him.

Alyse laughed; the piercing, shrieking sound reverberated across the empty street, coming from

131

everywhere and nowhere at once. Tom clamped his hands over his ears. Digging his nails into the side of his skull, he desperately fought to block it out. He closed his eyes reflexively.

Feeling somebody tugging on his arms, he relented, letting them drop back to his side, glad to find the sound had disappeared. He opened his eyes warily, wanting to find she had gone too. He took a startled breath as he noticed just how close she was to him. Mere inches away. Within touching distance.

"Why won't you just leave me alone?" he cried angrily.

"Who are you talking to?" someone asked from his left. He barely registered the question, much less who had uttered it, his entire focus trained upon her.

"I'll never leave you alone," Alyse whispered, her silky voice engulfing him, so different to the horrible sounds she'd produced before. "I'll always be here."

"But I don't want you here," Tom replied, voice quivering as her intimidating presence surrounded him.

"What do we do?" the same disembodied voice from his left asked.

"I don't know," another replied. "He won't move. Should we call someone?"

"Shut up," he said hoarsely, to everyone and no one in particular, wanting the entire world to silence and for everything to stop.

"They're right, you know. They can't see me. They never will be able to."

"If they can't see you, then why can I?" Tom asked angrily, shocking himself with that emotion.

Her eyes gleamed. "Because you're crazy. Because I let you. Because one day, you'll be here, like me."

She reached out, placing a hand on Mariana's shoulder. "They're insignificant. They don't need to see me.

132

The fun is in their inability to see me. Watching you struggle as they continually believe what you know is true. You're mad."

Mariana's eyes widened as a strange emotion overcame her. It felt as though strings of thorns were running through her veins. Scraping. Ripping. Tearing from the inside as they went. Dragging themselves across her body. Her breathing became shallow and her heart began to pound as pain radiated out from where the thorns touched. An intense wave of cold overcame her and she shivered. Pulling her hand away from Tom's wrist where she'd gently been tugging at his tightly clenched hand, she wrapped her arms around her frozen body, desperate to retain warmth.

Tom watched as Alyse held on to Mariana, not knowing what Alyse was doing to her. From the look on her face, he knew it was not pleasant. He'd had Alyse touch him before. He knew what she was capable of doing. The pain she was able to cause. The utter destruction that would always follow. In a moment of sheer insanity, his heart begging him to help Mariana as his mind screamed at him to stay still, he reached out and shoved Alyse away from Mariana.

To Oliver and Sebastian it looked as though Tom had attempted to attack thin air, but the moment he moved, the feelings which had come over Mariana vanished. Warmth flooded through her and the thorns disappeared. The pain they'd caused still radiated, angry and hot, burning as newly torn flesh.

Alyse laughed again. Her tongue darted out, licking her top lip, as if sweet nectar hung there. With Tom's rapid movements, the distance between the two had decreased and they stood close. Tom could feel her warm breath tickling his skin, soft strands of hair brushing gently against his cheek. Unable to look away from her, his eyes locked with pools of scarlet, flowing like molten lava. The world slipped away.

She reached out a hand and ran her fingers through his hair, playing with the strands. Tom found himself unable to move away from her once more, revulsion building up as she brushed against his skin. It was wrong, all wrong, she shouldn't be here and the revulsion intensified until he felt he might be sick. He jerked away from her outstretched hand, body seeming to convulse as he moved. She smiled once more, taking a few steps away from the stunned boy.

As though emerging from the cold, harsh depths of a murky lake, Tom came back to the present, taking in huge gulps of air as he did so.

Silence so heavy it rung in his ears hung in the air. There was no movement. No sound. The world had stopped. His friends stood still behind him, frightened and confused. Mariana clutched at her shoulders, arms locked tight around herself, eyes focused upon the floor, desperately avoiding looking at anyone. It was then that what Alyse had done came back to him.

"Mariana?" he asked, taking a step towards her, glad to see that his fine motor skills were back in working condition. "Are you ok?"

She looked up at him, eyes wild. "Uh...I have to go," she said, turning quickly. Tom reached out to grab her wrist and she stopped dead, not wanting or perhaps unable to move. She turned to look back at him and he could see the fear burning deep inside her. Right then he knew he wasn't crazy. She'd seen it too, or felt it, or something. But she knew it was real. She knew it wasn't in his head. "Mari?" he whispered, voice hoarse with the overwhelming joy that somebody else knew she was real. Mariana shook her head violently, wrenched her hand out of his grasp and walked away from the group as quickly as possible. Fear still quelling inside of her, though what had inspired this, she wasn't sure.

He watched her leave with a pained look upon his face, hoping she would be ok. Turning to his remaining friends, he felt Mariana was the least of his worries. Sebastian and Oliver looked at him in shock, not quite sure what to say or do.

"I suppose I should go too," Tom whispered, taking a step back. He hesitated as it looked as though Oliver was about to say something, but the boy only shook his head, not quite sure what to say and unable to gather his thoughts into a coherent sentence. "See you guys tomorrow."

He turned and walked down the path to his front door without so much as glancing at the barren apple tree where Alyse had stood. Opening the door, he slipped inside, disappearing from view.

Sebastian and Oliver let him go without a word, unable to think of what they could say. Neither could comprehend what had just happened, from their friend's odd reaction, to him seeing something none of them could, to the obvious fear that had gripped Mariana over nothing. It was all too surreal for the two to comprehend much less comment on, so remaining silent was the safer option for the moment, their questions unanswered but hanging in the air between them.

They continued down the road, walking passed Tom's house and heading towards their own homes. Despite not seeing Alyse beside the apple tree, both pointedly avoided gazing back at it.

Chapter Fifteen

Dropping his bag to the floor, Tom walked through the house towards his room, unable to concentrate on anything but what had happened moments ago. She'd been there, in front of him, so real...yet, only he had seen her. Though Mariana had felt Alyse's touch, she still hadn't seen the girl who had been following him for who knew how long now - it felt as though she'd been there forever.

He threw himself down upon the bed, slumping back against the pillows and letting his thoughts race forward. It was like having a thousand voices howling all at once, drowning under the thunder of their screams. She was real, she had to be. There was no other option. This wasn't a horror movie, it was real life, reality, and in reality everything was real, everything existed, everything could be seen. Even the smallest of particles could be seen somehow.

People weren't small though. Alyse wasn't small. She was living, breathing solid human form. One who had rapidly taken over Tom's life. In such a short amount of time nothing had come to exist but her, no matter how adamantly he tried to push her away. She was there, always there, forever intruding upon him. And that was what she was doing, he began to realise; intruding, breaking into what he kept sacred. Intimidating him with strange behaviors.

The more he mulled over her and the way things had changed the moment she entered his life, the angrier he become. Mariana's words from earlier rang through his mind, louder than the other voices, silencing their continual cries. *'I'd be angry if I were you...who does she think she is....'*

Not only had she attempted to intimidate and hurt him, but she had also hurt one of his closest friends. He couldn't explain quite how she had managed that with a mere touch but the wild look of fear in Mariana's eyes was one he couldn't seem to forget. There was very little he could explain about Alyse. None of it made sense. But he knew there had to be logical and obvious reasons to everything. It was simply his inability to understand that had to be clouding these reasons.

The more he thought about Alyse, the stronger the anger grew. Rage coursed through him, fueled by the fear he still felt coiled in his heart; the parasitic creature twitching, convulsing as if to remind him of its presence. He hated Alyse more than he had ever hated anyone and at that moment, he wished for her to appear, so he could take his hatred out on her.

Time slipped by as he continued to seethe. The day slunk away into twilight, shadows gathering unnoticed in the rapidly darkening room. Refusing to leave his room, Tom forced the anger to stay with him, gripping it tight like a child clinging to candy. He knew the moment he focused upon something else, anything else at all, the anger would slither away from him and he would be left with nothing but fear. Considering the way the past week had gone, Tom could only assume Alyse would return before long.

Chapter Sixteen

Silence engulfed the house as Angela finally went to bed, drifting off into a land of peaceful dreams. Darcy was away for the night so her room lay in silence, leaving the entire house still. Tom sat on his bed, having barely moved all evening, preferring to wait and stew in his own anger for her. The overhead light was off though the lamp at the side of his bed burned weakly, breaking up the heavy shadow. At some point his mum had come into the room, bringing dinner, assuming his refusal to come downstairs had to do with some physical ailment. She had been the one to flick the light on, commenting on the darkness of the room, before pulling the curtains shut and doing the motherly routine of checking her son's forehead for signs of a fever. She'd left him in silence and that was how Tom had been since her appearance. Silent. Waiting. Seething.

He regularly drifted into dreams fueled by anger he forced himself to feel, filling his mind with ways to confront her. He'd start awake at the climax of these dream snippets, hands clenched so tight he could feel the skin straining across his knuckles.

Jolting awake now, Tom glanced at his clock. The large flashing numbers let him know that it was 3am. Though he didn't want to, he knew he would have to sleep soon. Sighing, he stood up off the bed and began to change. Flinging his shirt onto the desk chair by the window, it was then that he noticed the curtains which had been shut before were flung wide open. The dark night beyond pressed in against the glass like a mouth gaping wide.

Knowing as soon as the sun rose he'd be rudely awoken by its blinding rays, Tom moved towards the curtains, unbuttoning his jeans as he went. Awkwardly slipping them down his legs, he hopped ungracefully, stumbling once, before finally kicking them off and into the corner. He grabbed a crumpled, worn shirt from the floor and slung it on, ready for bed the moment his curtains were drawn.

His eyes were drawn to the latch at the bottom of the window though he wasn't sure why. His window was always firmly locked when closed, as it was now, because the wooden frame had warped with age, leaving the window slightly open unless the closed latch held it down. Though this gap was pleasant in summer when the heat was stifling and a breeze could do wonders, in winter it was like the cold hand of death ghosting under. Eyes now focused upon the latch, he saw it quiver, before beginning to turn gently. Barely believing what he could see, he gaped as the window unlocked itself. Coming to rest at the side with a click, the window bounced up slightly, creating the familiar gap as cool night air rolled in.

Tom froze. Everything ceased to exist as his mind fought against a thousand thoughts racing against one another, desperately trying to be heard but gone too quickly for him to understand. The reasons in his mind moved too fast for him to focus on, becoming an indistinct blur of sound and noise with no meaning and no end.

Focusing on the white noise inside his mind and ignoring the angry bites of dread, Tom reached forward, ready to lock the window and pull the curtains shut when a hand came out of the darkness, pressing against the glass. Long fingernails tapped at the glass gently, rhythmically. The eerie sound sent shivers racing as fear plunged into him like icy hands grasping out. As he watched, the window began to slide up, the old wood squealing loudly in protest.

Tom stumbled backwards, knowing what would be coming through the window. Though he had anticipated her, terror still gripped him at the thought of seeing her once more, as it always seemed to. Her eyes flashed scarlet in the darkness, seeming to shine with their own luminescence. She crawled through the window, clawing her way into the room, slinking to the ground, her brilliant red eyes trained upon Tom.

Body uncurling, she stood up, now eye level with Tom.

His body shook and he nervously glanced around the room, looking for a way to escape her gaze.

"Previously so full of anger, Tom, and yet so full of fear," she murmured silkily.

"H-How did-"

He could feel heat radiating off her body. "I know everything, Tom. Every emotion, every thought...**everything**."

"Or you just think you know everything," Tom forced himself to say, trying to search inside him for the anger he'd felt before. *'She's not real, not really something to be afraid of'*, the voice in the back of his mind reassured, holding back the howls of fear the other voices so desperately tried to make him hear. *'Nobody could climb through the window,'* he reasoned, *'you're on the first floor. It's a dream. Just a dream. Like before, but much more realistic. Only a dream. It has to be a dream.'*

Alyse smiled. "Oh but Tom, I do know everything. I am connected to you. Right up here." She placed a slender finger upon his temple and caressed his forehead gently. "I'll always be right here."

With a great deal of effort and willpower, he forced his body to react to her touch. He reached up and grabbed her wrist, dragging that slender finger far away from his forehead. He held onto her wrist hard, nails digging into the soft flesh, drawing blood. "Don't touch me."

Her eyes seemed to glow with mirth. "Pretending to have courage. I almost prefer this over the fear."

"There's nothing to be afraid of," he said through gritted teeth, more to entice anger within him than as a show of any real wrath. The muscles in his jaw tensed almost painfully.

"And why is this?"

"Because you're not who you pretend to be," he replied, shocking himself with the simplicity of this reply.

"Then, who am I?" she said with equal simplicity. "Your

imagination? A dream?"

The anger Tom had felt before came bubbling up from wherever it had been hiding. Without thinking, his mouth began to form words he could barely comprehend, as though someone else was talking through him. "You're not a dream or a mythical creature or anything like that, you're just a girl. A sick and twisted girl who likes to pretend she's something else, likes to believe she's some messed up witch from a stupid legend. You've got no powers and you're not special. Obsessed with me for whatever unknown reason, but nothing more."

"I just like to play with you," she replied, still smiling.

"Like I said, you're sick and twisted," he said through gritted teeth. He still had hold of her wrist and he gripped harder, wanting to hurt her. Wanting to break her. Now that the gates had opened, his anger rushed forward. White hot flames of rage spewed forth, gathering momentum as his mouth pressed on. "Stop following me, leave me alone and stop breaking into my house! I wish I'd never gone into Rose House. What do you do, just hide out in there, waiting, hoping some stupid person will wander in and you can torment them?"

Her infuriating grin only spread wider and he could see an endless row of teeth glistening behind her parted lips. "I like this notion of yours. Tell me, if I'm just a girl, how do you explain the roses, the blood, everything that's happened?"

"I can't. Weird things happen when you're around but there must be a way to explain them. The supernatural doesn't exist. Myths and legends aren't real. You're just sick in the head and you need help," he spat. "Get the hell away from me."

The silence between them hung heavy in the air, his venomous words ringing loudly. "Are you quite finished, Tom?"

"Yes, I'm finished, with this and you," he said, letting go of her wrist as though it were a poisonous snake. He was happy to see he'd drawn blood, flecks of deep crimson marring her porcelain skin.

Bringing her wrist towards her mouth, Alyse's tongue darted out, dancing across her skin as she lapped up the droplets of blood. "So certain I'm the one who's wrong...but maybe it's you."

"I'm pretty sure you're the one who's wrong," Tom replied, eyes trained upon her. A part of him was still shocked at the way he was acting – though he had planned to take out his anger on her and frighten her away, he never actually believed he would've been able to. Some part of him had fully anticipated another internal panic attack resulting in him stricken by fear and left quivering in a corner of his room. This entire situation was a complete surprise to him, so much so that it almost felt as though somebody else was speaking through him. Adrenaline rushed through his veins and the courage to speak, to fight, had now become overwhelming. He no longer wanted to run in fear and hide, but rather, he wanted to fight, to confront and to destroy her. He wanted to hurt her the way she'd hurt him.

"And what if I really was a myth and you were in denial?" she questioned.

"Myths are called myths for a reason, they're not real."

Her tongue darted out to swirl around her left canine. "But I'm real Tom, I'm real,"

"Yeah, you're a real person, you're just not a myth," he said, though the fires of anger he had felt before were slowly leaving him. His heart had begun to race quite violently and he took a small step back away from her. The adrenaline he'd just felt, the adrenaline which had filled him with so much courage was rapidly turning sour and he could feel it fueling the cold hand of fear now.

"If I'm just a girl then why are you so afraid?" she said. "Why are you afraid, if I'm just like you?"

"I'm not afraid of you." Tom was sure she could almost hear his heart pounding against his chest by now. His stomach felt as though it were twisting in knots and he could feel sweat beginning to form on the palms of his hands.

She grinned. Her canines definitely looked longer than normal. In fact, something seemed odd about all of her teeth. Tom furrowed his eyebrows, trying to figure out what was so different. She seemed to shimmer out of view as he continued to stare, almost as though her entire form was changing. Tom blinked to bring her back into focus but, he couldn't.

He took another step backwards, confused. Everything else appeared to be solid, unchanged and yet he just couldn't focus upon her. *She's not real; she's just in my head* he thought for one fleeting moment, *it really was all just a horrible dream*, before remembering her pulse beneath his fingers and the flecks of blood that covered his fingertips.

"What's happening?" he said, more to himself, sure something was wrong with his eyesight.

"Tell me if I'm human now," she replied, though her voice sounded completely different. Her normal silken tone was there but...beneath that was something deeper, gravelly, almost as if an echo was present or somebody else was speaking with her. She was taller than Tom remembered her being and he wondered how he hadn't noticed before just how close to the ceiling she stood. At 6'1, Tom could just about reach the ceiling if he stretched.

He rubbed his eyes; the lack of sleep had to be causing him to hallucinate. *I must be dreaming*, he thought when he opened his eyes once more though the sight before him was more nightmarish. He opened his mouth to say something but found he couldn't speak. It was a nightmare. It had to be. He'd wake up any moment, drenched in sweat, bed sheets twisted round his ankles, completely alone in his own room. He'd wake up. He had to. Wake up.

"This isn't a nightmare, Tom," that strange voice whispered, the sound surrounding him. "This is completely real, I'm completely real."

Her body jerked, twisting left and right grotesquely, creating the illusion of some deformed puppet dancing at the hands of a psychopath. She dropped her head, bending forward, collapsing to the ground but continuing to shake violently. A horrible squelching sound filled the air. It reminded him of something from a documentary he'd once watched on fur farms – the sound of skin and flesh being ripped apart. His stomach turned violently as the sound continued and though he desperately wanted to run he found himself unable to even turn away from the girl before him.

Her back bulged and the ripping sounds made sense. Something black and slimy forced its way out of her torn flesh, rapidly growing, separating into two parts. Bursting through the black material of her dress, blood and gore dripped from what Tom could only describe as a pair of leathery wings. With her bent still, Tom could see her spine protruded bizarrely, almost as though it had been snapped into pieces, stretching the skin across it taut to the point of translucency. The coppery fragrance of blood which had filled the air was now overwhelmed with the smell of rotting flesh. Tom retched as the scent of death suffocated him. Blood pooled where her wings had formed and the skin was torn and shredded in parts revealing muscle and bone beneath.

What felt like an eternity of watching her squirm was over in moments; the room fell silent once more as Tom's retching subsided. Alyse's head remained bent, her straggly, sweat soaked hair completely covering her face, hiding her scarlet eyes from view. Tom waited for her to move, wondering, hoping whatever had happened to her in this nightmare world his mind so frighteningly conjured up might have killed her.

Alyse slowly began to uncurl. Keeping her head bent low, she stood up, now towering over Tom. The room seemed to warp around her, concrete and metal bending to encompass her unrecognizable form. Her hair had fallen away from her face and he could see that her facial features had also changed. High cheekbones strained against her

144

translucent skin as though attempting to rip through. Her lips were pulled back in a perpetual snarl and her teeth had morphed into razor sharp, jagged fangs. Her entire face seemed to have twisted into a grotesque mask, demonic and terrifying.

Tom found himself unable to not look at her eyes. Looking deep into scarlet almond-shaped eyes, the world stopped – there was no trace of humanity there. The scarlet irises seemed to have burst, allowing the blood within to spread, turning both eyes completely crimson. Her entire transformation seemed to be some bizarre, nightmarish mockery of a bad horror movie and though he reasoned it had to be a dream part of him knew this was real. The heavy smell of death. The heat burning off her. His mind could never have produced something this vivid.

Though her crimson eyes gave no indication, he knew she was looking straight at him. Tom watched the room warp as she stepped forward, the door completely vanishing to encompass the vast expanse of her. As she moved, her wings seemed to burst into flames, engulfing and spreading their way across her back until she was framed by their white hot intensity. Unbearable heat rippled through the room. And so the myth he'd read was complete – hellfire's flames lapped at her form.

"How about now, Tom?" she asked, in the echoic voice she had used before. "Do you still think I'm human or has this myth finally become reality for you?"

Tom's mind went blank and he found he had forgotten how to speak. *None of this is real*, the voice in the back of his mind reasoned, *you've fallen asleep and this is some terrible nightmare. Wake up!*

"This is no nightmare, Tom," she said. Alyse stood close enough for her breath to ghost across his cheeks. The smell of decay overwhelmed him, seeming to radiate off her. "This is all too real. The smell of death will linger in your room long after I leave tonight and you will know I'm real. I am the creature from these legends you so believe to not be true and yet here I stand."

She knelt down before him, bringing herself down to his eye level as he realized at some point he had collapsed to the ground. Extending her hand, she ran her fingers up and down his arm in an almost hypnotic manner. As she continued the movement, a searing hot pain began to eminent where her fingers touched. He could feel warm, sticky liquid trickling down his forearm, dripping off his fingers, running to the ground in rivulets. Her touched burned through his skin and he felt sure she would leave her mark upon his bones.

Unable to tear his gaze away from Alyse's eyes, Tom found himself lulled into a hypnotic trance. The world turned hazy behind her, flickering in and out of focus before slipping away completely, leaving he and Alyse to exist in a world of dark nothing.

Somehow he found himself away from Alyse, his room, everything that had happened. Standing at the end of a very long hallway, he gazed ahead. The hallway stretched out before him and he noticed thousands of doors on either side. It was a never ending stretch of doorways leading onto anywhere.

The hairs on the back of his neck stood on end and he became acutely aware of the fact that, though Alyse was not here now, she would be soon. His only way to escape was to make it to the end of the hallway. He began to slowly walk forward. The lights were dim though light exploded around each door, as though thousand watt bulbs hung above the eaves.

As he turned to look at a rather ornate door, it seemed to move out of the way so he was left staring at a blank wall. The door reappeared moments later. Tom continued on down the hallway, running now. More doors began to move, swapping places, dancing just out of his line of vision before coming back into place once more. Flashes of white light exploded around him as though a thousand cameras were taking pictures all at once and he shielded his eyes from the burning flashes.

The end of the hallway appeared before him and it was only by sheer chance he managed to prevent himself from running into the door. He opened it with a sigh of relief; sure he would be safely away from Alyse now. Brilliant white light flooded in, blinding him momentarily. As he closed his eyes, an arm wrapped around his waist. His breath hitching in his throat and his heart raced. He didn't need to open his eyes to know Alyse stood before him, holding him flush against her body. He could feel every contour pressing against him deliciously, every bone digging in viciously. He finally forced himself to open his eyes to find himself staring into pools of deep crimson. Her skin was flushed a strawberry colour and she seemed out of breath.

As he continued to stare the distance between the two diminished. Unable to stop himself, he leant forward and met her lips in a heated kiss. Her tongue darted out, running across his lips. Before he could do anything more, he felt her pull away and he sighed only to gasp moments later as he felt her lips upon his neck, nipping at the pulse point. Leaning into her kiss he threw his head back allowing her better access. He gasped once more, a mixture of shocked pain and pleasure as she nipped a bit harder, piercing his skin.

It felt as though a thousand razorblades were digging into his skin and he cried out in pain, wanting to pull away from her but unable to. Biting hard, she yanked her head back, ripping the flesh clean away. Blood trickled down the corners of her mouth and she licked her lips, enjoying every morsel of flesh and blood she had managed to grab.

Crashing to the ground in pain, Tom clamped a hand over the wound, feeling warm, sticky blood oozing out of the gaping hole she'd left behind. He closed his eyes in agony, only to open them once more and find himself, completely alone and unharmed, lying in bed with sunlight streaming in through the open window.

Chapter Seventeen

Tom stood in the bathroom, studying his neck in the mirror, looking for signs of what had happened last night. It seemed it really had been a dream as the skin along his neck was smooth, unbroken. Though he could still feel the pain of her bite, there was no way he could deny a lack of visible markings.

Deciding a shower would help clear the obvious nightmare from his mind, he unbuttoned his jeans, peeling them off his legs and kicking them away. As he lifted his shirt up over his head, pain danced down his left forearm and he gritted his teeth. He gingerly took his shirt off and looked down at the spot which ached. Running from wrist to elbow were long, deep scratches, red and sore, throbbing hot.

Stumbling backwards, feeling lightheaded, Tom sat down heavily on the edge of the bathtub. Memories of Alyse running her fingers up and down his arm came flooding back. There was no way he could explain the scratches. They had not been there yesterday.

The feeling of lightheadedness increased and he pushed himself down on to the floor, pressing his feverish forehead to the cold tiles. His mind raced as a thousand thoughts whirled, desperately trying to come up with any reason to explain the scratches no matter how ludicrous it may have seemed. Nothing could be as absurd as the thought of a myth actually haunting him.

He spent what felt like an eternity lying there, forehead pressed against the cold, white tiles. A hammering on the bathroom door brought him back to his senses and he quickly stood up.

"Tom, are you done yet?" his sister's voice floated through the door.

"Uh, just a minute," he said, nervously turning the shower on, aware that he had been locked in the bathroom for countless minutes in silence. He pulled off the rest of his clothes and slid into the shower, recoiling as scalding hot water danced across his skin. He allowed the water to burn him, hoping in some strange way it would burn away whatever Alyse had left behind. As the water cascaded down over his arm, the torn, scratched skin throbbed with pain, as if to keep Alyse on his mind.

With his skin red raw, he got out of the shower and wrapped a towel around his waist. Picking up his discarded clothes, he slung them over his arm to hide the deep cuts in case Darcy was waiting outside.

Opening the door, he came face to face with his mother instead. Though he had been preparing himself in case somebody was waiting for him behind the door, actually seeing somebody still took him by surprise.

"Alright?" she asked, looking warily at Tom.

Tom nodded quickly. "I'm fine, just a little tired that's all."

The look in her eyes clearly told him she didn't believe what he was saying, but she didn't press him for more information. As Tom took a step towards his room, Angela stood in front of him, blocking his path. "Tom I know something's going on. Please, just talk to me."

"Nothing's going on," he replied simply, avoiding eye contact, sure the moment he looked into her eyes and saw the concern there it would all come spilling forth. The need to say something, anything, bubbled away behind his lips and he could feel more rising inside him. He was about ready to explode.

"I'm really worried," she continued. "I know something's up, you're not good at hiding things from me. I just want to help you."

"It's fine, I don't need help," he continued. "I'm ok, I promise."

"I-"

"Seriously, I'm fine," he cut her off. Guilt. Instant guilt at snapping at her hit him and he wanted to apologise. He couldn't risk saying anything else. He wasn't sure what would come tumbling out of his mouth. Side stepping her, he walked into his room and slowly shut the door. As he did so, he looked into Angela's eyes. The words were there, forcing themselves against his gritted teeth and pursed lips, begging to be let free, but he held his tongue, too afraid or perhaps unable to voice anything more than raving madness. As he door closed, he felt another of those moments overcome him. He'd made a decision. He knew this one act had set in motion what was to come. And like moments were so wont to do, the time to change things would never come back.

Angela watched Tom disappear into his room. She now knew something was definitely wrong, but there was little else she could do. His friends were as unresponsive as he when she attempted to ask them. Mariana had briefly mentioned something about a girl when Angela had been at their house the week before, but she'd scurried out of the room before Angela could press further. Though Angela would not bring this up to Tom, she'd also heard him late in the night, muttering in his sleep, gripped deep within the throes of a nightmare.

Shaking her head, she pushed the thought away and continued down the hallway to the bedroom where she had been heading before the bathroom door had flung open. As she passed by Tom's doorway, she wrinkled her nose in disgusted as a pungent odor hit her. Though faint, it was slightly familiar. She vowed to buy a decent, strong air freshener and went about her business. It wasn't until a few hours later that she realized the fleeting yet pungent scent was similar to the smell of the squirrel they'd found in the attic a few years back – long dead, riddled with decay. The smell of death is impossible to forget.

Chapter Eighteen

Once dressed, Tom fled the house, keen to avoid his mum and any other acts of weirdness that might happen around her. As it was still early he had plenty of time to meet up with Oliver and Sebastian before school and describe what had happened. After mulling everything over, there was only one logical explanation for what had happened; Alyse and the myth had to be real, as illogical as it sounded.

The way he puzzled it out was: either everything was in his mind, or everything was real. He wanted it all to be a dream, a simple, yet horrifying dream and indeed, certain parts of his experience such as the endless corridor of doors had to have been a dream. The cuts on his arm however proved that something, at least one part of his entire ordeal had been real. They couldn't have randomly appeared; it was physically impossible and there was no way he could've done them to himself in his sleep. He'd thoroughly checked just in case he had hidden a ridiculously large knife under his bed and somehow forgotten about it. Of course, he hadn't, so this meant someone, or something had to have cut him. With his mind already attached to this explanation which he believed to be the most logical, it then became a concrete reality that Alyse had to have done this. He had a memory of it and everything. That meant that…she was real, the house was real, the myth was real and everything he had seen last night, what she had become, was also real.

Tom rung Oliver's bell twice, knowing he wouldn't disturb his mum who would probably already be at work.

"Yeah?" a gruff voice answered.

"Olli, it's me, come down, we have to go meet Seb, I've got something to show you guys," Tom replied, glancing around nervously.

"Tom is everything ok?" Oliver questioned, voice wavering slightly.

"No, look I'll explain when we meet Seb, just come

down," Tom begged.

"Ok, give me a few minutes and I'll be down."

Tom sat on the front step, waiting for Oliver. The cold morning air caused goose bumps to erupt across his exposed skin, despite the fact he wore a thick fleece hoody. Brown leaves rustled in the bitter wind. He felt cold, empty in the harsh grey light of a winter's morning as though the end of the world was about to hit, and he was the cause of it.

The door creaked open behind him and he lurched forward off the step, heart racing.

"Tom, I'm just opening the door," Oliver pointed out, nodding at the door. "What's wrong? You look like you haven't slept at all!"

"Let's go meet Seb," Tom replied simply, heading down the path and out of the front gate. Oliver followed, unease rising within him at Tom's strange behavior.

They silently walked one street on, Oliver desperately wanting to pry information out of Tom but resolutely holding his tongue. Seb's dad let the two into the house, puzzled as to why the boys would be there so early in the morning but not questioning this. He let them head up to Sebastian's room, knowing they would have a hell of a time waking up the boy who could sleep forever.

After numerous shakes, pokes and loud noises, Sebastian finally came to.

"Is everything ok?" he asked groggily, attempting to sit up but still lacking basic coordination.

"Tom has something to tell us," Oliver replied simply. Glancing back and forth between the two, Sebastian could tell that whatever Tom had to tell them was serious. He forced himself up out of bed and slowly began to get dressed.

Their attempts to sneak out of the house unnoticed were thwarted by Sebastian's mum who had prepared breakfast for all three the moment she'd noticed Tom and

Oliver on the front step. Any other normal day and her pancakes would be welcome but today Tom physically couldn't eat anything so Oliver and Sebastian ate enough for him as quickly as they could.

Ten minutes later all three were heading down the street towards the town's park which would be empty at this time in the morning.

"Should we stop and grab Mariana?" Sebastian asked as they passed the road leading down to her house. "She should probably be here too, she's part of all this."

"No, it's too dangerous," Tom replied, glancing from side to side as though he were part of some covert operation. "She can never know about this. The last thing I want is to involve her in it. Nobody can ever tell her what happens from here on. It's between us three. I don't want her involved or hurt or something."

"Mariana would kill you if she knew you thought something was too dangerous for her," Sebastian said.

"I don't care. At least she'll be safe," Tom said furtively. He wanted her kept as far away from all of this as possible. He would never be the cause of her fear again. He couldn't do that to her. And he knew somehow she'd be hurt worst of all in this. She couldn't be involved. He couldn't risk her. He couldn't lose her. "She'll understand. She'll be safe."

"Tom, what the hell is going on, seriously? You're making it sound like the end of the world."

"Not here, I'll tell you at the park," he replied simply.

The two followed Tom rather nervously, curious as to what he had to tell them, though both had an inkling of what it might be about. Reaching the park, all three made their way to the wooden gazebo in the far corner. Graffiti covered every inch of the gazebo, depicting who had been here last and what they had done along with insults and slurs.

Sebastian huddled in one corner of the gazebo trying to escape the bitter wind as Oliver sat on the floor. Tom paced

153

in front of the two.

"Come on Tom, we're here, what's up?" Sebastian pressed after a few moments of silence.

"Everything's real," he said simply.

Oliver raised an eyebrow. "Yes, I can see that."

"No, I mean, everything with Alyse, everything she says she is and everything the myth says she is, it's all real," he replied breathlessly before taking in a deep, shuddering breath.

Oliver hesitated. "What do you mean, it's real? Tom, it's not real, it's a myth. This girl pretending she's some psycho myth monster is real, but the actual myth part isn't."

"That's what I thought too," Tom replied, throwing himself onto the bench. "But it's not true. I mean, it is true, she is real, but so's the myth. She's the thing she said she was."

Oliver and Sebastian looked at Tom, both slightly confused and more than a little bit worried. Neither said anything. Neither knew what to say. There was nothing they could say.

"Don't you understand?" Tom pressed. "Everything the myth says about her, where she came from and what she is…it's all real. She showed me last night."

"How did she show you, Tom?" Oliver asked cautiously.

"Look at these." Tom rolled up his sleeve revealing the long, vibrant red gashes racing up and down his arm.

"Dude what the hell did she do to you?" Sebastian yelped. Leaping up out of his seat, he grabbed Tom's forearm and yanked it closer for a better look, ignoring the way Tom winced at his touch.

"She touched me last night and these happened," Tom replied as if it were the most logical explanation in the world.

Sebastian's eyes darted from the cuts on his arms to Tom's eyes and back again, not sure where to focus.

"Excuse me?"

"Yeah, I watched her transform last night and then she just…touched me. She ran her fingers down my arm and it was like she was just, touching me with a knife or something because these happened. But, they're not bad cuts or anything," Tom reasoned rapidly.

"Right, because that happens all the time," Sebastian replied, his voice dripping with sarcasm.

Kneeling on the ground before Tom, Oliver gently ran his fingers over the gashes, feeling the raised, jagged skin, examining them as Sebastian had. "Ok, Tom, start from the beginning. What exactly happened last night?"

Tom launched into the story of last night's happenings. Every moment was etched into his mind as vividly as if they were happening right there in front of him. He shuddered when describing her horrific transformation, the image of the creature she had become burned into his memory.

"But, how can you be sure that's all real when the other part was actually a dream?" Oliver asked once Tom finished his tale.

"Yeah, the doors and stuff were a dream, why couldn't this transformation be a dream too?"

"It could be, but then how did I get the cuts?" Tom asked almost petulantly, daring them to find an explanation.

"You could've done them to yourself in your sleep, maybe fighting off imaginary demons?"

Their thoughts were following the same paths his had. "With what? I looked all around when I woke up. There was nothing I could've cut myself with."

"Maybe you were sleepwalking, and you walked into the bathroom and found something sharp," Sebastian said, grasping at straws.

"There was nothing in the bathroom either. Guys, I've gone through every possible, logical thought in my head and the only one I keep coming back to is that she is really what

155

she says she is. That it wasn't a dream," Tom said with a shrug.

"Only that conclusion isn't logical at all, is it?" Oliver said carefully. "Tom, there are a thousand other possible explanations."

"And not one of them shows that Alyse is some psycho creature thing," Sebastian cut in. "If anything, they just prove she's a bit of a nutter."

"You didn't see what I saw," Tom said, voice heavy with emotion. "You didn't see what she became, what she was like up close."

Sebastian and Oliver shared one of their looks, both thinking everything and nothing at the same time. Neither knew what to say. Of all the things they'd expected Tom to tell them about Alyse, this certainly hadn't been it. "Thing is, if she is real, how do you explain that? You've always been the one to adamantly believe nothing supernatural or paranormal exists. And now you're telling us that you believe this girl is a witch from some story."

"Well, it took quite a bit of evidence to convince me." Tom bit back, frustration evident in his voice. "I'm all for her not being real, but she is."

"Is she, Tom, or do you just wish she was?"Oliver suggested cautiously.

"What the hell's that supposed to mean?"

Oliver stood up off the ground, brushing dry leaves and dirt off his jeans. He paced before Tom, trying to gather his words. "Just that, I don't know...this whole thing is a little bit messed up. It has been from the start. Maybe, you wish she was this psycho mythical creature or whatever, to make things easier?"

"Yeah because dealing with a myth is so much easier than dealing with a real person," Sebastian cut in dryly.

Oliver's shoulders tensed. "Shut up, Seb. I don't really know what to suggest, except to keep saying that no, she

156

isn't real Tom, she can't be."

"But she is, I've seen her!" Tom cried out, furious at the fact nobody would believe him. "I'll prove it to you!"

"How? We haven't seen her once, remember. We wouldn't even know what she looked like if she walked passed us on the street," Sebastian muttered. He was bent over, head in his hands, leg bouncing nervously.

Tom's eyes widened. "I know how I can show her to you!"

"How?"

"Simple, I'll take you into Rose House."

Silence surrounded the group.

"You what?" Sebastian asked, mouth agape.

"Yeah, it's perfect, we'll go into Rose house!" he said almost triumphantly.

"I don't think that's such a good idea. I mean, going into Rose House last time is what started all of this."

"Maybe it can be what ends it, then," Tom reasoned. "Or at least you guys will see her. You'll see that I'm not crazy and I'm not making any of this up."

"Tom, we don't think you-"

"Yes, you do," Tom interrupted, knowing what Oliver was going to say and not wanting to hear it. "I can see it in your eyes. Both of you. You think I've gone a bit loopy, confusing dreams with reality, wishing that some girl really was a paranormal anomaly. But it's not that, at all. It's real. She's real. And as frightening as it is, I can't escape that simple fact. She's haunting me, guys, literally haunting me. I don't know what to do to get rid of her when I'm the only one who's seen her. But maybe…maybe if you guys see her too, and you see that she's real, at least I'm not alone. Not anymore. Then, maybe we can get rid of her together."

Tom's voice was laced with desperation. He needed them. He needed them to believe him. He needed them to help. And the desperation in his voice made both feel so horrifically guilty. Though it was true they hadn't seen Alyse and neither of them believed there was anything supernatural about her at all, Tom did. And that guilt was further enhanced by the sly little voice at the back of their minds reminding them the only reason Tom had ever entered Rose House was because of them. Perhaps if he hadn't gone in there none of this would be happening right now. Maybe all of this was their fault.

If nothing else, maybe once Tom came to realize they couldn't see her he'd let them finally get the right people to help. And it was looking more and more like the right people wouldn't be there to look for a stalker.

"Fine," Oliver said after a few moments of silence. "We'll come with you into Rose House. Show us Alyse. We'll take it from there. Right, Seb, we'll go?"

Sebastian sighed. "Yeah, we'll come with you."

Chapter Nineteen

The day dragged as all three mentally prepared themselves for a trip into Rose House, unable to focus upon any class or conversation. Tom found it incredibly hard to not tell Mariana what their true plans were, and consequently spent most of his day avoiding her, knowing that if he did so much as mutter a quiet 'hello' to her, she would know he was hiding something. He could never lie to Mariana. Could never hide anything from her. And if she found out he was hiding something, she'd get it out of him. She'd insist on coming along. And then it would be his fault.

He couldn't help but notice the hurt look in her eyes as he hurried passed her at lunch, avoiding eye contact for too long. Or how she sat beneath their tree and waited for him the entire free period, glancing up at the school doors every few minutes as he watched from a window in the library. When this was over, he would have a small and fiery ball of wrath in the form of Mariana to deal with, but he knew it to be for the best. He'd rather deal with her fury than ever see her hurt, or the fear which had overcome her the previous day affect her again. He would rather do anything than see her hurt.

Despite the fact they had plenty of time to visit the house during the daytime, they chose to enter the house at twilight, to replicate the exact moment Tom had entered Rose Hose the first time around.

Standing just outside the gate however, all three realized how silly an idea this had been.

The setting sun caused shadows to form around the house, leaving parts of it hidden in darkness. Silhouettes and shadows flit beyond the windows and danced among the wooden frames. Though the street lights hadn't flickered on yet, the roses seemed to glimmer, as though lights were reflecting off thousands of tiny water droplets resting upon the petals of each rose.

"Look at the roses," Tom murmured, not quite sure why

he was speaking so quietly but knowing that he should.

"What about them?" Oliver replied, voice hushed.

Tom bit his lip. "I don't know. There's just something about them. They're not normal. Normal roses don't shimmer like that. The myth says the roses are her, like her blood and her power or something, and they're how she hypnotizes people…"

"Sounds pleasant," Sebastian said, wrinkling his nose in disgust. "Aren't myths wonderful things?"

"It isn't a myth, remember? It's real," Tom said, a slight edge to his voice. Neither boy commented on this, both holding onto their skepticism.

"Should we go on?" Oliver said after a few moments of awkward silence, with all three staring at the roses. Tom nodded and pushed the gate open. The gate swung open easily once more without a sound.

"Watch out for the thorns. They bleed."

"They bleed?" Sebastian asked in shock. "What do you mean 'they bleed'?"

Without bothering to explain, Tom grabbed a rose beside him, careful of the thorns and snapped it off, brandishing the torn stem at them. Droplets of viscous, scarlet liquid began to form at the broken end of the stem.

Oliver scrutinized the rose. "It looks like sap to me."

"That's what I thought, but smell it." Tom thrust the stem at Oliver, almost poking him in the eye with it. Oliver tentatively smelt the droplets forming. He wrinkled his nose as a familiar, coppery scent overwhelmed him.

"It actually does smell like blood," Oliver admitted, motioning for Sebastian to smell the rose too.

Bending forward, Sebastian inhaled deeply. And instantly regretted it. Wiping violently at his nose he attempted to rid himself of the coppery scent. "I guess, sort of."

"The myth says the roses bleed because her blood flows through them, they're part of her," Tom said, throwing the rose to the ground and continuing up the path. There was no need to explain what he had read about the roses on horticultural websites. Science always had a way of attributing logical explanations to the strange, the unexplainable, but Tom now knew the truth. And it all seemed to slot into place much easier than any scientific reasoning he had been grappling with.

"So, in theory, if you destroyed the roses you'd destroy her?" Oliver asked, following Tom up the path. It took him a few moments to realize his question made it seem as though he believed Tom. He shook his head to dislodge the thoughts.

"I suppose so," Tom reasoned. "But there are a handful of places all over the world where the roses are. I think you'd have to destroy all of them everywhere first."

"Sounds like some epic video game quest," Sebastian mused. "If we survive this let's create it; could be a best seller."

"Alyse won't kill us," Tom said simply. "She only wants me, I think."

Focusing on Tom's profile, Oliver scrutinized the strange calm that seemed to have consumed him. "Tom, you're surprisingly quite relaxed about this entire thing considering you've, supposedly, discovered this supernatural creature actually exists. And that she may very well kill you."

Tom paused mid stride, one foot partially airborne. This was perhaps the most calm he'd felt in the past few weeks, and that he should feel it now was almost laughable. He grinned and chuckled, before carrying on. "I know. It's strange. If I'm honest, the thought of it up until we got here terrified me, but now I don't know. I feel a lot calmer about the whole thing. I don't really understand why."

"Maybe...you're realizing it isn't real," Sebastian suggested hesitantly. "Maybe it was just a dream."

"I don't know anymore, Seb," Tom admitted. "It's why I want you guys to see her too. If it's real, and you see her then it's not just in my head, it's not a dream and I'm not going crazy."

"Stop saying that Tom, you're not going crazy," Oliver snapped. "Whatever's happening, I'm sure there are hundreds of explanations, so we'll find them all. But you're certainly not crazy!"

By this time they'd reach the porch and silence fell. Standing here once more, Tom was reminded of that fateful night barely more than a few weeks ago when he'd stood here, about to head in alone. Back when Alyse still existed only in the story. It was one of those moments, he realized, those life changing moments where a simple step could have you falling forward, catching fire and burning bright, or disappearing into nothing. And he seemed to have done everything and nothing all at once. "Weird to be standing here again."

"Yeah, seems like years since we made that bet," Sebastian added.

Tom clambered up the porch steps first, leaning against the door gently, hoping it would still be open. It was. He swung it open, shivering as the warped wood creaked in its too small frame.

The darkness was overwhelming as all three peered into the dank house. Tom flicked on his flashlight and walked into the shadowed house. The other two watched as darkness enveloped him. Had it not been for the pinprick of light coming from his flashlight, they would've lost sight of Tom completely.

Of course, what both failed to realize was though the inside of the house was bathed in pitch blackness, outside was rather light, with the sun still slowly setting. There should've been enough light to see basic shapes outlined in gloomy half light.

They followed him in, both flicking their flashlights on.

162

Unlike Tom's last jaunt in the house, he didn't waste time moving from room to room in exploration. The house held nothing of interest to him anymore. It was bleak and empty in comparison to her. She was all he could think about now and the anticipation of seeing her again, of proving her existence once and for all, left a giddy kind of excitement developing in his stomach.

"Where are we going?" Sebastian asked, as Tom headed for the stairs.

"I met Alyse in the master bedroom, the one I waved at you guys from," Tom explained. "I figured if we're going to find her at all she'll be in there."

Sebastian swung the flashlight's beam around the gloomy entrance hall. "I guess we won't be taking the scenic route?"

"There's not really much to see. The best room down here is the kitchen; it's got a great view of the garden."

"Can we see it quick?" Sebastian asked eagerly, as though he truly wanted to see the kitchen. Tom raised an eyebrow, the motion causing shadows to dance across his features.

"I guess," he replied with a shrug, turning from the stairs and heading towards the kitchen.

"What are you doing?" Oliver hissed the moment Tom was out of earshot.

"I'm not sure," Sebastian admitted. "I just, I don't know. I get the feeling we should keep Tom from going upstairs for as long as possible."

"Do you think there's really something up there, then?" Oliver asked, the hairs on the back of his neck standing on end as he glanced around furtively. Though he hadn't wanted to admit it the house did have a feeling of being occupied, as though someone was hiding in the shadows, watching their every move. Of course, this could have more to do with that primal fear of the dark and the unknown, and less to do with someone actually watching them. Stuck in this dark, unfamiliar house however, the latter was easier to believe.

"No, I don't think so," Sebastian said, though his voice quivered with uncertainty. "But I think once Tom realizes there's nothing up there for us to see, things could go quite horribly wrong. And then we've got to decide what to do once he does realize how much of this is actually inside his own mind."

"Almost makes me wish she was real. Either way, it's a bittersweet ending."

They followed Tom into the kitchen, both stopping at the sight of the garden spread out before them through the grimy kitchen windows. Thousands of roses pressed in against the glass, a sea of crimson spread out before them. The roses appeared to shimmer as they had done outside, seeming to sway hypnotically in a nonexistent breeze. Despite the gloomy light outside, the crimson petals burst with colour, perfectly visible in the dim twilight.

"You weren't lying about that view," Oliver whispered, almost in awe at the sheer magnitude of roses before them.

Tom leaned against the countertop, eyes sweeping across the garden, almost searching in between the roses for something. For the first time since they'd reached Rose House, he felt nervous. There was a feeling in the bottom of his stomach he couldn't quite explain. Like a whisper on a breeze his mind was telling him something he couldn't understand yet.

"L-lets go upstairs," he said, turning from the window. As he turned to the right, he caught movement out of the corner of his eye. Something large and agile was prowling through the roses. He shivered, knowing who it was, though he couldn't see the tell-tale red eyes.

His flashlight beam bobbed up and down as he headed back towards the stairs. Two similar beams bobbed beside him as Oliver and Sebastian followed. As one, the three climbed the staircase tentatively. Though rotting wood hadn't collapsed beneath Tom before, the fact three of them were on the stairs now meant more weight. Each creaking floorboard was as loud as a gunshot in the otherwise silent house, completely shattering the heavy hush weighing in around them. A hush so perfect it felt as though they were underwater, so deep sound physically could not penetrate.

Though Tom wouldn't admit it, his movements were slowing down partly due to care over the stairs, but mostly because nerves were setting in once more. He felt as though his insides had been replaced with ice and each step caused that chilled feeling to increase. The hairs on the back of his neck stood on end and goose bumps were forming across his flesh.

As they crept up the final few steps, Sebastian's flashlight reflected off something silver in Tom's hand. "Tom, what've you got there?"

Tom jumped at the sound of his name being called before looking down at his hand as if he hadn't realized he was holding anything. "Oh uh, just a precaution. Just in case." He held up a knife, its blade sharp enough to gleam in the sparse light.

"Shit, do you really thing you're going to need it?" Sebastian asked, eyes widening.

"It's just a precaution," Tom reasoned. He pushed the blade back into the knife's hilt. "See, it's safe and tucked away, but it's there, just in case."

"Aren't switchblades illegal?" Oliver asked, just as shocked as Sebastian. Tom had never been one to carry any weapon around with him. They'd all had it drilled into their minds how weapons could be turned on the person carrying them so were quite unwilling to put themselves in that situation. And it was Aysforth. Weapons and violence of any kind were almost never heard of. An unlucky fox would be shot every now and then if it strayed onto farming land but that was the extent of it.

"It's not a switchblade," Tom said. He sounded almost sad as he looked at the blade in his hands. "It was my dad's. I found it in some boxes of his a few months ago. I only held on to it because I thought it was kind of cool. Never thought I'd use it, but…I don't know, I just feel like I should have it while we're in here. Like I said, just in case."

Though neither Oliver nor Sebastian wanted to admit it, having a form of weapon was sort of soothing in a way, providing a false sense of security neither had felt since they'd entered Rose House. Not that it would be much good against a supernatural being if Alyse did exist, but again both were adamant the only real thing about Alyse was the fact she was a human girl. They now had an entirely different problem on their hands, though. What if Tom attacked a deeply disturbed, but undeniably human girl, on the pretense she was some frightening, mythical creature? Murder wasn't something they had planned for this evening's agenda, despite their strange entertainment. It never did end well for anyone involved.

They reached the top of the stairs and turned to the right, Tom in the lead, directing them towards the master suite. The air around them crackled with tension. Adrenalin coursed through veins as they approached a closed door. Thoughts of what could be behind it bombarded their minds. Fear. Darkness. Nothing. Everything. The idea of something unknown waiting on the other side caused hearts to race and Oliver could feel sweat beading on his forehead. Though both he and Sebastian were adamant Alyse was only a myth, the fear of the dark and the unknown intensified as they walked deep into the heart of the house. They could almost believe, standing here, in the gloom, hearts racing as their minds screamed at them to leave, that Alyse was real. The myth was real. Death awaited them beyond this door.

"This is it," Tom said, voice shaking, though he wasn't sure why he felt nervous when before he hadn't.

Oliver's eyes scanned across the door in front of him. Unnerving. "So this is where you first met her," he

166

whispered.

"It's where she found me," Tom replied, turning to look at his friend, momentarily blinded by the flashlight's glare.

"Like a cat chasing a mouse," Sebastian murmured.

"I guess she likes to play with her food." Though Tom had been trying for humor, the line fell flat.

"Open the door, Tom," Oliver said after a few moments. "Let's meet this girl, prove whatever she is and get out of here."

Tom gripped the handle and tugged it down, pushing the door backwards. They tentatively entered the room, eyes scanning every inch searching for something, anything that wasn't meant to be there. Unlike the rest of the house, this room was brilliantly lit by the full moon hanging low in the sky.

Oliver walked into the centre of the room and looked around slowly, turning on the spot. "That was surprisingly anticlimactic," he noted after a few moments of silence.

"I was honestly hoping she'd be here," Sebastian mused. He walked over to the bed and sat down heavily, a cloud of dust rising around him as the old sheets crinkled.

"So...where is she?" Oliver asked.

"I don't know," Tom replied after a few moments. "I know she's here somewhere but I don't know where."

Tom walked towards the window, staring down into the garden below, taking in the crimson sea of roses. "I was here, then I turned to leave and she was just there in front of me. The one day I actually want to see her and she's nowhere to be found."

"Maybe she only enjoys it when it's just you," Oliver suggested.

"What, you're saying she doesn't like an audience?" Sebastian scoffed. "Maybe she's just afraid of us. She knows Tom's easily fooled but neither of us will believe her bull."

Tom pressed his forehead against the cool glass, watching as his breath fogged up the windows. "You would if you saw what I saw," he whispered, barely loud enough for either to hear.

They stood in silence for what seemed like forever, waiting for something, anything to happen. By now any fear they had felt rapidly vanished, leaving Oliver and Sebastian feeling bored and slightly awkward. This was the part they had dreaded - finding nothing. Had they come up here and found a girl, hiding, waiting for them, they would've been able to prove to Tom she was just a girl. But they had found nothing, and now needed to somehow convince Tom she wasn't there. Never had been. The myth wasn't real and neither was this girl, human or not. It really was all in his mind. Tom's paranoia was now so great neither could deny they could no longer be enough help for him. Somebody else would need to be brought in. They didn't believe he was crazy, but something wasn't quite right. And if nothing else, he needed help bringing things back to the ordinary. Finding a supernatural being would've almost been easier than this, both quickly came to realize.

"Maybe we should go?" Sebastian asked after an eternity of silence.

"Yeah Tom, we can't just hang around here forever," Oliver added. "She's not going to come, probably because both of us are here. But, I'm sure we'll see her soon and then we'll help you deal with her."

Tom took a deep, pained breath. Desperation filled him as he tried to find a way of convincing them to stay. If they left the house now without either of them having seen her, he knew they never would see her. They never would believe him. He knew the thoughts racing through their minds, because he knew exactly what he would be thinking if the roles were reversed. From then on he would be deemed completely mad and the thought of this sent his mind reeling.

Closing his eyes, he begged her to appear. For once, his sanity rested solely upon seeing her, despite the insanity

168

she provoked.

"Tom?" Sebastian asked, taking a step closer to Tom, not sure whether the boy had been listening to their discussion. He knew the most important thing right now was to take Tom away from his house. The longer they stayed here the stronger he would pin his hopes upon her appearance.

"Ok, let's go," Tom finally murmured, sighing in defeat. He pushed himself away from the glass and turned back towards his friends. He froze in his tracks, staring blankly at the doorway. Leaning casually against the frame was Alyse, eyes glowing in the moonlight, a mix of silver and crimson. "She's here," he breathed, barely able to speak, throat constricting with fear. Beneath the fear lay a strong sense of relief. She was here. They'd have to believe him now.

Oliver and Sebastian spun round, glancing behind them into the gloom. Though the house was bathed in darkness, indistinct shapes lined the hallway just passed the bedroom door. Neither could see anything resembling a person.

"Where?" Oliver asked, moving towards the doorway.

"Stop!" Tom cried out. Oliver stopped dead. "Don't get too close to her."

"Tom, I can't even see her, what are you on about?" Oliver asked, looking around hoping she would jump out at him. He desperately wanted to see this girl, to help his friend whom he was starting to believe really was going mad, no matter how much he wished it not so.

"How can you not see her, she's right there in front of you, leaning against the door!"

"I have told you before, Tom," Alyse said slowly, voice thick like treacle. "Nobody can see me but you. Nobody will ever see me, but you.

"But they've felt you," Tom retorted venomously. "Mariana felt your presence, felt whatever you did to her. They felt you, so they know you're really there."

169

"Maybe, or maybe she was just humoring you," Alyse replied with mirth. "For all you know it could've just been a dream. You struggle so hard to define what is real and what is imaginary. Perhaps that scenario was also in your head?"

"It was real, I know it was, just like this is real, you're real and they **will** see you!"

"Who are you talking to?" Sebastian's gaze followed Tom's. His eyes fell upon the open doorway and the darkness that lay beyond it. He could faintly make out the worn carpet and the banister of the stairs. The corridor was completely empty aside from this.

Tom turned to Sebastian, an incredulously look on his face. "I'm talking to her. She's right there in front of you. Why can't either of you see her? She's real and she's there. I can see her. Please, just…tell me you can too!"

"No matter how much you beg and plead, they will never be able to see me," she said, a sadistic grin tugging at her lips. She took a step forward, delicately entering the room. Involuntarily, Tom took a step backwards, pressing himself into the glass behind him.

"Tom, what's wrong?" Sebastian asked, moving towards him.

Tom shook his head but didn't reply. "Why can I see you? If they can't, why can I?"

"Maybe there's something wrong with you," she said, ever so simplistically, as though the answer were staring him in the face.

"There's nothing wrong with me."

"I think there is," she whispered. Her voice was changing once more as it had done last night. He felt the words vibrate through the glass behind him and he shuddered.

"What's happening?" Oliver asked, voice rising an octave as he watched Tom stare blankly before him, conversing with nothing. His hands gripped the windowsill, clenching as hard as he could, his knuckles straining against the skin turning it papery white.

"She's changing," Tom murmured.

Her wings unfolded from behind her and the sound of bones cracking and breaking filled the room causing his stomach to turn. The temperature began to rise as heat emanated off her in waves and the heavy darkness which had once engulfed the house was rapidly banished by the light of the flames licking their way up over her skin.

"What is that smell?" Sebastian exclaimed, wrinkling his nose as a horrific scent filled the room.

Tom's eyes widened in surprise. "You can smell it too! It's her. It's what she smells like."

"It's what **death** smells like," Alyse said, voice amplified in the silent room.

"So you're dead?" Tom asked, desperately trying not to look into her crimson eyes though not sure where else to look either. During the transformation her clothes had been torn leaving behind barely enough cloth to cover her. This image was far from arousing, however, as her papery skin strained grotesquely across bare ribs and collar bones. Her hips protruded almost painfully and he wondered if it was possible for her skin to completely tear away. He could see every artery pulse with each beat of her heart and he could almost hear the rushing of blood as it raced through her.

"You've heard the tale. Burned. Cleansed in holy fire. Thou shalt never suffer a witch to live. But here I stand."

"If you're not human then what are you?" he asked, voice trembling.

Oliver and Sebastian watched as their friend spiraled downwards into insanity. His eyes were frighteningly wide, filled with fear, staring straight ahead at absolutely nothing. The colour had drained from his face leaving his skin ashen.

"Tom, I don't understand, wha-"

"Hush!" Alyse said venomously, turning to glare at

Oliver. The sound of cracking wood filled the room and Oliver collapsed to the floor. The floorboards beneath him had splintered and he found himself knee deep in floorboards, unable to pull himself out.

"Olli, you ok?" Sebastian asked, turning towards his friend.

Oliver gritted his teeth, straining against the wooden floor, trying to pull himself free. "I'm fine. Guess the place isn't as stable as we thought it was. I think I'm ok though. Just hurts."

"It wasn't the wood," Tom said, barely turning to look at Oliver.

"What?"

"It wasn't the wood, it was her. She caused the wood to break because you were talking. It's her way of warning you."

"Now, Tom, that's cheating," Alyse said patronizingly. "Giving them unfair advantages. It's more fun when they don't believe it's me. Men will continue to rationalize the world, when truth remains completely unknowable. Unbelievable. Too afraid that the illogical could hold presence in this world."

"At least there's proof you exist now," Tom said, a feeling of triumph slowly washing through him. "You caused the wood to splinter. You did that, nobody else."

There was a smile resting upon her lips behind which sharp, white teeth gleamed. "Did I really, Tom? Or is the wood, in fact, so old and rotten that any weight placed upon it caused it to splinter? Perhaps you use me as a supernatural explanation for something completely natural?"

"No, don't twist things!" he cried. "You said you did it! I saw you do it!"

"But they did not. They can neither see nor hear me. But both saw the wood splinter. And neither truly believes I did it. So in denial. So human."

"You never did tell me what you were," he said, forcing himself to keep her talking.

Flames licked across her skin, crackling and burning as they raced. If she was human, her skin would crack and peel, blacken under the fire. "I am your fears and nightmares in one. A soul so impure, burned in rage and wrath, fueled by lust for pain and man. I am in this, what I was in life. But now so much more than magic, potions, poisons, could have ever given me."

She took a step forward, the ground seeming to tremble beneath her. Her wings gently swayed back and forth, creating a current of air swirling through the room, carrying the scent of decay throughout.

"Oh, that smell's getting worse!" Sebastian exclaimed, wrinkling his nose and turning away from Oliver.

"Seb, what do we do?" Oliver whispered, as he continued to watch Tom converse with nothing. "We can't stay here much longer. It was a mistake coming here in the first place. I think it's just made him worse. Something's obviously really wrong with Tom and we need to get him home, or to a hospital, or somewhere, before he gets worse, if that's even possible."

"I know. Do you think, maybe, he really thinks he can see her?"

"I don't know," Oliver said, glancing nervously at his wild-eyed friend. "I really don't know."

A giggle burst its way forth from Alyse. "Your friends believe you to be insane."

"What?"

"They whisper in the corner like mice," she said. "They believe you have gone mad. You are seeing things. That you need help."

"Shut up, it's not true. I'm not crazy!"

He stepped sideways away from her direct line of vision and pushed himself into the corner, hoping to melt into the wood and disappear from those maddening eyes.

"You are." She stepped closer. "Crazy; that is why you see me. I am not real Tom, I have no substance, no reality. I cannot be seen by any but you. Just a figment of your imagination."

"You can't be. You have to be real!" he cried out. "The cuts, everything I saw yesterday. Everything that's happened, that's still happening. It's all real. You're real! This is real."

"Am I? Am I really real Tom, or is this in your head? Maybe I am nothing more than a way for you to explain away something wrong with you. Blame thrust upon somebody, or something, else." She grinned devilishly, obviously enjoying torturing him. She bit her lip, drawing blood with razor sharp teeth, staining her lips as dark red as her eyes.

Tom desperately tried to avert his gaze but was transfixed by the scarlet liquid pooling at the corner of her mouth. Gently dripping down over her lip, a trail of crimson stained her porcelain skin. She licked it delicately, enjoying the coppery taste. Her teeth glinted behind ruby lips, a terrifying surprise waiting beyond the barricade of hypnotic, addictive lips.

"I cannot wait to taste you, your blood, your sweet flesh, Tom," she said, the hairs on the back of his neck standing on end. He clamped his hands over his ears and shook his head violently.

"Shut up!" he cried frantically.

"You cannot tell the voices in your head to shut up. They remain there, a part of you…like me. Forever screaming. Forever heard."

"No, you're not in my head, you're real!" Tom cried, shaking his head though unable to look away from her, causing his vision to blur. "You're real! I'm not crazy and you're real."

"Tom!" Sebastian's voice broke through Tom's

174

disturbing break down.

Tom turned towards the direction of the voice and was surprised to see Sebastian stood a few feet away. In his fear and desperation he had forgotten about his best friends, had forgotten about where they were or anything that wasn't Alyse. She had rapidly become the only thing to exist. He could sort of see Oliver on the floor behind Sebastian, one foot still firmly stuck in the woodwork. A flashlight lay beside him, pointing directly at Alyse. Tom followed the light's direction, happy to see the beam created a shadow of Alyse on the opposite wall. If she was in his head, if she wasn't real, she wouldn't create a shadow – only things with a form, with substance could create shadows. Relief washed over him as his mind latched onto this idea, this unwavering proof he now held.

"Look at the wall!" Tom all but sobbed, pointing desperately. "Look at it and you'll see her. The light…it's creating shadows. Her shadow. On that wall."

"Tom, I don't think-"

"Please! Just look at the wall!"

Sebastian sighed and turned to the side. A semicircle of yellow light had formed on the wall, perfectly round and unbroken.

"There aren't any shadows, Tom" Oliver said gently, voice low, as if coming to him from a thousand miles away. "It's just a wall. There are no shadows. She's not here."

"I can't see any shadows either," Sebastian agreed reluctantly. "I'm sorry Tom, I really did want to see her, for you, but I can't. We need to go now; you're not feeling too well and I think we should get Olli to the hospital. He might be hurt."

"I'm fine," Oliver said but his voice quivered. "It's just a little cut."

Alyse giggled again; a sinister sound bouncing across the room. "It's not. A broken ankle. If left long enough, he will

175

meet us in death. It will be a feast then."

Tom shook his head violently as if to dislodge the very thought, banish it far away. "No!"

"We have to," Sebastian said, assuming Tom had been addressing him. "We have to go."

Sebastian extended a hand ready to help his friend up. Tom stood up slowly, unwillingly, body shaking as Alyse watched his every move, eyes hungry, blood still dripping from her lips.

"Ask the broken one if he smells what you and the other perceive to exist," Alyse said cryptically, as Tom went to take a step towards Sebastian. He stopped dead, glancing up at her and wishing instantly that he hadn't. In the few seconds he'd taken his eyes off her she had glided across the room and now stood beside him. Towering over him once more, the scent of decay bombarded his senses and it took all of his efforts not to throw up right there. "Ask him."

"O-Olli," Tom said tentatively. "Can you...smell that?"

"Smell what?" Oliver asked, looking up at Tom, teeth gritted in pain as his broken ankle throbbed beneath the woodwork. He knew it wasn't a little cut, and the pain was causing his vision to swim before him. He could feel hot, sticky liquid dripping down his leg and knew blood was pooling beneath him. But he also knew right now they needed to focus upon Tom and his rapidly deteriorating mental state more than anything. His pain could wait.

"There's a horrible smell in here, like Seb said earlier...can you smell it?" Tom pressed, acutely aware of how close Alyse stood; so close her breath caused strands of hair to dance gently across his cheek, tickling the back of his neck.

Oliver sniffed. "I can't smell anything, just dust and old wood."

"Are you serious?" Sebastian exclaimed, turning to look over his shoulder at Oliver in shock, as though he was the one who had suddenly lost his mind. "You can't smell that? It smells like something died in here!"

"I told you, it's her, it's the smell of decay," Tom said.

"It is the smell of death, Tom, but it is not me." Tom looked up, locking eyes with her. He couldn't understand what she meant. There was nothing else in the room that was dead beside her, and the smell only appeared when she was…like this. It had to be her. "It is not my death we await."

And suddenly, he understood. "You mean ours. We can **smell** our own death?" he said, disgust evident in his voice. A shiver ran down his spine as the thought began to set in. And then the anger from last night was back. She was planning to hurt Sebastian, to kill him. He wouldn't let her. He refused to be the reason why his best friend would lose his life. All of this was his fault. He had dragged them into this situation. Into Rose House. They were here because of him. And they were hurt because of him. They would not die because of him. He knew he had to fix it. He pulled the knife from his pocket and flipped the gleaming blade out of its hold.

Sebastian stared at the blade in Tom's hand. "Tom, what are you doing?"

"I'm going to stop her," he replied simply.

"You think this possible?" Tom jumped in shock; her voice was frighteningly close. She stood right beside him, centimeters away. Her teeth gleamed in the sparse light and he could see just how sharp they were. "Another attempted execution. Well here I stand, Tom, stop me."

He desperately willed himself to raise the blade and plunge it into the cavity where her heart should be, pulsing beneath the paper thin skin stretched taught across her chest. He could hear the rapid beating as it seemed to strain with each movement. Seconds ticked by without a reaction. Oliver and Sebastian tentatively watched on, not quite sure what Tom was planning, nervously expecting the worst but both frozen to the spot, unable to even comprehend what to do next.

Alyse grinned darkly. "You cannot," she giggled. "You will never hurt me because I exist as a part of you...I am you."

He remained mute, unable to reply. Her grin widened bizarrely, pulling her lips away from the gleaming fangs beneath; each silvery point now visible. She stepped forward, coming in between Tom and Sebastian, now facing the boy who could not see her. The heat of the flames engulfing her wings tickled across Tom's skin, white hot. He could barely see around Alyse to his friend though he managed to catch a glimpse of Sebastian's now incredibly wide eyes.

Sebastian gagged. "That smell, it's horrible!"

"It's her, she's right in front of you, Seb, move!" Tom begged, hoping his friend would take a step backwards.

The sound of retching filled the room as Sebastian doubled over, the smell overpowering him. "Stop it! You don't need to hurt him, he didn't do anything, it's me you want, leave him alone!" Tom screamed at Alyse, hoping to catch her attention but, for once, it seemed as though she didn't want him. He went to take a step forward, hoping to get around Alyse and in between her and Sebastian, but her wings burst out to either side, completely blocking his path, leaving him trapped.

"Tom, stop it," Oliver called out as Sebastian shakily stood back up. "We need to leave. You need to come back to us so we can leave."

"She's not real, Tom, she never has been and she never will be," Sebastian said, voice croaky from retching, looking Tom straight in the eye – though from Tom's perspective, he could not see this, Alyse completely blocking his view. "She isn't here now, and she never was. We'll help you see she isn't real. We will. Just come with us."

Tom clenched his fists, angry that neither of them was willing to believe him, even when Sebastian's life was on the line.

"Hear that? How they wish to help," she said, cocking her head to the side. "Such good companions, it is almost a pity you will lose both."

She raised her right hand and Tom recalled how her nails had dug into his own skin, sharper than any blade he had ever felt. Electric. Burning and intense. In that split second, Tom realized what she was about to do and forced himself to react. As her arm swept downwards towards Sebastian's chest, Tom leaped forward, blade held firmly in hand, plunging it deep into her back, directly between the juncture of both wings. His hand slipped between the skin, squelching, burying beneath the papery skin and muscle ripping across her back.

Deep, crimson almost black blood began to flow from the wound, coating his hands. He pulled the knife out of the wound and drew his hands away, not wanting to encounter her blood. He could feel it sliding across his own skin, slithering as though it were alive and he desperately tried to wipe it away, throwing the knife away from himself.

She spun towards him, eyes full of fire as blood continued to force its way out of wounds, dripping to the wooden floor and pooling at her feet. She stalked forward, and he hurriedly backed into the corner once more, sinking to his knees, hoping to disappear. Any anger and courage he had felt before rapidly vanished as those eyes bore into him, her anger and venom bursting through like an inferno. Blood drained from his flushed face and he shook violently. Despite the amount of blood gushing to the floor behind her, she didn't seem to weaken or even be affected by pain. If anything, it only enhanced her anger, her wrath.

"You will regret that," she said simply, grabbing his hands and pulling them out towards her. Turning them palms up, she raked her fingers down both of his wrists. Electricity burst across his skin where her fingertips touched. Blood spurted from open wounds, dripping down his fingers and onto the floorboards beneath him. Too shocked to move, he stared as the blood continued to drip, faster, forming into rivulets as the cuts deepened.

He looked up into her crimson eyes and noticed she had changed back into the girl he had first encountered, the terrifying nightmare seeming to have vanished. She leaned forward and kissed him, hard, on the lips, before completely vanishing. He licked his lips, tasting sickly sweet copper, remembering the blood which had covered her lips. Her own blood.

Oliver gaped at the sight before him. He hadn't had time to react before everything happened, and his mind still reeled over what he had seen. Unable to truly believe what had just happened. Tom had attacked Sebastian. A swift stab to the centre of his chest, before dragging the blade away. Sebastian had collapsed, and though Oliver didn't want to believe it, with the amount of blood flowing from the open wound, it looked fatal. He desperately fought to dig his phone from his pocket, struggling to reach it, fingers grazing against splintered wood as he scrabbled against his prison. His fingers grasped the sleek metal, praying it hadn't been damaged and would still work.

Mercifully, it had survived his fall and the impacting wood and he desperately rang emergency services. Dialing the number, he turned back to glance at Tom. As he did so, his heart stopped completely. In the window's glassy surface, a slight reflection had formed. Crimson eyes stared straight at him and a mouth full of fangs grinned wildly. Blood dripped from the corners of the mouth and a tongue darted out to catch falling drops. Expecting to see droplets of blood pooling on the floor, he let his eyes drifted downwards. Instead he saw his best friend, crouched in the corner, arms outstretched as though held by an invisible force. As he watched, deep gashes appeared along his wrists. It looked as though he'd slit them; an attempted suicide. But, he hadn't. Though still feeling light headed from the pain of his fall, Oliver could swear blind Tom hadn't done that to himself.

A rush of air hit him and he pulled backwards, wanting to hide away from whatever was passing. Seconds later, whatever he had felt was gone.

After a few moments of fear and confusion, he finally realized there was a far away voice talking to him down the phone line.

"Please, help," he frantically cried into the phone. "There's been an accident; I think my friend's dying."

Within minutes the sound of sirens wailing in the distance filled the air. Oliver closed his eyes in relief as the sirens wailed louder, approaching the house. The door crashed open and footsteps thudded on the old wood.

"Up here!" he cried desperately, voice croaky. Lightheadedness was rapidly creeping in on him. He had been trapped for quite some time now and he'd lost feeling in his leg, the wood cutting off the circulation. He knew something had broken in the fall though the agony he had been in earlier was slowly dwindling.

Paramedics burst through the doorway and into the room carrying stretchers and various pieces of equipment with them. As two raced towards him, Oliver shook his head violently "I'm fine, help them, help Seb!"

"It's fine, they'll help your friends, but you need help too," the paramedic soothed as Oliver continued to demand they help Sebastian and Tom though he felt himself weakening, unable to fight back. Pain shot through his entire being as the paramedics began to slowly shift the wood in an attempt to free him without causing any further damage. Stars burst before his eyes and the entire world began to fade. As the world turned black, a memory of those red eyes swam before him and he fell into fitful unconsciousness.

Chapter Twenty

Fire burst violently around Tom, surrounding him. He felt trapped by the heat, desperately wanting to hide away from the fire he knew to be Alyse. There was no escape. He shivered despite the unbearable heat.

"There is no way to escape me." Alyse's voice floated across the fire, seeming to carry the heat within it. "Like the fire I will consume. Ravage. Destroy."

With every word the flames seemed to swell, increasing in height and heat, overwhelming Tom. He collapsed to the ground as crimson flames danced closer. Closing his eyes, desperately trying to block out the image before him, he curled up under himself, creating a protective little niche in which he felt safe.

The white hot flames approached faster. Singeing his back. Burning the skin. Filling the air with the sickly smell of charred flesh as they engulfed Tom who remained curled up trying to hide within himself. Tom felt the flames consume him entirely, burning through to his very core, destroying everything he was until nothing remained

Tom's eyes burst open. Expecting to find himself faced with a wall of white hot flames, he was startled to find four very white walls and not much else. The smell of antiseptic hit him and he wrinkled his nose at the sterile, chemical aroma.

It took a few moments for Tom to fully understand where he was. At that moment, everything that had happened from the night before came rushing back. Was it the night before? Two nights? However recent it had occurred, the events came rushing back, bursting into his mind like a train colliding with the stars. Completely obliterating in its unbelivability.

Desperately wanting to know if both Sebastian and Oliver were ok, Tom attempted to get out of his hospital bed. Confused as to why his body wouldn't work, he expected to find wide, beige coloured straps wrapping around his arms and torso keeping him tied securely to the sides of the bed. No straps were found, however. There was no reason as to why he shouldn't be able to move

His wrists were wrapped in sterile, white bandages though Tom noticed droplets of scarlet along the metal bars beside his bed. He tried again to sit up, to climb out of bed but his body still refused to move. The most he could do was wrap his fingers around the metal bars of the bed, balling his hands into fists around the bars. Panic started to rise in his chest as his heart pounded faster. Sat here, unable to move from this bed he felt like a sitting duck, waiting for Alyse to come back and finish what she had started. Her ability to slither into any room unnoticed by all but Tom meant she could be outside, biding her time, ready to enter at any moment.

"Hey!" he cried as loud as he could, still pulling at his restraints. "Is anybody out there? Can you hear me? Hello!"

"I can hear you. They cannot, but I can," a familiar voice whispered from the corner. He whipped his head to the side, eyes wide, heart frantically beating against his chest, expecting to find Alyse beside him. The room was void of life; she was nowhere to be seen.

"Somebody, help me!" he called out, desperately hoping somebody would hear his cries. "Anybody!"

His wrists responded to the anger and fear coursing through him and his fists shook the metal bars on the side of his bed, causing them to clank loudly. The deafening sound bounced off the pristine walls.

"Nobody can help you now," the voice whispered, closer than before. He felt her breath ghosting across his face, causing the hairs on the back of his neck to stand on end and gooseflesh to erupt across his bare arms. Desperately wanting to pull away from her, he shook, bashing onto the metal bar repeatedly as he did so. The white bandages wrapped around his wrists began to turn crimson as his frantic movements disturbed the slowly healing cuts underneath, blood staining what was once white an angry red. "You belong to me. The only one to ever fight back."

The door swung open and three nurses came rushing into the room, appearing at his bedside and grabbing onto his forearms, trying to stop his violent thrashing.

"He needs sedating," one of the nurses said loudly, trying to be heard over Tom and his frantic pleas for help.

At the thought of being sent back into the dream world, Tom began to calm down. "No, please, don't send me back to sleep," he begged, lowering his voice to an almost inaudible level.

"We have to sedate you honey," one of the nurses whispered gently. "But it's ok, everything's better when you're asleep."

"No, it's not, she's there," he said, though he knew he was powerless to stop what was about to happen.

"She won't be there for much longer," the nurse whispered as Tom felt a long, thin needle slide deep into his skin. "She'll be gone soon."

"But, she'll take me with her," Tom muttered - he was rapidly losing the energy to communicate.

The nurse continued to whisper soothing words of nothing, holding onto Tom's arm, less to restrain and more to comfort him now.

"She's here," he managed to murmur before completely falling back into a thankfully dreamless sleep.

"Monitor his vitals," the nurse said the moment she was confident Tom was asleep. "I want twenty four hour watch on Mr. Leeson, like we should have had from the very start. He's a high risk patient who seems to still be in the throes of whatever hallucinations he is suffering."

"Has he been appointed a specialist yet?" one of the other nurses asked as he scribbled something onto the chart at the end of Tom's bed.

"He has. She should be here by tomorrow to start doing analysis and find out what's making him act like this," the nurse continued, glancing down at the sleeping boy before her. "And what caused him to murder his friend. Until then there's not much we can do for him except keep him sedated. Keep him safe."

Chapter Twenty-One

The next time Tom opened his eyes, the room was plunged in darkness. The blind had been pulled down across his window though sparse sunlight filtered through. This time he knew where he was. And his body, though heavy and sluggish, no longer seemed to be completely immobile.

His eyes slowly adjusted to the darkness and he began to distinguish various shapes in the room, illuminated by the meager light filtering in through the frosted glass panel in the door.

Just as his eyes had become accustomed to the sparse light, the door flung open. Dazzling white light flooded into the room. Tom closed his eyes, wincing as the brilliant light momentarily blinded him, flinching instinctively at whoever had entered the room.

"Good, you're awake," a very business-like voice said. Tom opened his eyes gently, getting them accustomed to the new lighting level in his room. He watched a woman in her late thirties stride into the room and shut the door behind her blocking off the light once more. Moments later, sunlight burst into the room as she threw the blinds up. The weather had seemed to clear since the incident at Rose House and the sun shone brightly in a cloudless sky; odd for late November but stranger things had happened, as he well knew.

"Who are you?" Tom managed to croak out, voice straining from lack of use; he'd obviously been sedated for a lot longer than he'd thought. Perhaps the weather wasn't so strange after all.

"I'm Dr. Helena Raleigh, I'm here to help you, Tom," she said, grabbing the only seat in the room and dragging it to his bedside.

"Right...help me with what?" he asked, slightly confused.

She spoke slowly, carefully choosing her words, eyes

flicking over his bandages quickly before returning to hold his gaze. "I'm here to help you with anything that may be troubling you, anything which led to what you did to yourself."

"But I didn't do it to myself," Tom protested.

"Yes, you did inform one of my colleagues about who had actually done this to you, Tom," she continued. "And that is also what I'm here to help you with."

Silence followed her remark. "So…my friends told you she's real?" he whispered, barely loud enough for her to hear.

"I have heard a lot about the strange events you have been experiencing," she said cautiously. Instantly Tom understood she was gently skirting around the issue.

Tom sighed, rolling his eyes and relaxing back into his pillow. "And you think I'm crazy just like everyone else does. Thanks Dr. Raleigh, but I really don't need a psychologist certifying me insane and shoving me into a padded cell."

"That is not what I'm here to do. We are not going to put you in a padded cell. I'm here to see what's going on and to help you however I can. I'm just here to help."

"Then stitch me up, tick all the little boxes saying I'm fine and let me out of this place. I want to see if Seb and Olli are ok." Tom attempted to cross his arms over his chest in indignation. As he tried to move, a sharp, searing pain made its way through his arm as he pulled on the IV attached to him. He settled for balling his hands into fists instead, the pain not worth the angry notion.

"Your friends did say you have a fiery personality," Helena noted, smiling. "You obviously feel relaxed in this environment if your personality is shining through. Unfortunately Tom, because of your self-harm, it's slightly more complicated than ticking boxes."

"I didn't do it myself, as I've told you already." Though he didn't want to admit it, she was right in what she had said before; he did feel comfortable in this environment. Despite having heard Alyse's voice before, he felt as though she couldn't get to him in here, as if he was completely protected from her in such a sterile, blank room. "Let me guess – it's all procedure?"

"There are an astonishing amount of procedures I do have to follow," Helena replied with a grin. "But they're helpful in the end." She waited for Tom to comment again but he remained silent. "So, Tom, tell me about Rose House."

"What do you want to know? It's an old, spooky looking house on the outskirts of town; my town that is, because I know I'm not in my town anymore," he said nonchalantly.

"How do you know you're not in your town?" Helena asked curiously.

"The view," he said, nodding towards the window. "I've been living in that town for almost 18 years and I know it pretty well. We don't have a clock tower like that."

Helena nodded. "So you're still quite aware of your surroundings."

"Like I said, I'm not crazy. I know who I am, where I am, how old I am, what year it is and who the Prime Minister is, if you'd like to ask me any of those questions," he said with a shrug.

"Ok, fine, you're not crazy, I get it Tom," Helena said with a gentle grin. "So, Rose House? I heard you're the expert on the house's myth?"

"I was till everything happened," he said snippily.

"So tell me what happened, then," she pressed. "In your own words."

"Nothing happened. I went into the house on a dare, met a girl there who likes to pretend she's the creature from the myth and then she became obsessed with me," Tom said. "She's been following me around and won't leave me alone. That's all."

188

"Ok," Helena said with a nod. He watched her write something down on a notepad. "Does she go to your school?"

"No, I've never seen her before," Tom replied. "She's the crazy one; she must've been hiding in that house for ages waiting for somebody to come in. Maybe you should find her."

"I'll make a note of it," Helena said. "Does anybody else know who she is, Tom?"

"I don't really know," Tom replied. "Nobody really saw her. She was good at staying out of the way."

"But you saw her a lot, am I right?" Helena queried.

"Yeah, but she was stalking me, she wanted me to see her," Tom said matter of factly.

"And she never did that when others were with you?" Helena pressed. "Stalk you while they were around?"

"Oh, she did, all the time," Tom said, stuttering as he thought of a way to cover this flaw in his explanation. "They just didn't notice her, or maybe she was still very good at remaining hidden, I just expected her to be there so I guess I noticed her." He wasn't quite sure why he was blatantly lying about Alyse to this woman; he just knew that telling her the truth about what Alyse was would not end well for him. Better to convince her Alyse was real and just a human being, than tell her the truth and risk being thrown into an asylum because nobody was willing to believe he might be telling the truth. Nobody was willing to believe that his hallucinations might just be real, for fear no rational explanation may exist.

"I suppose," Helena conceded with a nod. "Did you ever tell your family about her?"

"Nope, just my closest friends," Tom said.

"Why?"

"I guess I just assumed I could handle it myself." Tom shrugged. "And my friends were there too, so it wasn't like I

189

needed to tell my family. Why worry them?"

"Did she ever get violent towards you, Tom?" Helena asked.

He waved his wrists rather enthusiastically. "I'd call that violent, wouldn't you?"

"So, you're saying she attacked you then did those cuts herself?" Helena probed. "With what?"

"Um…" he stumbled. "My knife. Yeah, I had it with me because I knew she could be a bit crazy and I thought it would come in handy…just in case."

"And she used it against you?"

"Yeah," he replied lamely, knowing his lies were becoming less convincing.

Helena nodded slowly. "How come you didn't tell the police or somebody at school, if you knew she could be violent?"

"I don't know!" Tom cried exasperatedly. "I just didn't. I didn't want to. I thought I could get rid of her myself but obviously she was stronger than I thought and I couldn't."

Silence fell following Tom's outburst. "What's your life like at home, Tom?"

"Fine, normal, nothing interesting there," he replied, glaring at her.

"Do you get on well with your mother, and your sister?"

"Yeah, I guess. We fight sometimes but all families do. Nothing excessive," Tom said. "My mum is a hard working, upstanding citizen and all that, and Darcy's got coursework or whatever she pretends to do when she says she's at the library."

"So you don't see them much?" Helena asked, jotting something down.

"No, I see them loads," Tom said. "Well, I see them enough. I've got classes, things to do, homework, my own social life stuff like that anyway. And we all try to make sure we're home most nights for dinner so, yeah they're always around."

"Do you ever wish they weren't?"

"Not really, it's nice having them around…it's not like I get denied anything or treated badly," Tom said, rolling his eyes. "It's honestly just a normal family. Trust me."

"Do you have lots of friends?" she asked.

"I guess," he said warily, a little worried by the way she had suddenly stopped asking about Rose House and Alyse. "I've got a few close friends but I guess I get on well with everyone in my year."

"But you've only got a few you'd class as close?" Helena asked.

"Yeah, doesn't everybody? You know, outer circle, inner circle, all that?" Tom said, raising an eyebrow.

Helena nodded. "How many close friends would you say you've got."

"Three," Tom replied instantly. "I've got three close friends who I know will be there no matter what."

"And do you tell them everything?" she continued.

"Yes," he replied, again without hesitation. "Maybe not right away but eventually I tell them everything."

"Do you go to school with them or are they outside friends?" she asked.

"No we're all in the same year," Tom explained.

"What are their names, Tom?" Helena asked, as though she was genuinely interested in his social life.

"Sebastian, Oliver and Mariana," Tom replied.

"And they were with you, the night you went into the house?" Helena asked, jotting down a few notes as she spoke.

"You know they were," Tom replied, rolling his eyes. "You know both Sebastian and Olli were there with me and

Mariana wasn't. You also know that Olli got hurt when the floor collapsed beneath him. Just in case you were planning on asking me if anything happened while we were there."

Helena smiled. "So, you've got my questions answered ahead of time."

"From what you've asked me, it's not hard to see what's coming next," he said with a shrug. "Look, I know you have to ask me these questions. And I know you're not going to believe any of my answers-"

"Why do you think I won't believe your answers?" Helena asked, cutting into the tirade she knew was about to spill forth.

"I don't know," Tom replied, briefly avoiding eye contact. "Because you're searching for insanity, even though it's not there?"

"I don't think you're insane, Tom," she said, with a sigh. "I genuinely do not. I'm only here to help, to get you back on your feet and see where we can go from there. I'm not going to label you, or make you out to be something you are not."

Tom sighed heavily and leant back into his pillows, trying to get comfortable; it would be so much easier if his pillows weren't made of what appeared to be concrete. "What am I supposed to do when we're done today?" he suddenly asked. "It's not like I can keep myself entertained."

"Well, you've got the TV for hours of endless fun and you should have somebody coming in as soon as I leave to keep you company," Helena replied, glancing at a sheet of paper before her.

"One of my friends?" he asked, eyes glimmering.

"Um...no, a nurse," Helena said gently. "At the moment you are on a closed ward, meaning no visitors. Before you ask, no, I don't know how long you'll be here. However long it takes to sort everything out, I think."

"Oh, right, ok then," he said, defeated. "So, more questions?"

"Actually, I think I've asked enough for now," Helena said with a small smile. "I only wanted a preliminary meeting with you today; find out a little bit more. I'll be back again tomorrow though."

"Giving me something to look forward to, I see," he replied sarcastically.

"You'll grow to love me," She said with a smirk. "Do you have any questions for me?"

"Um, yeah, are my friends ok?" Tom asked, looking at her, eyebrow raised. "You haven't really mentioned them and, it just seems like something..."

"Well, Oliver's going to be fine," Helena said cautiously. "He broke his ankle and shin in the fall and there were quite a few deep cuts but they were stitched up, and they'll heal. He might need some rehabilitation once it's healed to get his balance back but other than that, he's fine."

"And Seb's ok, isn't he?" Tom pressed. "I mean, he wasn't hurt, I know that, but he's doing alright, yeah?"

Helena looked at Tom questioningly for a few moments. "Tom, what do you remember of that night, just before she attacked you, I mean?"

Tom furrowed his brow in concentration. "Um...I don't know. I know she was there, and I was talking to her. Sebastian said we should go and then...then she did this." He shook his wrists in Helena's direction.

"And that's it?" Helena pressed.

"Yeah, that's everything," he said, slightly confused. "Why? What am I missing?"

Helena pulled her chair closer to the bed and laid a hand upon Tom's forearm. "Tom, Sebastian was also...hurt...in the house. Quite badly."

"Is he ok?" Tom asked. Though he clearly remembered Oliver's accident, he couldn't remember Sebastian being hurt in any way.

Helena sighed. "Unfortunately, Tom, though the doctors did everything they could, Sebastian passed away."

It was as though Tom was twelve years old again, being woken up by his aunt in the middle of the night to tell him his father had finally passed away. Time had ceased to exist and all that remained was this desolate moment. The pit of his stomach seemed to have dropped and he felt completely empty. Cold washed over him and tears prickled at the corners of his eyes, spilling over before he could even register their appearance. His heart physically ached as the familiar sense of grief and loss came rushing back to him. This couldn't be happening. It wasn't real. This had to be another trick of Alyse's, or his mind's, or somebody's. Anybody's.

Tom closed his eyes, desperately trying to remember that crucial moment but continually drew a blank. Tears spilled faster down across his cheeks and he struggled to keep his breathing even and calm. "How did he die?" he asked through gritted teeth, attempting to hold back the sobs so eager to burst forth, though his voice still shook.

"Severe blood loss," she said gently. "But the doctors don't think he suffered." A gesture at sympathy and reassurance. It didn't matter that Tom knew dying was never completely painless. It didn't matter that he'd been told the same thing about his father, whom he'd seen suffer hours of agony. It didn't matter that he knew it was a lie. She still said it because that was what doctors did.

The memory came flooding back, barreling into him, knocking all breath and sense of time and place completely out of him. Alyse attacked Sebastian. He remembered the rage surging through him as he knew what she was about to do, remembered lunging forward, hoping to hurt her first. To stop her. He had been too late. The memory of her warm blood trickling down his arms, seeming to surge and sway of its own according, a separate, living entity crawling its way across his skin followed and he gagged as his insides revolted. Helena placed a shallow basin on his lap as he retched, emptying the sparse contents of his stomach into the plastic bowl. His hands began to shake and he clenched and unclenched his hands, wanting to rid himself of the memory of her blood.

His throat burned as the retching finally subsided, the stench of bile filling the room, clawing its way through his senses. Turning his head away from Helena, he glanced out of the window, wanting to look at anything but her as tears streamed down his cheeks. Never had he imagined one of his friends might actually die from this. With grief came another familiar emotion – guilt. It was as though the two existed hand in hand. When his father passed, he was convinced he was somehow responsible, as though the disease was his fault. Irrational, but convinced none the less. But now, the guilt was completely rational. Rightly placed. Rightly felt. Guilt consumed him as his mind focused upon the sole, important fact…Sebastian was gone and it was his fault.

"Do you remember what happened now?"

"Yes," he replied weakly, voice shaking with effort. His hands shook. His entire body shook. A dark cloud had descended over him in the moments since she'd told him and he felt cold all over, as if he would never be warm again. "I remember everything."

"Would you like to tell me?"

"She did it," he replied with a hiccup, his tears starting to get the better of him as they continued their steady stream. All pretenses had vanished as he openly cried in front of Helena, voice shaking. "She attacked him. She killed him. And it's all my fault."

"Why is it your fault?" she asked.

Tom took a deep breath, choking back a violent sob, knowing he needed to be coherent now as he tried to gather his thoughts and portray them to someone else. His mind was attempting to close, his body aching with loss but he needed to try and hold on to some clarity. At least until he'd said what he needed to. Then he could give in to his grief. "I told him to come into the house, I forced him to come inside and see her. If he hadn't listened to me, he wouldn't have…she wouldn't have been able to hurt him. He would have been fine."

"What did she attack him with, Tom?"

Tom closed his eyes. Memories swam before him and he could feel the cold wrapping itself tighter around him. "I don't know, same thing she attacked me with. Only I guess I was lucky enough to survive."

"So…she attacked him with your knife?" Helena scribbled something down on the sheet before her.

"I-I guess so."

"How did she get the knife, Tom?"

"I don't know."

"She must have gotten it from you at some point," Helena reasoned. "For her to have used it she must have taken it."

"I guess she did," he said, shaking his head in confusion. His story was rapidly unfolding before him, and he could barely muster the sense to put it back in to order. He didn't care. For the moment, his entire focus was on his grief consuming him. The feeling of loss was always there, had been there since his father's passing, but now it intensified, was renewed as a fresh grief was added to his loss. His mind still reeled with the shock and a quiet voice cried denial even as the rest of him knew it to not be so; Sebastian was dead and it was his fault. He may as well have killed him himself.

"See, the thing is Tom…the police found your knife beside you," Helena said.

"How nice of her to leave it behind," he said, anger building in his voice. Anger at Helena. Anger at Alyse. Anger at himself.

"But why would she leave it behind?"

"I don't know, maybe she's just that psychotic? Maybe she thought I wanted it back? A nice little gift," he said, voice shaking slightly. He clung to some form of reasoning, trying to keep a hold on his story.

"Ok, Tom," she replied, jotting something down. He mentally grasped at straws, trying to gather coherent thought as it ran away from him, seeing the cracks in his story forming, intensifying. He knew she could see right through it, but instead of seeing the truth, she only saw him hiding behind the thin veil of a lie. Tom realized, at that moment, that unless she saw Alyse as truth, not only in human form but also as the mythical being she was, he would be blamed for everything. Maybe if he could show her she was- no. That was what had brought him in the first place. That was what had caused Sebastian harm.

"You think she's in my head, don't you?" Tom asked, voice rising slightly. "You think all of this is in my mind, that I'm completely crazy, making it all up."

"No, Tom-"

"Yes you do!" he cried violently, fear now mixing with his feelings of grief and loss. He was rapidly realizing he now had something else to lose alongside Sebastian. "You're going to try and blame me for everything, convinced she isn't real but she is. I know she is! I've seen her, seen everything she's done to me!"

"Tom, calm down."

"No!" he screamed. "Don't tell me to calm down. I know what you're trying to do. You're going to blame me for Sebastian's death. I didn't do it, she did! Ask Olli, he was there, he saw everything, I know he did. I saw it in his eyes...he saw something! Just ask him, please!"

"Tom, calm-"

"Ask Olli what he saw that night!" Tom cut in, voice shrill.

Helena recapped her pen and gathered up sheets of

paper filled with scribbled writing. Slipping them into a folder, she stood up. "Unfortunately, Tom, I'm going to have to end the session here," she sighed. "I have another appointment. But I will be back tomorrow, and every day, to help you. Hopefully I can show you I'm just trying to help."

"Then believe me, and you can help me," he said weakly. Tear continued to course down his cheeks and his voice shook with sobs and emotion. She squeezed his hand gently and walked out of the room, leaving him alone once more.

As promised, a nurse soon came to join him, sitting in the chair beside his bed. She tried to strike up a conversation with Tom but he pointedly ignored any question she asked. He could see in her eyes, she believed he was crazy too, completely to blame for Sebastian's death. She was here to contain the crazy; keep it from getting out. Continuing to stare out of the window, he allowed the tears to fall, allowed himself to cry. Grief. Anger. Fear. All three emotions wrestled against one another, desperately wanting to be heard, to be felt, and his mind raced with thoughts. The cold clung tightly to him as the emptiness of loss demanded to be felt. Six years had been erased in a moment and he was a frightened little boy again. He wanted to wake up from a horrific nightmare and find out everything was fine. Find out Sebastian was fine.

Day drifted into night unnoticed and he would find himself immersed in bouts of tears as loss settled itself permanently in his chest. Nurses came and went, supplying him with food and various medications. He knew each one shared the same thought; he was completely insane; a murderer.

Chapter Twenty-Two

"We're going to remove some of the IVs attached to your arms today," Helena said with a smile during their next session.

"So you don't think I'm dangerous enough to warrant needing to be steadily sedated then," Tom replied with a smirk. "Good-o!"

Helena stood to his right, gently removing a needle from the top of his hand. Tom brought his arms up to his chest, bending his elbows gingerly, wincing as the joints ached from disuse. He'd been trying not to move his arms as much whilst he'd been hooked to the various drips as each tug on the line caused pinpricks of pain to shoot across his arms and just wasn't worth it.

"Feels nice to be able to move properly again?" Helena asked, smiling as she watched him stretch out his arms.

"I guess," he said. "It certainly beats being hooked up to a thousand machines."

"Tom, we're just taking care of you," Helena explained gently. "Now, tell me how you're feeling today."

"Hungry, the food in here is absolutely rubbish. And the blue pill they keep giving me makes me feel really sick," he complained.

She threw a half smile his way as she dug a pen out of her bag "Not what I was referring to. But I'll let the chef know he displeases you."

"You could always make me happy by getting me McDonalds," he said with a shrug.

"I'll bear that in mind for your birthday," she said. "Seriously though, how are you feeling?"

"I'm fine, I suppose. Well, as fine as I could be," he replied with a shrug. "Considering I'm stuck in a locked room with everyone around me thinking I'm insane. And potentially a murderer."

"They don't think that."

"Of course they do, you can read it in their expression," he said with a shrug. "I may be 'crazy' but I'm pretty good at reading people."

"Does it bother you that they might think you're crazy?"

"Well, it certainly doesn't fill me with butterflies," Tom replied. "It's the murder part that bothers me. I'd never kill my best friend."

Helena watched Tom in silence for a few moments, noting his body language and facial expressions. Aside from crying, he hadn't expressed his feelings around Sebastian's death to Helena. Not that she couldn't read his emotions quite clearly from the way he reacted as he spoke – his guilt almost radiated off him, and this was the emotion which concerned her most. "Do you think I think you're crazy?"

"I know you think I'm not right," he said. "I can see that from the questions you ask and the way you write down the things I say. If it's particularly juicy you underline it a few times. That's always exciting. Plus, if you thought I was completely normal you wouldn't be here questioning me like this, would you?"

"And you genuinely don't think I could be here because I want to help?" she pressed.

"I guess, I don't really know anymore," he replied with a shrug. "I'm sure you've got your questions ready for me, so go ahead, ask them."

"Did you ever have an imaginary friend as a child, Tom?" Helena asked, brushing a strand of hair away from her face.

"I don't think so," he replied.

"What do you mean?"

"Well, a lot of my memories have Mariana in them, and I'm pretty sure she's real, unless you've got a bombshell you'd like to drop on me?" he said dryly. "But no. No imaginary friend."

"Where you quite creative as a child, can you remember?" she pressed.

"You mean like arts and crafts, or in the imaginary able to make a game out of nothing way?"

"Imaginary," she confirmed. "Did you spend a lot of your time playing imaginary games, alone or with Mariana?"

"Yeah, I did," he replied. "It was easier to create a new game, a new place, anything really for us to play in. There wasn't much else to do. Surprisingly, children don't have complex thoughts."

"So did you find the real world boring in comparison to these imaginary places?"

Tom paused, wary, weighing up the best way to continue. "I suppose I did. I don't really know. I guess they could only ever be more interesting than where we were. I mean, anything could happen. It's like day dreaming, only you believe it more as a kid. It's almost real."

"But you always knew it wasn't?"

"Well, I suppose so," he said cautiously, thinking carefully about his answer; her pen was poised above her notepad so he knew she was heading towards something interesting. He could almost see the sparks of anticipation flying between paper and pen. "I know I spent a lot of time thinking about these other places and imagining all this stuff, but I never thought it was more real than where I was. Why, are there kids who can't tell the difference?"

"It's not that they can't," she attempted to explain. "Just that, for whatever reason, this imaginary place can seem more comforting than real life and they would rather find themselves in this place."

"That's a bad thing?" he asked. He'd discovered early on that the more questions he asked her, the longer he could prolong an almost meaningless discussion, keeping her preoccupied and away from psychoanalyzing him.

"No not at all, creativity and imagination are both key attributes to healthy psychological development, just sometimes, it can worry."

"But why would anybody even worry about that?" Tom pushed – it was a game he now knew well. "Kids just have active imaginations."

"Sometimes, very rarely, it can be a sign of some kind of psychological disorder," Helena explained. "But once something is expressed in a movie or on TV, everybody assumes it is a common occurrence and then want to rule it out."

"Does that happen often, neurotic mothers bring kids with imaginary friends and the like in to see psychiatrists?"

"Enough," she replied. "I suppose they just want the best for their chi-."

"Hang on," Tom cut in, glancing at her suspiciously. Half way through her explanation, the pennies had started to fall and something clicked into place – he could almost see the exact line of discussion she was working them towards, and he had walked right into it. "Are you asking me about all of this imaginary nonsense because you still think Alyse is in my head?"

"It's an angle I ha-"

"No, you are, aren't you?" he pressed, with a smirk. "You're wondering if the two are connected. If she's just in my head. Perhaps my strong imagination as a kid is still very active now. It would be an interesting twist. Or maybe it would be exactly what you want."

"Tom, it's not like that," she said reasonably. "Just asking questions."

"Because you think I'm an insane murderer," he said with a sigh, disappointed both at not being able to avoid her probing questions and also that she was still trying to push for the 'its-all-in-my-head' angle. He'd been hoping for something a little different by now.

"Well, I don't Tom, and I'm trying to prove that, along with helping you in any way," Helena said matter-of-factly before cracking a grin. "Though you do make it difficult sometimes."

Tom smiled weakly back at her. "Sorry. It's not as though I've had practice with situations like this before."

"I do understand, you know," Helena said gently.

Tom nodded in response, feeling no need to verbally reply. She couldn't understand. Not really. But he felt no need to contradict her. They sat in silence before a thought occurred to Tom. "Is there…any way I could see my mum?" he asked, though he held no hope for a positive response; the almost mocking pleasure he had felt before had quickly dissipated, leaving him desolate and empty.

"Unfortunately, not yet, Tom," she said sympathetically. "I know you want to see them. I can imagine it's a bit difficult being locked in here alone without your family."

"Is there any reason I can't see her?" he asked. "I mean, I'm locked up, having tried to supposedly commit suicide, I've just found out my friend's dead, and I've supposedly killed him. I'd kind of like to see my mum."

"I know, you will soon," Helena said gently. "But that's all I can say on the matter. I'm sorry."

Tom slumped back against his pillows. Though he had known he'd be denied the right to see them, he had still hoped that maybe, just maybe, there would be a slight chance. Evidently not. After four sessions it was apparent she wasn't closer to believing his innocence, meaning the rest of the world still doubted him.

"Aside from your parents, and Oliver, is there anybody else you want to see in particular?" Helena asked.

He contemplated answering this question, knowing what would follow. He debated lying, saying no, avoiding the looks and the horribly obvious and awkward questions that would follow. Tom sighed and decided on the truth instead; there were enough lies floating around as it were. "It'd be nice to see Mariana again."

Helena nodded. "You haven't mentioned her much. Tell me more about Mariana."

"What do you want to know?"

"Anything you'd like to tell me about her," Helena replied with a small grin.

"There's not really too much to tell. She's one of my oldest friends; our parents are friends so we grew up together, played together things like that. I guess we were always going to be friends."

"Just friends?" Helena asked. She watched as Tom's cheeks flushed scarlet and he avoided looking at her. "Nothing more?"

"I really, really don't want to discuss the intricate detail of whatever me and Mariana may or may not have had before this whole crazy thing," Tom said, still refusing to make eye contact with Helena.

"What did she think when you told her about all of this?" Helena asked, ignoring Tom's statement.

He grinned. "She called me crazy then spent most of the time apologizing. It was funny."

"But you weren't mad at her?"

"Well, at first, yeah I was furious," he explained. "But you can't really stay mad at Mari for too long. She gets this angry look in her eyes and she's so tiny, it's just cu-uh...funny."

"So why, of all people, did you not want Mariana coming to Rose House with you that night?" Helena questioned

"I didn't want her getting involved," he replied simply. "Guess I wanted to protect her. I couldn't stand her being hurt. Looks like I made the right choice."

Helena nodded, looking at him questioningly before scribbling notes into her notepad. He knew what she was trying to hint at by asking questions about Mariana, but he wouldn't even consider that thought anymore. He was locked in here and he would probably never see her again, they'd never have the chance to see what could have been. Maybe this was the best way he could protect her, after all, being locked away completely. Though it killed him inside to know this, he'd also known, deep down, as soon as their moment had passed, it never would come round again.

"Do you believe in hell, Tom?" Another session of never ending question was upon him. It was almost comical how predictable her questions were becoming. Perhaps he had watched one too many forensic dramas on TV and their predictability led in this fact. Or maybe he just knew where she was leading these sessions to. He was almost tempted to compile a template list of answers and simply point to them. It made no difference what he said; the outcome was always the same. Weeks slowly trickled by and he was still locked away from the world in this small, white room.

He thought for a few moments. "I suppose. I don't really know. I guess there must be something out there. People who do horrible things must go somewhere." Tom bit his lip gently. If there was a place for evil to go, where did Alyse exist? She was hell itself…what would become of her for the terrible things she had done, not only to Sebastian but the thousands of people before him? Could she die…again?

He had decided, if no judicial system would help, he would take matters into his own hands and bring about her punishment. He had already wounded her once, proving she could be hurt. He just needed to find a way to hurt her enough. If she could be hurt enough, maybe she could be eradicated. Based on the stories, burning hadn't helped, if anything it had made her stronger – had they known that during her trial this entire event could have been avoided. So there must be another way to stop her, to destroy her. The

205

knife had cut so cleanly through her skin, piercing deep into the flesh like soft butter until it hit something hard, possibly bone. And it had hurt her. Though there had only been anger in her eyes, he'd seen the pain hiding behind it; he'd heard the choked gasp as the knife sunk into her back.

Locked in this ward, however, he knew it would be impossible, unless she happened to have some inane allergy to sterilization and would keel over at the mere sight of an empty hospital room. But this then did leave the question, what would happen to somebody who was already dead, once they were killed again?

"So you do believe in life after death?" she pressed, noting his blank gaze as he became lost in thought.

"I guess," he replied with a shrug, coming back to the immediate conversation, still subconsciously trying to think of a way to get revenge on Alyse. "I mean, I assume something else is there; it would be nice to know we don't just stop when we die. That everyone I've lost is still here, somehow."

"Like Sebastian?"

"Yes, like Sebastian," he said through gritted teeth. "Like my brutally, painfully murdered best friend."

"How do you know he suffered pain?" she asks momentarily distracted from her previous questioning.

He looked pointedly at her, maintaining eye contact, something he hadn't done for most of the session. "I was there, I saw her physically plunge her uh…the knife…my knife…into his chest. I may not be the expert but I'm assuming that would hurt, a lot."

She nodded gently, whether in agreement or encouragement, Tom could not tell. In truth, her nodding irritated him; she reminded him of one of those nodding dog figurines, head continually bobbing up and down, swayed by an invisible force. "Do you believe in heaven as well then, Tom?"

He could feel tension and anger starting to quell in the

pit of his stomach and he wanted to ignore her completely, move the session along to some other line of questioning. But he knew her well enough by now to know she wouldn't move along. "Yes," he all but spat. "I do believe in some form of heaven. My dad's there." He waited. Questioning could go either way now; would she cling to the idea of heaven and hell or would she spring upon his father's passing? It all depended on which would make him seem more crazy, more unhinged. More likely to kill.

"Which one do you think you'd go to, Tom?" Helena asked.

Of course, this was completely the more insane route. "How should I know?"

"Well, just, thinking about your life so far and the way you see these two places, which one do you think you belong in?" she pressed, nodding her head as she spoke once more; he wondered briefly what would happen if he flicked her on the forehead – would she bob faster, or would it simply result in him being put into restrains faster than he could blink?

"I don't know," he reiterated. "I've not done anything bad, so I'd say heaven. I know you look at me and think differently – as I'm sure a lot of people do. But I guess I'd go some place good."

"What about the devil, demons, creatures like that, do you believe they exist?" she asked, writing furiously as she spoke.

He furrowed his eyebrows in confusion, watching her as she scribbled away, planning his answer. The idea of 'the devil' had never seemed real to him and demons had always been stories, ways to frighten people into behaving. But Alyse had proven this untrue. She wasn't human, as her transformation had proven, and the way she looked suggested she was demonic, if books and movies were anything to go by. And that smell, so strong, almost sickly sweet in its decay. His instinct told him she was wrong, evil, surrounded by the impulse to run, protect himself from her. "I don't believe in the devil," he began carefully, mindful of the words he used and how she may construe them. "At least, not a guy with a pointy tail and a pitchfork, running around prodding people into doing bad things. I do think there's…something…out there, that is bad in some way. A force, I suppose. I don't know about demons."

"Well, do you think they're real?"

"I don't know," he repeated. "I suppose they could be another dark force."

She seemed to be toying with a thought, her pen nib tapping gently on to the paper before her as she turned the idea over in her mind. "Have you ever had any contact, from these dark forces? Have you ever had a dark force tell you to do something?"

"No, as I said, I'm not crazy," he replied, turning away from her, bored with the questions – they had started out so positive, too. He'd almost expected her to keep him guessing, but here was the predictability he had come to know so well.

"What about voices, do you hear any voices?" she asked.

"Ok, stop," he blurted, gesturing with his hands to silence her. "You keep asking me about hell and demons and all of this. Why? I'm not religious, so it's not something I've ever really been surrounded by. And I can't think of anything bad I've done…can you?"

He watched as her eyes lowered back towards her paper, jotting something down quickly, avoiding eye contact. Looking back up, she calmly returned his gaze. "It isn't my place to judge you, Tom. What do you think?"

"You want me to confess to murder, don't you?" he said with a shake of his head. He was frustrated; he was frustrated by the same questions over and over leading him back to the same place with her, and he was frustrated with her. He was frustrated with the fact she wouldn't diagnose him yet. If she thought he was crazy then fine, have him committed, locked up, strapped to a chair and shocked in to submission. But if she thought he wasn't, if she truly thought he wasn't crazy, he wasn't a killer then let him go. Let him see his family again. Something more than this same stalemate, round and round of questioning and accusations. Something needed to happen. "You want me to break down, say I do think I'll go to hell because I murdered my best friend. I'm not going to do that though! I didn't murder him, I'd never hurt him. So I don't think I'm going to hell, and if I am, I won't be going because of that, because I didn't do it!"

"The situation-"

"Forget the situation, or how it looks. Voices haven't been whispering to me, I've not been dancing with the devil or whatever you think I've been doing, and I haven't murdered anybody," he said in exasperation. "You said you spoke to Olli, he must have told you this!"

"We did indeed speak to Oliver," she said carefully choosing her words. Always so careful about the damning things she said.

"And, what did he say?" Tom asked, watching her with hope. He vividly remembered looking into Oliver's eyes at one moment and seeing absolute fear. He knew Oliver had seen Alyse, however briefly. He knew she was real. Oliver had to have told them this, it was his only hope and he clung to it desperately.

She took a deep breath. "Tom, Oliver said in his official statement nobody else was in the house, but you three."

"So...what did he see?" Tom asked, heart sinking as fear welled up inside him, his only hope dashed. Not for one second did he believe Oliver had told them the truth. But then, lying on this side of the accused crazy train, he could instantly see why Oliver would have lied about it. It was mad of him to think Oliver would've said anything else.

"The amount of pain he was in meant he found it difficult to focus, but he does remember clearly seeing you fatally attacking Sebastian with your knife," she said, maintaining eye contact with Tom as she spoke.

Tom shook his head violently – he'd started to accept Oliver lying about not seeing Alyse, but he couldn't accept Oliver accusing him of hurting Sebastian. Oliver had to know this lie could surely get him in a lot of trouble. He could've come up with something else, something better. Oliver was the brainy one, the one with the cunning plans and detailed ideas. He was the story teller. He had to have a better lie up his sleeve. "No. no, he's wrong! Talk to him again!" he cried. Tom could feel fear curling itself around him, burying deep in the pit of his stomach, icy tendrils stretching across his entire body. "Ask him again, he's not remembering it right, he saw something else, I know he did!"

"Tom, he didn't," she said with a tone of finality. "He didn't see anything else, because there was nothing else to see. I know it's confusing."

"No, it's not. It's pretty simple, I didn't do it, she did!" he screamed in desperation, pounding his fists against the metal bars surrounding his bed, causing them to clatter noisily. He could feel tears prickling at the corners of his eyes as emotion overcame him. "She did it, I saw her, she was there, she was real, she hurt him and I didn't. I never would. Ask Olli again, he's wrong! She was there!"

Helena pressed a button on her pager as Tom continued to desperately beg her to believe him. His screams increased into hysterical sobs of fear, tears rolling down across his cheeks, as four nurses raced into the room. They held him firmly in place whilst one of the nurse produced a syringe and injected Tom with a clear substance; he knew it to be a tranquilizer of some kind as the anger began to leave him.

"I'll be back tomorrow Tom," Helena said gently, as she gathered her stuff. His eyes began to droop, drifting off into a dreamless sleep as she exited the room.

"Is it that time again?" Tom asked as Helena walked into his room the next day.

"What do you mean?" Helena asked with a slight smile, sitting down in the seat beside his bed.

"I didn't realize it was question time already," he replied sarcastically.

"Tom, our sessions are at this time every other day," she said matter-of-factly. "And no matter how much you hate them and hate seeing me, they will always be at this time, every other day."

"It's not like I have a clock or any way of telling the time," he replied, sarcasm biting its way through his tone of voice; he couldn't be bothered with her today, with any of it, really. Part of him was starting to toy with the idea of simply confessing to murder and pleading insanity – anything to get him out of this room.

"It is a bit plain in here," she said, glancing around at the bare, white walls. "At least you've got a TV."

"Then my life must be complete," he replied dryly, though his scathing sarcasm wasn't as harsh as usual, as though he had given up on communicating.

"You seem a little down today, Tom," Helena noted as she took out her ever present silver pen and notepad. "Anything you want to talk about?"

He contemplated a witty retort in response to what he saw as an incredibly stupid question but couldn't muster enough energy to bother with this. "No," he replied simply after moments of contemplative silence. "I don't want to talk today."

"That's a shame," she sighed gently. "I was hoping you'd like to take the opportunity to talk during this session."

"What's the point in even talking?" he replied with a defeated sigh. "No matter what I say, it's not going to change anything. You're going to believe what you want to believe, you're going to interpret what I say however you want to and nobody is going to bother actually listening to me and what I've got to say."

"I've explained all of this to you so many times, Tom," she said, with a sigh of her own. "Things aren't like that."

"But they are," he cut in, not wanting to listen to another of her speeches. He took a deep breath, knowing once he began his tirade he would not be able to stop. The thoughts had been bubbling away inside of him since the moment his sessions had begun. He couldn't contain them any longer, particularly as she genuinely, wrongly, seemed to believe she was open and willing to help him. "They are exactly like that because, no matter how hard you try to be unbiased or whatever, you're looking at me, you're judging me and you're seeing what you want to. The rest of the world is as well. The doctors and nurses who come in here every single day judge me, see me as a murderer, a bad person. No matter what I say, they're not going to stop looking at me like that. My own mum probably thinks the same thing and god only knows my friends must do as well. I've not done anything wrong, except be in the wrong place at the wrong time.

I didn't ask for any of this and I certainly didn't want my best friend to get hurt. But no matter what I do or say from now on, nothing will change because you will all hold on so tightly to your notions and judgments. I guess it's just human nature. Even if you sign that bit of paper waiting at the end, check all the boxes that say 'sane and innocent' and let me walk out of here without a shred of accusation or anything hanging over me, everyone would still think I'd done it. Don't think your helping me, because you're not. You're doing your job, you're getting paid and you couldn't give a damn what happens to me as long as your pay check is signed. Talk to me all you want, ask me all of your questions and I'll answer, fine. But, please stop pretending you're doing it for me as we all know you're not. Now you're just being patronizing."

The silence which followed Tom's diatribe was heavy and awkward. He turned away from Helena, unable to maintain eye contact after all he had said. He had wanted to say more, wanted to say something that would visibly hurt her, but he found himself unable to do this. She may have upset him but even he wasn't that cruel. Or if he was, his mind was unable to think of something spiteful enough to say to convey the hurt he wanted her to feel. And it was all for no other reason than because he wanted to. He wanted somebody else to feel as bad as he currently felt. None of this was her fault, after all, and he knew all of this. He could already feel the guilt burying itself deep into his gut, slowly starting to consume him. An apology was forming on the tip of his tongue and it took all of his energy just to bite it back. He would not apologise for any of this. It needed to be said. He needed to let it out.

"Are you finished, Tom?" she asked after a few moments of silence. He nodded resolutely. "You're right, people will judge you. And it is human nature to do so. Unfortunately, people will always remember the bad, even if it is all untrue; they think there's no smoke without fire. That's why I'm here and you can choose to believe it or not but I genuinely do want to help."

He shrugged in response, unable to conjure a reply to this, having said everything he needed to already. "Can we get on with the session?"

Nodding her head in agreement, Helena produced another sheet, filled with another set of inane questions Tom resigned himself to answering. Hours seemed to drag by and with every question he answered the feeling of emptiness spread through him. It was as though he had finally resigned himself to this place, to be stuck here. She may be genuinely interested in helping him, but that didn't change the fact that he believed she couldn't help. At least, not in the way he needed her to. Particularly not now, following Olli's statement.

As the questions finally petered out and their session drew to a close, a thought hit Tom. Perhaps it was a long shot, but it was worth a try. "Doc," he said, cautiously, testing the waters.

"Yes, Tom?" she replied, the ever present calming smile lighting up her features once more; it was her 'shrink face' – the expression she automatically reverted back to when working with Tom. It reminded him of his 'customer service face' he'd perfected last summer working in retail. A façade, of course, but a large grin that screamed 'I'm happy to help' at any potential customer. Even If they didn't deserve it.

"I, um, have a request," he said slowly, not quite sure how to word what he wanted to say. She nodded in encouragement. "I know it's a bit of a long shot, but, I was wondering...is there any way I could go to Sebastian's funeral? I know you all think I'm the reason why he's dead, and maybe I shouldn't go, but I want to pay my respects to him. He was my best friend, after all."

Helena stared at Tom, not quite sure how to respond. Of all the things she had expected him to ask, this hadn't even occurred to her. Reeling in shock, she forced her mind to produce a coherent reply.

"I know I shouldn't go," Tom said, before Helena could reply. It was as though his mind was convincing him to keep pressing the issue; the more he asked maybe the more likely she'd be to agree. He had seen her façade slip, and he wanted to avoid the inevitable no. "I know, it's probably a really bad idea, but, please?"

"Tom, what date is it?" she asked, forehead furrowed in contemplation. He could see she was clearly confused about something.

"Why does that matter?" he asked. That was the last thing he had expected her to say. "Can I go though, please?"

"Just, answer me this one question. Humor me. What date is it?" she pressed, a hint of urgency in her voice.

He nodded slowly, in agreement. "Um, well there aren't any calendars in here either," he said slowly. "So I don't know exactly, but it's definitely end of November. Actually, I think it's mid-December, somewhere around there. Yeah, because we went into Rose House three weeks after Halloween, and I've been here, about two or three weeks I'd say, so that would make sense."

His voice dropped towards the end of the sentence, finding it hard to continue having noticed the puzzled expression upon her face. She seemed to stare right through him, eyes gazing intently, piercing into his mind and reading the multitude of thoughts swarming throughout. As she watched him, her hand began to race furiously across the page, writing down a thousand incriminating things without her needing to glance at the page. Shifting uncomfortably under her gaze, he dropped his eyes to the floor, unable to maintain eye contact. He picked at the skin around his thumb, jagged nails tearing at the skin, causing flecks of blood to dot the surface.

Finally, the hairs on the back of his neck relaxed as her gaze shifted away from him. Looking up, he found her staring down at her notes, contemplating.

She sighed, took a deep breath and looked back up at Tom. The look in her eyes let him know she had something difficult to tell him, he could feel the sympathy radiating off her in waves. He groaned inwardly and rolled his eyes; why she couldn't just say no, he'd never understand. Put him out of his misery and just let him get on with his day. Not that he had much more to do than watch mindless soaps and quiz shows on TV – the number of channels he received had been severely restricted.

"Unfortunately, Tom, you won't be able to go to Sebastian's funeral," she began slowly.

Tom sighed, shoulders slumping slightly. Though he had known she was going to say no, it seemed a small part of him had been hoping for a positive answer. "You don't think it's a good idea, then?"

"It's not that," she continued, carefully choosing her words. "This is going to be hard for you to adjust to, Tom but

I must ask you to listen to me very carefully, and though it will be difficult, you need to trust me."

"There's nothing I can do about it, if you say no," Tom said with a shrug, trying to hide his disappointment.

"Tom, there's a reason why you can't go to Sebastian's funeral, and it's not because I don't think it's a good idea," she said. She paused for a moment, gathering her thoughts. Tom waited for the psychobabble that would follow; reasons why it wouldn't be beneficial to himself, the healing process, rules, regulations and such. It didn't matter as the answer was a solid no. "It's because, well…the funeral's already happened."

"But wouldn't there have been an autopsy, because you guys think I murdered him?" he asked, trying hard to force the image of Sebastian on the autopsy table, being sliced open, dissected and probed, as far away from his mind as possible. "That happened quickly."

"Yes, there indeed would have been an autopsy as there were grounds to believe it was a homicide," she continued. "Like I said, this will be difficult for you, but you need to trust me. Sebastian's funeral happened just over five months ago, that's why you physically cannot go."

Tom stared at Helena in amusement, not quite sure what game she was playing or what she hoped to achieve from this activity of hers. He raised an eyebrow in disbelief, and shook his head. Helena mistook this as confusion and took a breath, preparing herself for the oncoming torrent of abusive, confused and possibly fearful comments Tom would undoubtedly produce. It surprised her to hear a snort of laugher coming from the boy, a grin spreading across his features.

"You expect me to believe that I've been here five months?" he said, shoulders shaking gently with laughter. "I've only been here two weeks or so. I may not know as much as you, but I know how long I've been in this bed. Is this some kind of strange exercise we're doing to 'help' me?"

"Tom, this isn't an exercise," she said gently. "You really have been here for five months, almost six, actually."

"But, that's impossible," he said, eyebrows furrowing in confusion. "I couldn't have been here that long. There's just no way."

"It is, Tom," she said gently, though more forcefully than before. "You have been here for almost five months. And you have been making fantastic progress. I'm not sure why you don't realize just how long you've been here."

"So you're telling me I've somehow lost five months?" he asked, still unable to quite understand what he was being told. "It's May? And my family hasn't even been in to see me once? I've been alone in here for five months. That's pretty shitty, don't you think?"

"There's more to it, Tom," Helena said, voice hitching as she spoke. She coughed, attempting to cover the nerves bubbling forth. She couldn't understand just how this factor had been missed or why Tom was so confused about the date. Aside from the hallucination, there had been no other strange or abnormal occurrences, no other afflictions. All of her preliminary tests had confirmed this. But now, there was a new complication; how and why had time stopped for him? When he had first arrived, one of the things she was required to establish was whether he knew when and where he was. And he had. He knew the date, the year, who he was, where he was. He knew the basics. It had all been clear. Whether this had been a simple fluke or, at the time of questioning, a moment of lucidity in an otherwise confused and turbulent mind was a complete mystery. A mystery she needed to desperately solve. It may be the key to Tom's current mental state and could affect the entire case.

"Oh really? I can't wait to hear the next absurd thing you're about to tell me!" he replied sarcastically.

Knowing his sarcasm was a way to hide the fear and confusion he felt, Helena ignored his response. She could feel her entire profile and the months of hard work unraveling in front of her, and all because of what seemed like a simple oversight. One date, and everything was destroyed. "Tom, it's not May, either. It's the end of October, October 22nd, to be exact."

He looked at her, complete silence echoing through his mind. "But that's impossible," he said carefully, after a few moments. "That means we've gone back in time. I didn't go into Rose House until Halloween. Never would've thought a stupid dare would lead to all of this!" he muttered angrily, glaring at nothing. "First I've lost five months and now we've travelled back in time? It's starting to feel like The Twilight Zone in here."

Helena smiled, though the movement did not reach her eyes. "Of course you haven't time travelled, Tom," she said sadly. "I'm going to give you a breakdown of what I have come to understand happened to you over the past year, from what both you and your friends have told me. I know this is going to be very hard to accept. You may feel it absurd or untrue, but please believe me, I only tell you this because it is the truth. Because I think I might be able to help you even more, now that I know this and I think, knowing this will help you too. You went into Rose House for the first time almost a year ago, on Halloween 2010. Around mid December of that year, your friends noticed you were receiving bright red roses. Here and there, one would appear, in your locker, on your lunch tray and so on.

After break, you told them how you believed somebody was stalking you, a girl who had been in Rose House. You mentioned that she believed herself to be a creature from an old myth you had researched. Though skeptical, your friends listened to you, informed you to go to the police as they feared she might be dangerous. You refused."

Helena paused, studying Tom's expression intently. Though looking at her, it was clear he did not see her; he seemed to be staring at the wall behind her, at nothing. She could tell he was listening though, the confused expression and slight movements of his hands curling around the metal bars and releasing after a few seconds a clear indication of his distress.

She took a deep breath and continued. "There were a few incidents where you suffered panic attacks and mood swings which you attributed to this stalker, though your friends never happened to see her. In April, around the 17th, Oliver believes, you told both of them how you though she was actually this person in the myth, this creature. You told them, in detail, how she had transformed in front of you. You then proceeded to convince them to enter the house with you. On the 19th all three of you went into the House. You then woke up here, five days later, on the 24th."

"And I've been here ever since," he added, voice quiet. Helena nodded in agreement, letting silence fall once more as he contemplated the situation. A thousand thoughts should have been bombarding him at once, and yet...his mind was silent. There were too many thoughts to grasp at once. "How am I supposed to believe you, when I don't even know the exact date?" he spat out. There were too many emotions for him to feel, so he listened to the one that was the easiest to deal with; anger. "You could be telling me anything."

"But why would I do that? What would I benefit from doing that to you?"

"I don't know," he bit back. "I don't know why you'd do it, but it can't be true. It's impossible. Time doesn't move like that. You don't just lose months and days. It doesn't just disappear. It has to be...I have to...somewhere-"

"I don't have any answers as to why this has happened, yet," she said gently. "But it has; and I will find the answer for you. I will help you as best I can, and I will continue helping you."

"I still don't believe you," he said stubbornly, though his voice waivered, as though unsure of what to think. She could see the desperation building in his eyes as he clung to some form of logic, needing her to be lying. To be making it all up.

This was his last ditch attempt to hold on to his own perceived truth and if she was right about this, then what else was she right about?

Tom watched as Helena pulled a sleek, black mobile phone from her pocket and held it in front of him. Pressing a button, the screen was illuminated, instantly flooding with colour as a picture of a vibrant sunset replaced the empty screen. In big, bold numbers across the top half of the screen was a digital clock, reading 15:29. Beneath that, in a calligraphic script was the date, reading October 15th 2011.

He turned away from her, from the phone clearly showing the date to him. He wanted to argue, accuse her of doctoring the date on her phone as part of this elaborate plan to confuse him for whatever reason. He knew there was no point. No matter what he said, he had no reason not to believe her. As she had said, what would be the point of doing this to him if it wasn't true?

Closing his eyes, Tom willed away the tears. Up until this point he had been able to convince himself that Alyse had to be real as did everything that had happened. There was no reason to believe otherwise - he was acutely aware of the rest of the world and nothing else had changed. He hadn't heard voices, seen apparitions, felt strange things. He'd been sane. He'd been here. It had all been real. At least, he had thought it was.

He could no longer believe this. Nothing made sense. Time had completely run away from him. Three weeks had somehow become an entire year and he could barely remember any of it. If time could so easily be lost, what else could have been lost? Thoughts? Memories? Actions? Maybe he had...

He shoulders slumped and he looked straight at Helena. He could feel everything he'd clung to, everything he'd so strongly believed, slip away from him. "Fine, I guess I'm crazy, and I guess I killed him. I killed my best friend, and I didn't even realize I did it. I'm crazy." He paused, taking a deep breath, emotionally drained and unable to feel anything anymore. Confusion and fear clawed at the back of his mind but he was too exhausted to acknowledge them. Too desolate to feel anything. All he could do was give up. Give in. They'd won. "Please fix me."

Chapter Twenty Three

Tom liked the pills. There were so many of them to take, so many pretty colours doing so many wonderful things to him. He never wanted them to stop

The blue ones made the world seem sharper; come into clearer focus. They helped him note the passing of every single day, slow and torturous; the sands of time oozing languidly down through the hourglass of life. They made him realize just how obvious his time lapse was – the erratic ringing of bells and strange flickering of light he could remember from his first few months, or days, or however he remember it now became an obvious routine of lights out at 10pm and the tolling of lunch bells at 1.

The red ones calmed him down. They kept the feelings of anxiety and fear firmly away, allowing his mind to wander free from these emotions. From any emotion. He couldn't remember what it felt like to feel anything anymore. His heart, his mind, his emotional existence was firmly locked behind an iron door, held in place by his army of little red pills. They were his militia, his battalion. They would fight back the demon emotion.

The white ones were his favourite. They made him forget. He would be given them in the early hours of the evening before drifting off into a quiet, dreamless state, where nightmares would not be able to haunt him. During the day he could easily suppress the memories, but at night his unconscious self, the evil thing that it was, would push those thoughts forward into his dreams. He knew, without a doubt, without the white ones he would go mad. Madder than he already was, of course.

Combined, they kept him in a comfortable, dream-like state of nothing, unable to feel or notice anything. In the real world, but not quite. It made things easier. Combined, they curled around him, protected him. They became him, and he became the pills. He couldn't exist without them. He couldn't find peace without them. Without the pills, he would be nothing but madness and pain. Without the pills, he would not exist.

Tom fell into a routine of ease as the days began to pass. The revelation had shocked him into submission, destroyed everything he thought he had known and forced him to consider everything Helena had told him to be true. From then, he had cooperated, allowed her to make him believe Alyse was a figment of his imagination. She was a part of him, the darker side, a way for him to present the dark thoughts swirling around in his mind without any direct consequence upon himself. He was a living case of Jekyll and Hyde; only, not contained within the fantasy realm of books. Unlike the story, there was no neat, simple ending, and there were plenty of consequences.

Naturally, a court case was held though it had to be postponed on a number of occasions due to Tom's lack of lucidity – during the time he was still convinced Alyse was real. They called these 'episodes' and their entire trial, their plea of insanity was only helped by these 'episodes'. How exactly could somebody be accountable for murder if they honestly believed there was some kind of hellish beast at hand, working her evil will on others? How could anyone be accountable for their actions, if they didn't even know what day or month it was?

Then, of course, with his acceptance of the truth, and admitting the only logical explanation as to what had happened, the case could proceed. Tom's confusion on the passing of time, along with various testimonies and the considerable evidence stacked against him had a verdict of 'guilty' returned by the jury. Fortunately, or not, Tom sometimes wondered, due to his 'episodes' and various hallucinations, instead of being sent to a high security correctional facility, he was sent to a 'special place' for the criminally insane. Or, as they liked to call it, a Psychiatric Secure Unit; legal terms, of course. The term 'insane' could apparently be considered as offensive; because naturally being seen as a prisoner was the highest standing in society, and 'insane' only tarnished this good reputation. He felt insane was a more fitting word, though - talking to nobody, reveling in their crimes, obsessed with blood, sex and death, no remorse felt by some, no memory or recollection for others. Yeah, they were insane.

Tom never thought he'd miss the hospital he had been kept prisoner in before, yet he longed for the days of never ending solitude, of a decent TV and the chance to at least be partially convinced he was normal. Though, unsurprisingly, he soon found out that had been another 'special' hospital for the psychotic. Perhaps prison would have been better for him. Or perhaps he really was as insane as every other person in here.

Chapter Twenty Four

He sat across from Helena once more, tentatively resting an elbow on the frigid metal surface of the table between them. He wrote today's date out, in full, in a small notebook that had been placed before him. Though pens and sharp pencils were forbidden he was allowed the use of a soft, almost mushy crayon. Procedures you see, no sharp objects and all of that, lest he suddenly decide his dire predicament was too much and shoved it point first as hard as he could into his eye. And boy was that something he'd considered more than once. Like right now.

Whether it was the place itself or his actual insanity suggesting this, he couldn't determine. Though, it probably was because he was insane. This was all because he was insane. Mustn't forget that, this isn't a holiday camp, you're just a crazy little flower. He chuckled to himself.

The pages of the notebook were filled with dates, one on each line, marking down the passage of time. It had been an idea of Helena's, to combat the paranoia he had begun to feel at the thought of losing days again. It was a natural fear, she'd reasoned, with pity in her eyes – a look he was starting to hate more than this hospital. Only natural, she'd said. After all, it was a scary thing, losing so much time. It wasn't like gaps in his memory forming after a few too many alcopops they'd convinced Sebastian's brother to buy them when he was fourteen and they'd all been happy, and normal. And alive. No, it was much worse.

The notebook was good. This way, he could keep track of every single day as it passed. Though he did not meet with Helena every day, the nurses would still bring the book to him, once a day, in order to keep up this routine. Once a day. He didn't know the time. Just that the sun was always up, always shining through the shatter resistant windows – nobody was getting out of here through those.

"Never forget," he murmured as he pressed the purple tip onto the paper, causing pieces of crayon to flake off.

"Can't forget."

The waxy crayon slipped through his fingers and he closed the book, sliding it across the table towards Helena. "How are you doing today, Tom?"

"Fine," he replied sullenly, glancing out of the high window and avoiding eye contact.

"Anything you want to tell me about?" she pressed with a gentle smile.

"Nope," he replied just as sullenly, arms folded across his chest, finishing this perfect image of teenage defiance and boredom. "Same old story, different day. Still crazy, still stuck in here, can't remember anything though I know I did it all. Don't really want to remember."

"Do you wish you could get out of here?" she asked.

"I'd be lying if I said I didn't," he replied seriously, looking her straight in the eye for the first time this session. He couldn't help it; she irritated him to no end. "But that's never going to happen and if it does, I'll only be going to prison; from captivity to captivity."

"How do you feel about that, Tom?" she asked.

"I don't feel anything," he replied simply. "It doesn't matter what I feel, because nothing will change. This is it now." An awkward silence fell quickly between the two. Despite the countless months they'd spent together, a rapport had not formed and Tom still resented Helena deeply. He knew he always would; loathing had coiled itself firmly within his heart, directed towards her, spitting and hissing like a poisonous snake. And though none of this was her fault - if anything she was a key figure in caring for Tom's wellbeing, he knew he would blame her endlessly for this. She was the one who had brought the entire world crashing down around him. She was the one who had destroyed all hope of ever leaving here, of ever being normal again.

He'd never know she was the one who'd also greatly reduced his sentence and helped keep him away from maximum security and isolation. But she knew what she had done for Tom. And that was enough for her.

"Is it time for my medication now?"

Chapter Twenty Five

Miles away, on a familiar, grassy plane, underneath an old tree, Oliver sat, back resting against the trunk. Weak sunlight filtered down through the leaves, dappling upon the ground. It was a sign that spring was truly here with summer fast on its heels and yet Oliver still felt cold. He'd been cold since the moment he was carried out of Rose House, delirious and in pain.

Sitting alone underneath the tree he watched as fellow classmates filled the grounds, writing in books, swapping gifts and promises to stay in touch, smiling, laughing genuinely happy. End of year was literally days away and there was little left for the graduating class to do other than enjoy the last few weeks of adolescence before entering the real world of University, work and the mundane banality of day to day life. They hugged and cried and clung on to one another, not wanting to say goodbye. The shadows of final exams loomed ahead, of demon A Levels, of standardized testing – a two hour snapshot into two years worth of learning that would tell very little of what they knew, of who they were, and yet they were forced to sit through if they wanted any semblance of a good future, so they'd been told. But now, in the heat of spring, with good friends and tearful goodbyes, most could temporarily forget the demons lurking ahead.

Despite all of this, Oliver felt neither happy nor anxious for this to come. If anything, he desperately wanted to turn back time, go back to before anything had happened, before he'd even moved to this school. When things were simple.

A shadow momentarily fell across him, as somebody sat down heavily beside him, briefly blocking out the sunlight.

He didn't need to look to know that it was Mariana. Nobody would come near him anymore, not since…

They sat in silence, neither knowing what to say to the other. Since what had happened with Sebastian and Tom, neither had spoken. It had been almost a year of no communication, not knowing what to say or how to be friends, how to be normal. Perhaps there was no way to be normal. Their lives, touched by madness and murder, could never again exist without the memory of these. After all, how easily can you forget watching somebody you love descend into insanity, or die before your eyes? They couldn't exist once the delicate balance of their lives had been so completely shattered, and so they had simply stopped existing. Drifted. Moved away from each other, and everyone else.

"I heard you're leaving," Mariana finally murmured, tugging at blades of grass nervously.

"Yeah."

"When are you going?" Mariana asked, not wanting to let the silence return. She had things to say, things she needed him to hear. She couldn't let what was possibly the last time she'd ever speak to him pass by without saying what she needed to.

"Tomorrow night," he said.

"But, what about-"

"I'll be back for our exams," he cut in, not wanting to hear the question, knowing she was forcing some form of care or interest. "But I'm not staying any longer than I have to."

"Where are you going?" she pressed.

"Brighton. I've got a conditional offer at a good University and it's a good town, great night life. Lots of boys." He tried to smile at her, attempted some form of humor, some kind of jest, but his once illuminating smile was barely a flickering candle and it didn't reach his eyes.

Mariana sighed heavily. "You weren't even going to say goodbye, were you?"

Oliver turned and looked at her for the first time in what seemed like years. He instantly noticed how much older she looked, as though she'd aged ten years in the time that had passed. Her eyes held a maturity to them he had never seen before and her skin, so rosy in the past was sallow, drained of colour. He desperately wanted to hug her, make her feel better and promise her everything would be fine, everything was going to be perfect, they'd be best friends again, she'd go down and visit him and they'd dance and they'd drink and they'd find people to fall in love with and forget everything that had happened in the darkness of Aysforth. They'd be happy and free and they'd just forget.

But he knew he couldn't do it, because it would be a lie. The lives they'd once led, full of promise and hope and future and freedom, were tainted now. All they could hope to do was move forward, move away, and perhaps bring back as much normality as possible.

"We haven't spoken, Mariana. Not since what happened. I didn't think it would be appropriate."

"We were friends once," she said quietly, pulling at the grass more forcefully. "I still would've liked to know."

"Now you do," he replied simply. The awful, awkward silence fell once more, leaving both squirming uncomfortably. There was no emotion between them. No feelings of friendship or care. There was simply a blank expanse of nothingness.

"You know, I miss them too," Mariana said tentatively, after what seemed like an endless amount of silence. Thinking about what she had lost, Sebastian…Tom…she couldn't cry anymore. The past year had been spent so lost in tears over everything, that she honestly believed she'd never be able to cry again. Never be able to feel anything, ever again, except the loss of her best friends. Her everything. Her Tom.

"Please, Mariana, I don't want to talk about it," he sighed in frustration, glaring at the building in front of him, not wanting to take out his anger on her. "I've talked enough about what happened, or didn't happen. I just want to forget it."

"But you can't forget it," she replied. "We can't forget it, because nobody here has forgotten it."

"Why do you think I'm leaving?" he retorted sarcastically.

"Yes, but I'm not, I'm stuck here," she replied, anger causing her voice to hitch. "You can run away from everything that happened, but I can't. Sebastian's dead, Tom's crazy and you're running away. You all turned out to be fantastic friends."

"Maybe you should blame the one who turned crazy, and not me, ah?" he replied angrily biting back at her accusation. In that moment he hated her. She hadn't been in that house, she hadn't seen what happened. Tom had wanted to protect her, to keep her away from everything. She could go on thinking they'd all left her but right up until the end Tom had loved her, had protected her. They all had. And here she was accusing him of something he had no control over. How could she blame him for wanting to run away? How could she not want to escape?

"I don't think he's crazy," she said so quiet it was barely audible.

"Yes, because a sane person does exactly what Tom did," Oliver said sarcastically, shaking his head in disbelief. "We all know why you refuse to believe he truly did lose his mind. The boy you loved, Mariana, doesn't exist anymore. I don't know what happened, or why it did, but he's not in there. He's long gone now."

A blush spread quickly across Mariana's cheeks. It was more than just the fact he knew how she felt for Tom; everybody knew, really, had always known, except for her, and Tom. They'd not realized until it was too late, far too late. Until nothing could ever happen. No, it wasn't anything to do with that. It was that Oliver believed she was grasping at straws, not seeing the truth, or what he believed to be true.

Mariana remained silent, knowing he would ridicule her for the thought she was entertaining. Not that it mattered, he was leaving tomorrow. He would never be a part of her life again. Her heart sank at this thought. He hadn't been part of her life for the past year, but he'd been there, a familiar blanket of warmth and now he'd be gone. Unless…

"But what if he didn't do it?" she whispered.

Oliver turned to her in disbelief, eyes widening comically in shock, trying to gather the words to reply. "What are you on about?"

"What if he didn't do it?" she repeated, biting her lip nervously, unsure of how he would react.

"Then who did, magic fairies?" he replied. "I saw him do it, Mari. I saw him kill Seb. Maybe he wasn't sane when he did it, but I still saw him do it."

She glared at Oliver. "That's a lie, I know it is."

Oliver blinked rapidly, eyebrows furrowing in confusion. "What?"

"I said, that's a lie," she repeated, voice gaining strength. "When you were in the hospital, you were talking. You said you saw something in the house, someone else. You saw her eyes. Red eyes."

"You mean to tell me you're going to believe the mad ramblings of somebody on enough pain medication to knock out a small elephant?" Oliver replied, raising an eyebrow skeptically, though she could see a flicker of something hiding in obsidian eyes. "Yes, because that is completely reliable evidence. You've got a case on your hands there, call Scotland Yard."

"I know you saw something, Olli, just like I know I felt something that day outside Tom's house," she continued, ignoring his sarcasm though the scathing retort hung on her tongue. "I know there is something else out there, just like I'm sure you do. You may be running away to escape the people here, but I know a part of you is also running away, just in case."

"In case what?" Oliver retorted, turning away from her. "I go crazy too?"

"Oliver, now you're just being deliberately spiteful," Mariana said testily. "You know as well as I do what you saw. And I also know how you're feeling about it. You can ignore it and run away from it for as long as you want. But I can't actually handle Tom locked up in there, being accused of Sebastian's death when he didn't do it. I hope you're ok with that at least. If you're not then no matter where you run to it will always haunt you."

She glared at Oliver once before getting to her knees, attempting to stand up.

"Wait," he finally sighed in exasperation. She sat back down almost triumphantly, looking up at him in expectation. She could feel the fire of something indescribable starting to burn inside of her – it was brief, flickering, but it was there. "Fine. If you want to know, yes, I saw something. I don't know what it was, I only saw it in the window. Probably a reflection or trick of the light or…something. And I was in so much pain I could barely understand what was going on. So it doesn't matter anyway. But…there was something."

"I knew it," Mariana said. The fire inside was burning brighter now. Building in heat and propelling her forward. Before she'd been clinging to her own beliefs, but now…now she had something else to support her.

Oliver sighed. There were so many things he wanted to say to her, but the words would not come to him. So he said whatever he could to push the situation away. "Mari, whatever it was, it was nothing. Tom still did what he did and Seb's still dead. Yes, there might be something weird, but it doesn't change the situation. Nothing can. Nothing will bring them back so we just need to move on."

"But it has to change it, somehow," she said. "We both know something else is there, it has to mean something." At that moment a bell sounded out across the green and pupils began heading towards the iron gates. Oliver stood up laboriously and flung his bag on his shoulder.

"I have to go now, I've got a few things I still need to pack," he said, helping Mariana up as he did. "I probably won't see you again."

"One day you will," she said with a weak smile, though both knew this would never happen.

"Please, Mari, be careful and don't do anything stupid," he whispered. "Whatever we saw doesn't matter. You need to let it go. Let them both go and move on. I love you Mari, you're like a sister, but I can't watch another person get destroyed by this. Don't be stupid."

"Olli, I," she stopped, unable to think of a response. She nodded and they awkwardly embraced, a final goodbye, before Oliver turned and walked away.

He may have been running away, but Mariana would not, especially now that she knew she wasn't the only one to doubt what had happened. She watched him leave and she felt desperation rise within her. She was now truly alone in all of this, having lost her three closest friends to madness, murder and fear. Having lost it all in so short a time. And her Tom…her sweet, sarcastic, loveable Tom…he wasn't insane. She'd felt, in that one moment, that something else was there, and if only he had trusted her that final day, spoken to her as she waited for him, maybe she could've changed everything. Maybe she could've helped him. Guilt weighed heavy upon her and she stifled a sob – it seemed she still could cry. She bit back the tears and closed her eyes as her mind drifted back to Tom, and the last moment they had shared beneath this tree.

The fire continued to burn as tears gently dripped down her cheeks. She stood at the precipice of something monumental. She would get Tom back, if she had to descend into the deepest levels of madness herself. She would find him again.

Chapter Twenty Six

He wasn't quite sure when he became acutely aware of the fact he was being watched. It wasn't as though the feeling had suddenly hit him. In fact, it had been building gradually for a number of weeks, yet now he finally became aware of it. The hairs on the back of his neck rose as he felt eyes trained upon him and a delicate shiver ran down his spine, as though ghostly fingers were dancing across his skin.

They were always being watched in this place – never a moment alone, away from the prying, hawk like eyes of the nurses swarming about, controlling and stifling the patients. Never a moment of solitude. Constantly being scrutinized. Eyes, always on him, on them. Eyes desperate for something to watch, something to catch, something to see. He knew they were waiting for one of them to snap, for the pressure to get too much, leading to a catastrophic melt down. They craved it, desired somebody's insane emotions to come bubbling forth, bursting out of them like an explosion. Maybe they'd take out a few of the other patients too and there would be a blood bath. A messy finale to a boring day.

This, however, was different. He was being watched, but not by the vultures, skulking along the outskirts of the room, waiting. And it wasn't a patient whose eyes were trained upon him – having been here long enough he could sense the stares of the insane and there had been many since his arrival. Fresh meat and they could smell it, they still could. He was an outsider, not one of them, and yet still locked in here. Neither criminal nor insane, he didn't belong, and they could sense it. They knew it. He wasn't like them.

The gaze trained upon him was neither patient nor nurse, nor anybody he could see. He felt sure whoever it was could see right through him, read his mind.

He looked around, eyes carefully searching every corner of the room, finding nobody watching him, nobody crouching in the shadows, nobody even remotely interested in him in any way. There was nobody there. It was in his head. And this was always the truth. It was in his head.

Tom stood up and headed across the room to the bathrooms, where an orderly stood guarding the door. Though he may not have been considered dangerous, as none of the patients were, there were of course a number of security measures in place to ensure they didn't become dangerous. Avoiding eye contact, he slipped inside the bathroom and pulled the door shut behind him. There were no mirrors, the reflective glass obviously too much of a hazard to those desperately seeking to end their own lives...or the lives of others. In fact, very few mirrors existed within the complex. If it wasn't for the need to shave on a regular basis, Tom felt certain he would never have seen his reflection.

As he entered the stall directly in front of him, something flashed in the corner of his periphery vision. Turning to the side, he saw nothing. Assuming it was a trick of the light or his mind playing tricks on him, he shrugged it off and carried on. Once done he headed towards the sink to wash his hands. He turned the cold water tap on, but nothing came out. Sighing in frustration he turned it further, till it should have been fully open with water gushing out into the porcelain basin. Still nothing. The same happened with the hot water.

It was then that a strange creaking sound filled the room, quietly at first but rapidly building in volume until it became a deafening drone. He covered his ears with his hands, wincing at the volume of the noise as it reverberated through the room, causing the ground to shake. As quickly as it had started, it vanished and the lack of noise within the room felt like an insurmountable amount of pressure weighing down on him. The silence didn't last for long as water began to gurgle out of the taps in front of him. He bent over to wash his hands but recoiled instantly in disgust. The water flowing from the taps was not crystal clear as he had been expecting it to be. Instead, it was a crimson colour, staining the sides of the porcelain sink a faded pink. The smell of iron and copper hit him and he wrinkled his nose in disgust. Fighting to turn the taps off, he desperately wanted to rid the room of that smell.

He managed to turn the cold water tap off; however the hot water tap would not turn. He shoved his entire body weight into attempting to turn said tap but it still wouldn't move. He leaped back with a gasp and a string of profanities as the metal scalded his hand; the tap seemed to have become red hot in a matter of moments and as he watched, the red water began to bubble and froth, steam rising up from it. The smell of copper increased in magnitude, overpowering his senses. He felt sick and slightly dizzy as the smell took over and he raced back into the stall, emptying the contents of his stomach.

There was a hammering on the door, the orderly demanding he come out. He flung the stall door back open, ready to demand the orderly do something about what had to be a faulty tap, only to find both taps off, the sink pristinely white once more, and the smell having completely vanished.

The orderly shoved Tom out of the bathroom and back into the common area as his mind still raced regarding what had happened. He knew he wasn't hallucinating; it had been real if the burn on his hand was anything to go by. Maybe he needed stronger medication. It wasn't anything else. There couldn't have been anything else. Everything was fine. Everything was normal.

Chapter Twenty Seven

"Ok Tom, tell me again what happened," Helena probed calmly.

"I've already told you twice," Tom sighed. "The story isn't going to change.

"I know you've already told me, but you've told me what you believe happened. Give me just the facts; start from the beginning and don't interpret what happened."

Tom rolled his eyes and slumped back into his chair. "Fine. I went into the bathroom. I went to wash my hands. The tap wouldn't turn."

"But I thought they did turn?" Helena interrupted.

"Right, yes, they did turn. Both turned, but no water came out. Then there was a really loud noise."

"What was this noise?"

"I don't know," he conceded with a shrug. "I think-"

"No, we'll do the thinking after," she said. "Just hard facts for now."

Tom glared at her, not appreciating the interruptions. He hated it when she interrupted him. "Fine," he said through gritted teeth. "There was a loud noise. Then, the noise stopped and the taps started running, but the water was red. I turned the cold tap off but the hot tap wouldn't turn. It became really hot and the red water was boiling. It smelt really bad. I threw up then when I came back out it had all stopped."

"How did it stop, did you turn it off?" Helena asked.

"No, I was too busy being sick to turn it off," he replied sarcastically.

"Then, how did it turn off?" she pressed. "Taps can't turn themselves off. Was somebody else in the bathroom?"

"No, I was alone. You know it's one person at a time unless someone accompanies you in," he said matter-of-

238

factly.

"And nobody accompanied you?" she asked. "Nobody could have come in without you noticing?"

"No, nobody could've come in without me noticing, and nobody was in there with me. I was completely alone, and if you don't believe me, you can ask the guy who was standing guard outside," Tom said through gritted teeth; sometimes her questions were beyond pointless. "That's a point, he came in. Maybe he turned them off?"

"So then what did happen?" she said.

"I. Don't. Know," he replied, frustration bubbling.

"I'm just trying to help you piece together the event in a logical manner," she said gently. "I know it's a bit confusing, but there is a logical explanation."

"Would you like to give it to me, then?" he asked with a sigh. "Just tell me what happened and we can get on with our lives."

"Do you think it was a hallucination?" Helena asked, ignoring his request.

"No," he replied firmly. "I know it was real."

"All of it?" she pressed.

He stared at her. "Well, from the incredibly tender burn running across my palm, yes, I'm sure it was all real."

"What could've made the water run red?" Helena asked.

"I don't know. Rusty pipes? Bad connections? Something like that; but I'm not a plumber so I couldn't diagnose the piping for you," he said with a shrug.

"Ok, so there is a logical explanation for the discoloration," she said, her voice lilting slightly. "What about the smell? What did it smell like?"

"It was horrible, and really strong," he said, wrinkling his nose as he remembered the smell. "I don't know, it's a bit hard to describe. It smelt like something was rotting, but there was like, a chemical smell to it. Like when a rusty penny or something."

"Like copper?" Helena asked, watching him intently. "Or...blood?"

"I guess you could say it smelled like that," he said with a shrug. "It was really sickly."

"What do you think caused it?" she asked, eyes still trained upon him in an unnerving manner.

"Again... I don't know. You said copper so, rusty pipes?" he replied with a shrug.

She nodded intently, jotting down a few notes quickly. "How do you feel about the entire experience?" she asked after a few moments. "Is there any part of you that doubts the explanation you've suggested?"

"No," he replied quickly, shaking his head. "There was nothing else to it."

"Do you believe that, a hundred percent?" she pressed. "Be honest with me Tom."

He sighed in exasperation. "Fine, maybe some part of me thinks it was a little bit too weird for such a simple explanation. But considering everything I've seen before, or thought I'd seen, or whatever, you can't blame me for that shadow of doubt."

"So, that doubt is still there," she said with a nod. "Is it as strong as it once was?"

"No," he replied. "And I can say that with complete honesty. For a moment, I did think maybe it was something else. But I know it's not the real reason. I know what is real, or at least what I think is real, but it's more likely to be real than – well, you know what I mean."

"I do," she said with a smile. "You're making a lot of progress Tom. You've attributed a logical explanation to a strange occurrence and you believe that explanation. Sometimes things do happen that we can't explain at the time, but there is an explanation."

Tom nodded, not quite sure what to respond with, or if she was even expecting a response. He'd been seeing her for so long he often knew when to reply, and what answer she was looking for. It was rare he found himself needing to lie to Helena, but he knew sometimes the truth would be more hassle than it was worth, so stretching it just a little bit was worth it. It was necessary. And it wasn't as though he was lying; it was still the truth, just perhaps not the whole truth, or a stretched variation.

He wasn't lying, not now at least. He did believe there was a logical explanation, and he was willing to accept it as fact. But, there was still a big part of him that doubted it, even if that part was completely wrong.

"Ok, so you'll be on slightly different medication for the next week, just some pain medication for your hand. You might feel a bit drowsy at first, but it's temporary," she said with a smile.

Tom stood up to leave the consultation room. An orderly lingered just outside the room ready to accompany Tom back to his own. At the door he turned back to look at her. "Did you ever find out what was wrong with the water?" he asked nonchalantly.

"Not yet," she conceded. "They're still looking into it. It hasn't happened since so they're wondering if there was a buildup of debris or something in the pipes and you were unlucky enough to have to put up with it."

Tom nodded, accepting her explanation and leaving the room. The fact that they couldn't find a concrete explanation had slightly unnerved him. The part of his mind still focused upon the idea of Something Else accepted this explanation as a reason to panic.

Chapter Twenty Eight

"How's your hand?" the orderly asked as she and Tom walked back to his room.

"Oh, it's ok, stinging a bit I guess," he said, glancing down at his right palm, covered in gauze strips. The skin throbbed angrily underneath and he could almost see the blistering, red skin of his palm as it slowly healed itself.

The orderly nodded. "Someone's going to come and give you something for the pain in about an hour or so, just before dinner. Can you bare it until then?"

"Yeah, it's fine," Tom said with a slight smile. Though all the staff within the complex were professional and conducted themselves in an appropriate manner, many still treated the patients as animals in a lab. Whether it was their mental state, or their criminal past, Tom could never decipher, but it affected their view regardless. All they'd ever see him as was a murderer, a monster. But there were those, however, who still treated them as individuals, as human beings, particularly patients lucid enough to appreciate that kind of attitude. It made a nice change from the scrutiny he normally received.

She opened the door for him and allowed him to walk inside first. She followed him in and glanced around the room briefly; a quick check to make sure everything was in order. Just in case.

"So, yeah, about an hour or so somebody will come and get you for dinner, give you some pain relief and that. It will probably be me but I'm not sure. We're having scheduling issues today," she smiled at him before starting to back out of the room; that was how they all left the patients, never turning their back on them. Staff never turned their back on patients. It must have been something they were taught – don't turn your back on the crazies or they might get you. Maybe it made sense; he could understand why someone might take the opportunity, should it arise. There were certainly times when he wanted to attack one of the members of staff. Not that he would ever admit it to anyone of course, most sane people didn't freely admit to wanting to kill someone. Though he was sure they'd all felt it at one point. The human race could be rather irritating at times.

"I like your drawings, by the way," she said with a smile as she slipped through the doorway. "You're a pretty good artist."

"Thanks," Tom said, with a slight smile. He had been provided with paper and soft crayons – for pens and pencils of any form were too dangerous for the patients to be trusted with – upon his arrival and these had often kept him thoroughly entertained for hours. Though the place was not particularly inspiring, he always found something too sketch, albeit roughly, due to the useless nature of these horrid crayons. Many of his drawings focused on the people he missed most. People he hadn't been able to see in a very long time. His family, his best friends…and beautiful emerald eyes. He missed her the most, though he knew she probably despised him now. Nobody cared about the criminally insane.

He made his way to the desk, wanting to once again sketch her eyes. Every time he attempted to draw them, they were never quite right; he didn't have the right shade of green, that was a given, there would never be a shade of green brilliant enough to really capture her sparkle. But the shape was still wrong. And he needed to perfect them, before the memory of her eyes faded even more. He was already finding it hard to remember her smile. The longer he was here the harder he was finding it to remember anything of his past life.

His heart began to pound harder than it had before as his eyes landed upon the drawings scattered across his desk. Drawings that were clearly not his own. He stood glaring down at what he saw, unsure as to whether what he was seeing was real.

Strewn across the table were four sheets of paper, each with the same image upon them; a single, red rose drawn from a variety of angles and positions. He traced the outline of one with his index finger, the texture of the waxy crayon resembling that of a rose petal. Pulling his hand away as though he had been burned, he rubbed his fingertips together, eager to remove the waxy residue. The crayon had stained his fingertips a pale shade of red, almost resembling blood stains.

He gathered the drawings into a pile and placed them on the edge of the table. He wanted to show them to Helena, see if she could find a reasonable explanation as to how drawings he hadn't done managed to find their way into his locked room. Because he certainly couldn't find one.

No. There must be one. There had to be one. His mind grasped at straws, desperately racing through ideas and potential explanations. There had to be one. It was so simple. It would be staring him in the face.

They were only drawings. Nothing dangerous. Nothing ominous. Nothing to worry about, just images on sheets of paper. Nothing. Nothing at all. Nothing.

At that moment the hairs on the back of his neck began to rise and the feeling of being watched returned. He refused to let it affect him, refused to turn round only to be confronted with nothing more than an irrational sensation.

"There's nothing there," he whispered to himself. "You would've heard the door unlocking if anybody had come in."

He closed his eyes tight and took a deep, calming breath. Opening them once more, the calm which had come over him quickly vanished, only to be replaced with heart stopping fear. He let out a shrill cry before covering his mouth with both hands, desperate to prevent the scream from escaping. The gauze bandage around his palm brushed against his lips and he could smell the antiseptic cream through the cover. Sat on the bed before him, eyes blazing crimson, sat the girl who had plagued so many of his thoughts since that fateful night.

Though the medication he took was meant to prevent him from dreaming, he would often still dream of her. Her blazing eyes would glare through the blackness at him as she crept ever closer, radiating a burning heat and a fiery anger directed towards him. Though in these dreams she never managed to approach him, he could still feel the fire within, desperately trying to consume him. He never saw anything more than her crimson eyes; nothing else could break through his drugged haze.

This was no dream, however. She looked real, and the heat rising within the room certainly felt real, if the sweat beading across his skin was anything to go by. He stumbled backwards, knocking crayons off the desk, causing them to clatter to the floor.

She stood up, gliding across the small room, closing the gap between them. Her teeth gleamed in the partial light filtering through the high window. The locked, barred window. The air around her seemed to ripple and the temperature in the room rose faster.

Tom's heart pounded against his ribcage, adrenaline and fear coursing through his veins. Part of his mind clung to the rational idea that none of this was real. It was all in his head. None of this could be real because it wasn't logical and reality existed in a logical state. What was, and what was not. What existed, and what did not. What could be and what could not be. She could not be. And she certainly could not be here. In this room. This secure, locked room to which nobody had access.

"Missed me, Tom?" she asked, voice silken, hypnotizing. "It has certainly been too long."

"You're not real," he found himself saying, void of control, knowing he shouldn't engage this hallucination but finding it impossible not to. He knew that if he spoke to it, he would be giving it power over him. But he was a slave to the primal centre of his brain where fear was rapidly taking over. "None of this is real."

"I see we still cling to this ridiculous hope?" she said with a pout, the effect of which was ruined by the hideously sharp, lethal teeth. "I had hoped our last encounter had been enough conviction for you. To prove I exist, as a part of you."

"No, you're in my head," Tom said, grasping onto the idea blossoming deep within his mind. "You're in my head. You're not real. You're a part of me. You're a manifestation of myself and a way for me to blame my own wrongdoings on someone else. My alibi. You were never real."

"Do you truly believe that, Tom?" she asked with a smirk.

"I believe it because it's true," Tom replied, maintaining eye contact with the girl he knew wasn't really there. Helena had told him to say this to himself, if the manifestation ever returned. He needed to remind himself of what she really was until the hallucination eased and he could get help. He had to turn away from it. He had to try.

"Then if I exist solely within your mind, how am I able to physically hurt you?" she asked, a mirthless grin spread across her dangerous features.

"You never did, I did it to myself," he replied, repeating words he had come to know by heart as the months of therapy ticked by. "I hurt myself and blamed it on you, a thing that doesn't exist."

"And nothing exists within this space now, with which you could hurt yourself, correct?" she asked with a devious smirk.

"No, there isn't," he conceded. "That's why I'm not going to hurt myself, because I can't. It's simple."

She closed the gap between the two completely and grasped his wrist. She clung tightly to his pale wrist, nails gouging deep into the skin. "So how is this occurring?" she asked, a sadistic smile twisting across her porcelain

246

features. "How are you being hurt if nothing within your room can hurt you?"

Tom bit his lip, trying to prevent himself from screaming out in pain. Blood was pooling around her fingertips, running in rivulets down his skin from where her nails dug in. The pain blossomed around her fingernails, swirling out along his skin, dancing up his arms and burying into his mind. The taste of copper filled his mouth as his teeth pierced through his lip, drawing blood. The pain was nothing in comparison to the feeling of her hands on him. Hands which didn't exist. Hands which couldn't possibly be there. None of this could be happening. It wasn't.

"Is this not real, Tom?" she asked, increasing the pressure with which her nails punctured his skin.

"I'm doing it to myself," he reasoned, words muffled as he spoke, still biting his lip. Still trying not to cry out in pain. To scream. To beg for it to stop. "I'm hurting myself."

"Cease with reason and accept truth," she whispered menacingly. "You could not do this to yourself and you know this. I am real, and I am here, watching you, hunting you."

"If you're so desperate to hunt me why don't you just kill me while you've got me here?" he begged, hating the way he sounded so desperate and yet needing to say something, anything, to get out of this. To stop this rapid decline. He was peddling backwards into the hallucination that had clouded his life for a year. The drug addled haze was gone now. The pills couldn't help him. "Why haven't you killed me already?"

"Because I like to play first," she replied, her menacing tone enhanced by the hint of childish glee and the manic excitement building within her crimson eyes.

She released his wrist from her grasp, and he stumbled at the loss of support. He wrapped the hem of his shirt around his bleeding wrist, applying pressure to the wounds. Though blood trickled out of the half moon gashes across his scarred wrists, it was evident they were nothing more than superficial cuts.

"They come to take you away," she said, a maddening edge to her voice as she took a step backwards, away from Tom. She smiled serenely at him, "but I will return later. I tire of playing."

She turned to look at the door, waiting expectantly. Rather than turning to see what had captured her attention, he watched her, waiting for something to happen. If she was right, someone was about to open that door, and he needed to see what would happen next, what she would do. It could be the final step in his mind's acceptance of her as imaginary. He needed to know she was just in his mind.

Sure enough, a key scraped the lock of the door before swinging it open. Tom's eyes remained focused on Alyse, however. Though never having taken his eyes away from her, he suddenly became aware of the fact she was no longer there. It was as though she literally vanished into thin air, or was perhaps dancing with the dust motes floating high above him. He hadn't noticed her disappearance but it felt as though she hadn't suddenly vanished; rather, she just faded away.

"Tom?" a voice said, breaking through his thoughts. "Did you hear me? It's dinner time, let's g- oh what happened to your arm?"

He glanced down staring at the stained hem of his shirt and the little droplets of blood pooling at the edges of angry, red welts. He was acutely aware of a sharp pain stemming from each welt but his mind was focused elsewhere.

"I don't know," he said, bemused, unable to explain what had happened. The cuts were perfect half moons, as though he had dug his nails into his own wrist, but his nails were bitten down. Logic escaped him as he desperately searched for an explanation. "I don't know," he repeated. "What happened?"

The orderly carefully walked into the room, examining Tom and his immediate surroundings for a weapon of any kind. He knew a second orderly had to be in the room, looking through his things, searching for anything he shouldn't have. Papers rustled and the sheets on his bed were lifted. But they would never find anything.

"How did you do that, Tom?" she asked gently.

"I don't know," he said, shaking his head. The more he searched for a simple explanation, the more extraordinary and unbelievable they became in his mind. A haze seemed to have descended across his field of vision and the orderly faded in and out of view. His legs started to feel weak as the panic rose within him. "I feel dizzy," he managed to mutter. His knees gave way and he sank to the floor, clutching his wrist and disturbing the blood beginning to clot. His eyes closed and he welcomed the comforting frigidity of the tiled floor against his feverish skin.

Chapter Twenty Nine

The world came back into focus with a bang as his eyes flew open. He glanced around the room, searching for something though he couldn't quite remember what. The room looked unfamiliar, but the whitewashed walls and heavy scent of disinfectant let him know he was still in the hospital. Lights flared above him, filling the room with an almost blindingly white light

Footsteps clicked down the hallway, coming towards him, their sound filling the empty room, echoing intensely. He flinched but fought the impulse to close his eyes and shy away from whoever approached. The fear soon subsided as Helena came into view, her hair slightly disheveled and the blouse she had worn earlier in the day considerably more wrinkled.

"You're awake," she said quietly, glancing down into his open eyes. He nodded, not quite sure how to respond to such an obvious observation. "I hadn't expected you to wake up this evening."

"Where am I?" he asked, his voice quivering.

"You're in a secluded part of the hospital," Helena replied. "It's like a hospital wing, I suppose."

"A hospital within a hospital," he muttered. "Sounds confusing."

"Not as confusing as what happened to you earlier this evening," Helena said as she sat down on a chair beside his bed. "Do you want to tell me about any of it?"

Tom stared at her blankly. It was almost as if the past few months hadn't happened and he was back in his very first hospital bed, when her analyses of him had just begun. The déjà vu he was feeling was unnerving, if nothing else. "I am still in the same hospital, right…the criminal one?" he asked, wanting to make sure he hadn't had another time lapse and somehow dreamed up the past few months. It wouldn't have been the strangest thing to happen to him today. If today had really happened. Maybe he was losing his mind again. It felt like that.

"Yes Tom," she said gently. "You're still in the same hospital. You've only been unconscious for about an hour. But the circumstances meant I was needed, so I've had to come back, to be here when you woke up."

"Oh," he said, mentally sighing with relief.

"So, do you want to tell me what happened?" she asked again, this time more firmly, to prevent him avoiding the question.

"I passed out," he said with a shrug. Despite the months he had spent in Helena's care, he still attempted to brush off every question with a simple answer.

"Yes, you did," she conceded. "No medical explanation could be found to indicate why you may have fainted."

"Loss of blood?" he offered, glancing down at his wrist which was wrapped in thin bandages once more. He wondered if these cuts would scar too. It would be a nice addition to his rapidly expanding collection of battle scars.

"Though the cuts on your wrist are interesting, and slightly perturbing, they are superficial cuts," she said. "They're very shallow cuts; by the time you were brought here your blood had already clotted, closing the wounds. You barely lost any blood."

"Well that's my only explanation," Tom said with a shrug.

"Tom, I think we both know that's not true," Helena said gently. "I've known you long enough to know when you're trying to conceal something. That's what I'm paid to do, after all."

He ducked his head, avoiding Helena's eyes. He hated her more than he could ever express right now, and her incredibly irritating knack of seeing right through him. "I'm not concealing anything."

"Why were there drawings of roses in your room?" she

asked, avoiding the cat and mouse question game that could've ensued.

"I was going to ask you the same question," he replied. Emotion flickered briefly in her eyes before she managed to regain her stoic composure. Remaining silent, she encouraged him to continue. "They weren't there when I came to see you earlier, but when I got back to my room, there were loads of them. The orderly pointed them out."

"How did she do that?" Helena asked curiously.

The question threw him. It seemed rather unusual. What was she expecting him to say – she sung to him whilst doing a small jive? He could feel his jaw clenching as he tried so hard to contain the sarcastic response building in his mind. "She said I was good at drawing," he finally said. "I know I'm a good artist, so I just assumed she meant my own drawings, the ones you've seen. But these are perfect drawings. I'm not that good. I know they're not mine."

"Could you have done them in your sleep perhaps? Or while not entirely focused?" she asked. "They could have been done by you; you just might not remember it."

"Have a proper look at them," he said, venom lacing his tone. "They're perfectly drawn and actually look realistic. All I've got is wax crayons and there is no way these were drawn just using the cheap crayons I've been given."

Helena paused. She could feel Tom's irritation coming off him in waves and knew if she phrased the next question wrong he would shut down completely and her entire evening would have been cut short for nothing. Sometimes, though she wouldn't admit it out loud, all she wanted to do was give up on him. "If you didn't do them, who did?"

"I don't know," he said. "Somebody looking to play a sick joke. Nobody but staff has access to my room so that's suspicious in itself, wouldn't you say?"

"Do you really think any of the staff here would do that?" she asked, a hint of disbelief evident in her tone.

"Well they don't exactly think of us as normal people in here, do they?" he replied sarcastically. "Maybe they're using us for entertainment. I suppose they need to find it somewhere; looking after a bunch of crazies isn't going to be much fun. Let's poke the mentally deranged animals in their cages and see what happens. That kind of thing."

"It still doesn't explain why anybody would do that," she said. "No matter how sadistic you believe the staff to be, they won't attempt to harm your recovery. A stunt like that could cause you to relapse, let alone what it would do for their professional career. I know you still refuse to believe we are all here to help you, but Tom, we are here to care for your wellbeing and nothing more."

He scoffed and raised his eyebrow at her choice of words.

"You need to tell me the truth, Tom," she said, after a few moments of silence. "I need to know what happened in your room. If you are having a relapse, it may be an indication that your dosage isn't quite right."

"So if it all starts happening again, this time it's just because of the pills I'm taking?" he asked, incredulously. "All because of the pills I'm taking to supposedly stop everything?"

"Medicine requires a delicate balance in conjunction with the body's natural composition. A slight increase in one thing could affect underlying issues, bringing any problems to the surface," she conceded. "But it's just one cause. I'm not saying it would definitely be because of your medication, but it could be making it worse."

"Well that just seems completely pointless," he scoffed, wrinkling his nose in disgust.

"So I take it something did happen then?" she pressed.

He glared at her. "Fine, yes, something strange happened. I thought I saw Alyse. I know I didn't, I know she's just a part of me and I confronted her and told her this, like you said I should do if I ever see her again. I accepted her as a part of me and all that. But I did see her."

"And the cuts…were they because of her?" Helena asked, as she jotted something down on a notepad Tom hadn't noticed her carrying.

"Yes," he sighed, giving in. "She grabbed my arm, or I grabbed my arm, or something. I don't quite know how it works. But nails dug into my skin and that's what those cuts are."

Helena nodded slowly. "How vivid was she? Was she actually there, or did you see her in your mind's eyes, like we discussed?"

He thought about it for a moment, trying to recall his last meeting with her. "She seemed quite vivid, like she was really there," he finally replied. "But I don't know."

"Did she say anything?"

He furrowed his eyebrows in mock contemplation. She'd said plenty, but perhaps he could skim over this one small detail. "Not that I can remember."

She nodded once more, taking down a few more notes and glancing across the page, obviously deep in thought. "How long did you see her for?" Helena asked.

Tom shrugged. "Not long, it only felt like five minutes, but I don't have any clocks in the room so I don't know."

The nodding continued, though she now looked him in the eye as opposed to focusing upon her scrawled writing. He wondered briefly whether she ever got neck cramp from all the nodding and shaking. He stifled a laugh – now was not the time for inappropriate humor, he had to remind himself. "It's interesting that you should see her again," Helena began, dislodging the thoughts from his mind. "But, the fact that you don't seem to remember much about your encounter and that you're trying to rationalize what you saw is a very good sign."

"But I still saw her," he said, shoulders slumping slightly in defeat. This was the route of the problem. The real reason why he was trying to hide so much. He'd been in here for what felt like an eternity and it had all been worth it when he'd been improving. But now he was right back to square one. "I'm back to where I started because I still saw her. I was still afraid of her. I still thought she was going to hurt me."

"The fear is still there because that part of your mind which was so convinced she actually existed is still there. It hasn't gone away, we simply understand it better," Helena reasoned. "Seeing something which we know shouldn't be there is going to frighten us. And considering everything that has happened, being afraid is a natural response. But does it feel like the fear could take over?"

He bit his lip, considering the response. Her appearance had caused fear to consume him, and he knew it could take over, just like it had done before. He also knew that wasn't what she wanted to hear, and though he had finally told her mostly what had happened, a part of him was reluctant to say this. In that moment, he knew he would never fully be honest with Helena. He would never fully tell her the truth. And no matter how many sessions he had with her, this would never change. "No," he replied, after a few moments. "It doesn't feel like it could take over. It doesn't feel like it did before."

She half smiled at his response and nodded her head again. She was beginning to remind him of a bobble headed dog he had once seen in the rear view window of a car. It was almost comical, really. In a deeply annoying sort of way.

"Are you sure that's everything that happened?" she asked. "There's nothing else you need to tell me? Nothing that could be vital in helping you recover further?"

Tom hesitated. "No, that's everything," he said after a few moments. Telling her everything wouldn't make much difference in this scenario. If anything it could make things worse. It was easier to keep things hidden, out of view and away from the world. She knew enough to make things better, to prevent him from seeing Alyse again. She knew enough to restore the blissful unknown and that was all he wanted. She knew all she needed to.

"Ok," Helena said. "I'm going to alter the dosage of your medication slightly, increasing it. Not by much, just a little bit more. There shouldn't be any side effects but we are going to keep a close eye on you, just in case. I'll be here most of the evening anyway."

Tom barely registered what she had said; it hardly mattered as they had complete control over his medication anyway. They could literally do whatever they pleased, prescribe him any number of drugs and there was nothing he could do about it except hope they'd send him into blissful oblivion. He was powerless, but the numbness that came with each drug was a welcome relief. Maybe if they hurt rather than healed he might have objected, but there was nothing wrong with being numb, with feeling nothing at all.

She handed him a cup of water and a little paper pot with two bright blue pills in them. He knocked them back and took a gulp of water, forcing the rather large pills down his throat, anticipating the silence to come.

"If you're feeling better, we'll go back to your room now," Helena said, standing up and motioning to an orderly standing just by the doorway.

A slight twinge of fear caused Tom's heart to skip a beat and he glanced around the room, trying to think of a way to prevent this return. The fear subsided, however, as the active ingredient within the pills he'd just ingested slowly began to course through his system. He nodded mutely and stood up off the bed.

By the time they reached his room, all emotion seemed to have been taken away, replaced with a blank nothingness. He felt nothing; no fear, no anxiety, no emotion. He felt as blank as the whitewashed walls surrounding him. He liked feeling like this.

Chapter Thirty

Tom couldn't remember closing his eyes. He couldn't remember falling asleep and he certainly couldn't remember the moment the world slipped away and he began to dream. But he was dreaming now. He hadn't been able to dream for so long. This world felt too foreign to him.

The blank ceiling he had been staring at in the sparse moonlight filtering in through barred windows had suddenly become engulfed in white hot flames. Sparks rained down upon him, burning his skin, the acrid smell of charred flesh filling the room, choking him. The flames leaped higher, causing the paint across the walls and ceiling to curl and melt under the intense heat.

Though he had been lying on his back looking at the ceiling it now appeared as though his world had turned upside down. He was looking down at the ceiling, watching the flames race across it as they would across a wooden floor. The flames he had been sure were falling down upon him were actually leaping up to burn him.

He couldn't move. He couldn't scream. He was trapped with nowhere to go as the flames rose higher around him. The searing, burning pain engulfed him, seeming to probe far beneath his skin to the bone. As the flames climbed higher, however, he became aware of their true temperature. What he had thought was searing hot was ice cold, yet it burned the same way.

In the centre of the fire sat a body. Though he couldn't see it, he knew she was the source of the ice cold fire, of the paradox which was attempting to consume him. Or confuse him. The fire was made up of her, appearing red hot but actually cold inside.

His eyes remained fixed upon her body. He couldn't turn away from her, knowing that the moment he did, something bad would happen to him. She could only burn cold for so long before it reached him, but perhaps he could prevent whatever was to come for a little bit longer.

As he watched, she slowly began to move, perhaps aware of his eyes trained upon her. She lifted her head agonizingly slowly. Her body twisted grotesquely, moving in a broken and jerky manner, as though her bones were too weak to support her weight. She curled her entire body backwards, bending unnaturally far until her head rested completely upon her back. Though now looking directly up at him, her eyes remained closed. Tom knew he should've felt relieved by this but his mind and body begged for her to open her eyes, to look at him. He knew who she was; he didn't need to see the eyes to know that, but he needed her to look at him. He needed to see her. And he needed her to see him.

A smile played upon her lips and blood trickled down from the corners, creating a bizarre, puppet like affect. Her tongue darted out, licking up the droplets of blood like fine wine, not wanting them to drip away. As she did this, the blood smeared across her lips, staining them a deep scarlet. The same colour as her roses. Those damned roses.

Finally, her eyelids began to flutter and he braced himself for those scarlet eyes. He knew this was the end, and that she was the harbinger of death but he needed to see them. She was a part of him and he needed to see his own death.

Her eyes opened and his heart stopped. He had expected to see scarlet eyes, so dark and haunting, emotionless and burning through him. Instead, the eyes staring back at him were hazel and full of fear. They weren't her eyes, they were his. He was looking down into his own eyes.

He woke up gently, eyes slowly flickering open, serenely returning to the land of the living. His eyes adjusted to the darkness, sparse moonlight illuminating various objects around the room, so normal and unimposing. A direct contradiction to the dream he had just left.

"Do you now see why I do not exist solely within your mind?" a silky voice whispered through the darkness, wrapping around him almost soothingly.

"I don't understand," he replied. There was no fear.

"You do, you understand now," the voice continued, closer this time. "You understand I am who you believed me to be."

"I'm not afraid of you."

"The dead don't fear anything," she whispered. He could feel her breath ghosting across his neck. "They have nothing to fear when they no longer feel."

"Oh," he replied simply. "Am I dead?

"Not yet," she said. "But you will be."

With that, the room blazed with light, burning so brilliantly he had to shield his eyes. He was unable to turn away from the source of the light as it seemed to come from all around him.

Alyse stood before him, her scarlet eyes burning through him, dark and terrifying as he had remembered them to be. Fear began to consume him once more as he looked at her. Though he remembered her transformed figure to be terrifying, seeing the ordinary girl in front of him with a gleam of darkness behind those awful eyes was even more terrifying than he could have ever realized. He almost wished to see the grotesque smile, the razor sharp teeth and the impossible wings, rather than this ordinary girl, normal in every way except for the bloodlust pounding through her crimson eyes.

The stench of decay was overpowering and though he felt sick, the need to be sick was no longer there, as though all human reactions had been taken away from him.

"And so it ends," she whispered, her sonorous voice sending shivers racing down his spine. "What have you become, Tom? Crazy? Or are you sane? Regardless, now you know...I am real. Everything they told you was in your head is all real."

As she spoke, her sharp teeth grazed against the delicate skin across his jugular. He knew she was doing it on purpose; an act of his death to come, a rehearsal.

The pain he anticipated racing through his body as teeth dug into his skin never came. He waited for it, but they remained locked in this strange embrace as lethargy overcame him. Something was about to happen, something he hadn't expected. He thought this would be death, but it seemed for him, as for Alyse, death would not be the end. Finally he managed to close his eyes. Everything went black and he knew it was over.

Chapter Thirty-One

The bed was made; the room was neat and tidy. Everything was in its place. But the boy was missing.

"How could he have just vanished?" Helena glared at the orderlies as they tore the room apart, searching for anything; any indication at all as to where Tom may have gone. "There are bars on the window and his door is locked! He couldn't have escaped by himself and he certainly couldn't have gotten far."

Behind her stood a warden and a police officer - both were communicating with members of their team through radios. The moment Tom's room had been found empty all forces had been gathered to conduct a search, to find him. A disappearance so soon after his relapse could only indicate something bad. It was no coincidence.

"They haven't found him anywhere on the grounds," the police officer said to Helena. "We're expanding our search to include the immediate area now. There is no trace of him so far. Nothing on CCTV and nobody has seen or heard anything out of the ordinary."

"That's impossible. The amount of cameras and video equipment in this hospital, something must have picked up his image," she said with exasperation. "He's not just disappeared."

"You can see the tapes for yourself," the officer replied. "But according to my team there is nothing of the boy or anything suspicious on any of them."

A murmur of surprise from one of the orderlies caught Helena's attention and she turned away from the exasperated officer.

"I think I found something," the orderly said, standing up slowly. Helena entered the room and walked over to the orderly.

Helena felt her stomach flip. "That's impossible." Resting behind the headboard was a perfectly formed red rose, its colour so vivid as to render the whiteness of the wall beside it dull in comparison. Each petal seemed to shimmer despite the fact the rose rested in partial darkness, hidden in shadow from any light source. Scattered on the floor around it were rose petals, all of the same shimmering colour.

As they watched, the rose petals began to rapidly curl up and decay, leaving behind nothing more than dry husks; a shadow of their former selves.

Epilogue

Eyes stare out from among the shadows. The darkness is all around, encompassing, encroaching. Suffocating and heavy, the light could never penetrate down here. There is no light amongst the darkness. There is only shadow. There is only the vast expanse of emptiness, of darkness.

He's here. With me. She knows it. And she will never give up. But I will never give him up. He is one of mine now, and nothing she can do will ever take him away. She will die before I relent.

About the Author

Born in Malta, Chloe Testa now lives in Surrey, dividing her time between writing novels and teaching English with almost no time to sleep in between the two. She is a lover of great books, good company and bad puns.

For information, details, giveaways and to sample other selected works of hers, visit www.chloetesta.com.

7118907R00147

Printed in Great Britain
by Amazon.co.uk, Ltd.,
Marston Gate.